L.T. RICHARDS

Our
SECRET LIFE
Full Immersion

Acknowledgments

We would like to thank our friends, who have been instrumental in developing this book. They have been inspirational and supportive. We would like to thank a few people who were key in reviewing *Our Secret Lives: Full Immersion* and providing constructive feedback in its development.

Thank you:

BL

VO

KG

RD

The sequel to *Our Awakening* brought even more excitement and thrill. Ryan and Ginger found themselves diving into unforgettable adventures with close friends, each new experience pushing their boundaries. The deeper they ventured, the more they realized how vast and uncharted the world around them truly was, leaving them both unprepared and fascinated by the unknown.

With each encounter, their friendships fueled a desire to explore further, taking them deeper into the swinging lifestyle. The allure of it all sparked curiosity that led them toward even darker, more mysterious paths they never thought they'd tread.

Their journey continues in *Full Immersion*, where the excitement only intensifies.

Table Of Content

Prologue

In *Our Secret Life: Our Awakening*, Ryan and Ginger's world transformed the moment they embraced a daring lifestyle shift that electrified their relationship. What began as a nerve-racking, off-premise meet-and-greet quickly escalated into thrilling house parties that pushed their boundaries and unleashed passions they never thought possible. Every step they took deepened their connection, fueling a desire neither could have anticipated.

That first encounter didn't come easy. Anxiety and doubt gripped them both, but fate had other plans. A chance meeting with an unexpected couple shattered their hesitation, and the floodgates of excitement burst open. The experience was exhilarating, awakening something raw and primal inside them. They were hooked.

Over the next few years, they forged friendships that transcended the typical boundaries of casual encounters. Wine festivals became playgrounds for flirtation, house parties were filled with sensuality, and even the most mundane moments in public were tinged with a thrilling undercurrent. A simple wink across a crowded room was enough to send sparks flying and their hearts racing, knowing the night held the promise of more. Every stolen glance was a tease, a precursor to what awaited them when they returned home, their libidos ignited like wildfire.

Yet, the risk of exposure loomed over them. Ryan and Ginger lived in constant fear of their best friends discovering the truth about their double lives. Their secrecy tightened like a vice, especially when nosy questions arose about their unusual absences. The tension reached its peak when they accidentally crossed paths with swinger friends in public. The awkward moments of explaining how they knew these strangers sent their hearts pounding in their chests, adrenaline fueling their need to keep everything hidden.

But beyond the sexual awakening, something far deeper blossomed between Ryan and Ginger. They explored not only new pleasures but also parts of themselves they never knew existed. Each learned how to satisfy the other in ways that hadn't been possible before, taking lessons from their newfound partners and bringing them home to heighten their intimacy.

Still, the struggle to balance their secret life with their public one gnawed at them. The thrill of the lifestyle was undeniable, but the constant fear of being discovered haunted every interaction. The stakes were high, and keeping their hidden world separate from friends and family was the ultimate challenge.

CHAPTER 1

Vanilla Time

Ginger

By now, Ryan and I had been in the swinging lifestyle for a few years, but the past year especially had been a whirlwind of new friends and tons of parties. When Mercedes and Chet, our best vanilla friends who were also our neighbors, came dangerously close to finding out our secret, I decided I needed some time to refocus on life outside of swinging.

That decision solidified about six weeks after our last play party when Kathy, who'd hosted the party along with her boyfriend, called with some interesting news: She was pregnant. And she was convinced it was Ryan's. Except . . . Ryan had gotten a vasectomy a few years ago. Apparently, Kathy's boyfriend had lied to her about being sterile from a young age. Even though we knew it couldn't have been Ryan's, and the truth had eventually come out, I was still annoyed at him for being so careless about condoms. After that, I seriously needed some vanilla time.

A couple of weeks later, we sat outside with Chet and Mercedes around their firepit, drinking some wine, laughing about what was happening in our lives, and simply enjoying our time together. We really liked our vanilla friends and feared losing them if they ever learned about our alternative lifestyle. So, we always had to be careful about what we said.

After a few bottles of wine, Mercedes said, "Sooo, it seems like your daughter had a pretty wild party a few months ago. How beat-up was the house when you got home?"

Crap. That hadn't been our daughter's party. We had hosted a swingers-style house party for my fortieth birthday two years ago, and what a party it was. I looked at Ryan but then realized I had to say something quickly. I feigned anger.

"She said it was only supposed to be a few friends, and it grew bigger than she expected. She said they were leaving when we called her, and there were only a few stragglers left by the time we got home."

Mercedes leered at me, as though she knew I was lying but couldn't prove it. "Anytime you need me to go and break up a party, just let me know."

We laughed it off, but Ryan and I exchanged a glance, and I was sure we were both envisioning the horror of Mercedes walking in and catching us.

We continued to talk about other things such as boats, birthdays, and other celebrations coming up. We laughed quite a bit, as we usually do with them. Mercedes talked about her new job, and some of the people she'd met, and how we had to meet them. They sounded like fun.

Before it got too late, we made plans to see them for dinner the following week, and then we helped them clean up and gave our good-night hugs. Ryan held my hand as we walked home. I stared at the road most of the way there, replaying the conversation from the night.

"She knows!" I blurted out when we were halfway home.

Ryan laughed. "I think she's just fishing. Don't get worked up over it. If she really knew, she would have asked more questions."

Maybe he's right. But I still couldn't help but think she suspected.

Chet and Mercedes were the kind of friends you could only dream of meeting. They meant the world to us, and I didn't know what we'd do if we lost them over this.

Over the next several weeks, we spent time with them on many occasions, going to dinner, seeing movies, or just hanging out, and there weren't any more suspicious questions. I started to believe it had all been in my head.

Late one afternoon, I answered a knock at the door and found Mercedes standing there. I opened the door, and before I could say a word, she excitedly said, "There's this eighties band playing at the Hitching Post this weekend. We should go see it. I heard they're really good."

The Hitching Post? My stomach sank. Several of our lifestyle friends liked to go there, and there were frequent meet and greets there. I just stared at her.

"Is everything all right?" Mercedes scrunched her eyebrows together.

She knows. How could she know? *Crap, she must know.*

"Ginger?" Mercedes waved a hand in front of my face.

I snapped out of it. "Yeah, I'm here. That sounds great. What time?"

"The band starts at nine, so let's get some dinner there before it starts so we can get a good seat." She grinned and hugged me. "It's going to be so much fun! I need to get to the store. Just wanted to quickly stop by to see if you could make it."

"I'll let Ryan know." I stared at Mercedes as she walked to her car. *What does she know? And how?*

As soon as she was gone, I rushed into the garage, where Ryan was tinkering with something.

"She knows! Mercedes knows!"

Ryan looked up, startled. "Mercedes knows what?"

"She just asked us if we wanted to go to the Hitching Post to see an eighties band. She's never asked us to go with her to see a band before. And why there?"

Ryan laughed. "Maybe she wants to see that band, and that's where they're playing." He paused, his expression turning thoughtful. "She was quite curious about what we've been up to."

"Yes! That's why I'm thinking she knows something."

Ryan held up his hands to calm me down. "If she knows, then there's nothing we can do about it. Let's just go see the band with them, and if we see anyone else we know, we can say hi and limit it to a hug and a handshake."

I nodded and agreed. What else could I do?

Mercedes suggested we carpool to the Hitching Post and volunteered to drive. So, if we were outed, we couldn't hide from her and Chet. But I didn't have a good reason to turn her down, so I agreed.

That evening, she sent me a text to ask what I was wearing. "Are you dressing up in an eighties theme or just nice club clothes?"

I texted her back: "It will get hot in that place. Not much for cooling, so I'll just wear some club clothes."

A moment later, she called me on the phone.

"Hey," I said. "What's up?"

"Have you been to this place before?"

Shit. I didn't know how to answer. *Tell her the truth, I guess?*

"Yeah, Ryan and I went there to see a band about a year ago. It isn't a very attractive place, but it was fun with a dance floor. I definitely remember it getting hot and stuffy in there."

Whew, I think I dodged that.

"Oh, okay. I haven't been there in probably fifteen years, so I wasn't sure if anything changed. All right, we'll pick you up around seven. This is going to be fun."

It felt like we were playing with fire. I went downstairs and told Ryan I needed a pregame drink. He shook up some tequila with ice and poured us both a shot.

"If anyone we know comes up to us, just shoot me," I said before throwing back the shot.

"It will be all right, sweetie." He put his arm around my shoulders and gave me a squeeze. "If we meet anyone we know, we'll just play it off like they're old friends."

"Okay." I held my arms around him for a full hug, which helped me feel better.

Mercedes and Chet arrived right at seven to pick us up, and off we drove to the Hitching Post. The billboard outside announced the Endeavors band as entertainment for the night.

"I've heard a lot of good reviews for this band. I think we'll have a good time," Mercedes said.

"I've heard the name, but we've never seen them," I responded.

We walked in, and I let Mercedes pick a table so she wouldn't suspect how well we knew the place. Unfortunately, the table she picked just happened to be near where the meet and greets usually happened.

I pointed to the back. "How about a table in the back where we can talk over the music? This area might get really crowded."

Mercedes agreed, and we went to a large corner booth in the back of the tavern, where others couldn't easily see us.

We ordered food and drinks, and chatted. The crowd picked up after eight, but I didn't recognize anyone so far. We might be lucky after all. I relaxed a little more as we ordered more drinks and watched the band set up.

By the time the band started at nine, I still hadn't recognized anyone in the crowd. The four of us hit the dance floor for a few great eighties songs. The singer was outstanding.

As we returned to our table for a break, a couple approached us and asked if we remembered them.

It took a second before I did. Our daughters were in cheerleading together. "Terri, right?"

16

"Yeah, you remembered! This is my husband, Allen."

It was all coming back to me. Our daughter had also dated their son for a little while. I looked back at our table. "Let me introduce you to my husband, Ryan, and our friends, Chet and Mercedes," I said, leading them to our table.

Terri narrowed her eyes at Mercedes. "You look familiar."

Mercedes smiled. "We've lived in the same town all our life."

"I'm sure we've bumped into each other. It's such a small town." She looked at me. "I saw you out here dancing and remembered your daughter telling us how much we'd get along, so I thought we'd say hi."

"Would you like to join us?" Mercedes asked.

"Thanks, but a few of our friends and Terri's sister are on the other side of the bar," Allen said. "Maybe we can go out sometime soon?"

"Sure, that would be great. Let me get your phone number." I got Terri's number and sent mine to her.

"Allen and I are usually at the Boat House every Friday night to sing karaoke. Stop by sometime," said Terri.

"Sounds great," I said. "We'll do that."

They went to their table, and we returned to our booth. As we sat down, Mercedes asked, "How do you know them?"

Ryan raised his hands and shook his head, not knowing either.

"Our daughters were in cheerleading together, and I saw her once in a while. And our daughter dated their son too."

"It's such a small world around here," Chet said.

The band played some more nostalgic music, and I grabbed Mercedes's arm to go back on the floor to dance. The guys stayed in the booth. Mercedes was a great dancer. I wished I'd gotten out to dance more when I was younger, because I couldn't move anywhere close to the way she did.

Terri came up to us with a woman who I assumed was her sister and started dancing. We laughed and danced a lot. I'd been so worried about coming here with Mercedes, but now I was glad she had asked us. The band was really good, and we were having so much fun. After many more songs, dancing, and laughing, we made our way back to our table. I needed something to cool down. Luckily, the guys had ice water waiting.

I sat on Ryan's lap and gave him a kiss.

"Hey, hey, hey, this is a public place," Mercedes quipped. "Clean it up."

"Mercedes, lighten up, we're in a dark corner," I said.

Even she laughed at that.

It was nearly midnight now, and the four of us decided to head home. It had been a really fun night, and I was glad I didn't ruin it by worrying. When Mercedes and Chet dropped us off at home, I asked about getting together next weekend too, but Mercedes would be away on some work-related travel, so we said we'd figure something out after she was back. Then Ryan and I went inside and straight to bed.

The next morning, I got a text from Terri. They were glad to meet us and were hoping we could go to the Boat House next Friday. The Boat House was a run-down, cheap bar in our small town. They had karaoke on Friday and Saturday nights. Most people drank so much that it didn't matter how well anyone sang.

Ryan agreed to go, and we said we'd meet around eight o'clock. Terri and I texted each other all week and got to know each other a little more. She seemed like a lot of fun.

The question was, how far did we want to take it with them?

What am I thinking? Am I now going to think of everyone we meet in a sexual way? Ryan did that enough for the both of us. I pushed the thought away, but I couldn't help but smile, thinking of how much this lifestyle had opened me up and brought more excitement to our lives.

CHAPTER 2

A Sizzling Hot Tub

$\mathcal{T}$he week flew by. On Friday, as I waited for Ryan to come home from work, I thought back to whether Allen and Terri had given any signal about their interests. They had approached us and wanted to get to know us, but was it just because our kids knew each other?

Ryan came home around 6:30, and I had dinner ready for us. I poured some wine into Ryan's glass as we sat down to eat.

"Have you given any thought to whether Allen and Terri are lifestyle-friendly?"

Ryan stopped with his fork halfway to his mouth. "I can't believe *you* are asking that."

"Believe me, so am I."

"I'm hoping they are." He flashed a devilish grin before taking a bite of food.

Terri was knock-out gorgeous, so I figured Ryan would want her. She was thin, with huge breasts, and even though she wore her hair in a large eighties style, it suited her.

"Let's not push it on them and just get to know them like vanilla friends. Remember, their son and our daughter are still friends," I said.

Ryan agreed. It still didn't stop me from wondering whether I'd be interested in Allen. He wasn't as tall as Ryan, had an average build, and his blonde hair had some gray that added to his Southern gentleman aura. *Hmm . . . he's definitely handsome.*

Stop it. I reminded myself that we would get to know them like vanilla friends.

Ryan and I did the dishes, then changed into clothing appropriate for the Boat House, which just meant jeans and a simple polo for Ryan, and a nice low-cut blouse for me.

When we arrived at the bar, Terri and Allen waved us over to a table. We exchanged hugs and sat down. I was a little surprised that we were hugging already, but I went with it.

We ordered some drinks, and then the karaoke DJ called Terri's name to sing. She sang beautifully and swayed with the music. Ryan and Allen were both focused on her—and her tight jeans.

Terri returned and told Ryan and me to pick a song, but neither of us sang very well. We chatted about our town, kids, and interests. I grew more attached to them as we found their interests similar to ours, and they seemed like a lot of fun. Then, the DJ called up both Allen and Terri for a duet. I was impressed. We applauded when they finished.

We were the only ones applauding, as most were into their drinks and talking. They came back to the table and thanked us for being their only fans. We spent a couple of hours talking and enjoying our drinks, and Terri and Allen sang a few more songs.

Around 10:00, Terri leaned over the table so we could hear her over the music. "Would you two like to go back to our hot tub for a few more drinks?"

Ryan looked over at me, smiling. I knew what his answer would be, but he waited for me to decide. I thought for a second, then said, "Sure. Let us go home to get our swimsuits, and we'll be right over."

Allen gave Ryan their address as they paid our bar tab. *That was kind of them.* Then we got up and walked out.

Terri gave me another hug. "This is great. We'll see you in a little bit."

"Don't worry about bringing any beer," Allen said. "I have some on tap."

Ryan and I got in our car and drove home.

"Where will this lead?" I asked.

"I don't know, but they're fun. We won't instigate anything; we'll just let them set the pace."

That made sense. I was contemplating this very thing happening earlier in the day, but now that there was actual potential for more happening, I was worried that if we took this hot tub experience too far, it could ruin a potential friendship, or might come back to haunt our daughter.

We went home, put our swimsuits on, and grabbed some beach towels, plus shorts for the ride home. Terri and Allen only lived a few minutes away from us. They'd been so close this whole time, and we never knew.

When we arrived, the back gate was open. We walked through and around the side. Ryan called out a hello.

"Come on around. We're on the deck!" Terri yelled.

Terri was in her bikini, bringing out towels as we walked up to their beautiful deck. It was brown with white trim and stretched the length of their house, with the hot tub enclosed in a large screened gazebo.

We followed Terri into the gazebo, where she set down her towels, and we set our beach bag on a bench next to the spa. We then followed Terri into the house, where Allen brought Ryan a draft beer.

Ryan took the amber beverage with a smile. "Wow, with service like this, we need to come by more often."

Terri quipped, "Sounds great. The door is always open."

Ryan was focused on Terri's gorgeous breasts nearly falling out of her top, so I nudged him and gave him a look to put his eyes back in their sockets.

He just smiled and gave an almost imperceptible shrug.

Allen looked to me. "What would you like to drink?"

"I'll just have the same wine Terri is drinking."

Terri poured her white Zinfandel into a glass, filling it to the brim. She handed it to me, then grabbed the bottle. "Okay. Let's go."

Allen followed us to the hot tub with a pitcher of beer in hand. We all climbed into the hot water, and each of us found a corner of the hot tub to sit.

They had some good eighties music playing, and the temperature was perfect. We chatted some more about life in town, how gossipy everyone was, and our kids' high school experience. Then, after an hour and two more drinks, Terri excitedly said, "Let's play a game."

Ryan and I looked at each other, knowing where this would probably lead.

"Okay," I said. "What type of game do you want to play?"

"We like to play truth or dare in the hot tub."

Ryan grinned. "That sounds fun. What are the rules?"

"No rules, fuck the rules. We just play how we want."

Ryan glanced at me, and then back to Terri. "Okay, so what if I dare you to make out with Ginger?"

There was a long pause, during which a smile slowly spread across Terri's face.

"Okay, we gotta know," Terri said, glancing to Allen, then between me and Ryan. "Are you guys swingers?"

I wanted to sink to the bottom of the hot tub. I was sure there was guilt written all over my face.

Ryan just sat there with a straight face and asked, "Why are you asking that?"

Terri blushed. "Well, most of your daughter's friends know, and they gossip, so our son told us."

Our daughter's friends know? How…?

I didn't know how to respond, and Ryan didn't seem to either.

"You are, aren't you?" Terri continued. "We knew it."

"Terri, we don't fit into any category per se, but we have some fun friends that we go out with now and then." I'd basically just admitted that we were guilty as charged.

Terri then started asking a ton of questions, like how you could be with another person when your spouse was there, and whether there was jealousy. Ryan and I answered all of her questions honestly. There was no putting this cat back in the bag, so honesty seemed the best policy.

At first, Allen was just sitting there listening to us, but then he looked to Ryan. "Just so I understand what you're saying, you're good with watching another guy fuck your wife?"

I got the sense he wasn't as enthusiastic about this as Terri.

"I enjoy watching the excitement on her face when she gets pleased. I actually get a little turned on watching her with another guy, especially when she looks at me, or if I'm involved too. It's something that really requires security in a relationship, and you can't really comprehend what I'm saying unless you take the plunge. No pun intended." Ryan winked at Terri and laughed.

Terri and I laughed, and even Allen smiled a bit. I still wasn't sure Allen was really sold on the idea. Terri seemed intrigued and asked how we got into it.

I went on with our story and how we're still figuring things out, but we enjoyed meeting a lot of great friends. We emphasized that it's not all about sex. It's about the electricity and relationships you create with friends on an entirely new level.

"Are Chet and Mercedes swingers?" Terri asked.

I quickly replied, "Absolutely not, and please don't say anything to them."

Terri and Allen promised they wouldn't tell anyone. We sipped our drinks in silence for a minute, and then Terri's devilish grin returned.

"So, what about that game of truth or dare?"

Ryan replied with zero reluctance, "I'm game."

I was a bit hesitant, as I wasn't sure how Allen would take watching Terri with Ryan, but agreed.

"Sure, this could be fun," Allen said. He had a hint of reservation in his tone, but if it became awkward, I made up my mind that we would back off for the evening.

"And you're sure about no rules?" Ryan asked.

"No rules. There are no rules," Terri quickly responded.

Terri had lust written all over her face. She wanted Ryan desperately, but then again, Ryan was quite attractive. I kept thinking how her eyes would light up once she wrapped her hands around Ryan's cock.

"Sooo, without rules, it can get pretty crazy," Ryan said. "Especially with my mind."

Allen said, "Okay, if it's a dare that's out of line, then we can all vote on it."

We collectively agreed.

"Great," Terri said. "I'll go first. Ginger, truth or dare?"

"Dare." I had already spilled enough truth.

"Okay, take off your top."

"I'm wearing a one piece." I smirked, realizing it was going to come off anyhow.

"Okay, take off the entire thing. I'll do the same. And don't even think about asking for a vote, because I don't think the men will side with you."

Wow. If I didn't know better, I'd think she's been planning this for a long time. Maybe I *didn't* know better.

The stupid grin on Ryan's face told me Terri was right, and he wouldn't support me with this one. I complied with removing my swimsuit and set it on the stairs next to the spa. Terri took off her top and bottoms and put them on the side of the hot tub.

"There we go, much more comfortable." She sat back down in the water, her breasts slightly submerged and swaying with the motion of the water. Ryan couldn't keep his eyes off them.

"Ryan, truth or dare?" Terri called out.

"Dare," he said, quickly reaching to untie his swimsuit.

Of course he would.

"Oh no, you don't know what I'm going to ask," Terri said, and he stopped. After a moment full of anticipation, she continued. "While standing up, face us and slowly remove your swim trunks."

I burst out with laughter. Ryan looked at Allen and said, "I think we need to vote on this."

"I don't want to see his junk," Allen chided.

"Oh, I do!" Terri exclaimed with a lustful and almost starving look in her eyes.

Everyone looked to me. *Payback's a bitch.*

"Sorry, sweetie. You didn't have my back." Besides, I liked seeing his package.

Ryan stood up, untied his swim trunks, and slowly slid them down. He stepped out of them and tossed them on the steps by my own swimsuit. The warm hot tub definitely had him hanging low, and I could tell the excitement of our little game had stimulated him

28

already. Terri was staring at him like a cat staring down her prey.

"Okay, you can sit down now," Allen grumbled.

Terri gulped down some wine. "Wow, okay. Allen, truth or dare?"

Apparently, no-rules truth or dare meant Terri was running the show.

"Dare," he responded.

Terri said, "Go run around the house five times."

I thought Ryan was going to choke on his beer. I burst out with laughter also.

"I'm not going to run around the house while you three are naked in the spa," he whined as we continued laughing.

I was confident Ryan wanted to have Allen go for a run, but I had to support Allen. "I don't want him to work up too much of a sweat."

Terri laughed and said, "Okay, take off your trunks instead."

"Wow, your enthusiasm toward me is overwhelming."

Terri muttered, "I see *your* junk every day."

I laughed. "Come on, Terri, you should always enjoy your husband."

"See, listen to her. Thank you, Ginger." Allen smiled, threw his swim trunks on the deck, and raised his beer toward me. I returned the gesture.

I figured if this was going anywhere, I'd better win some points with Allen.

"Okay, Ryan, it's your turn," Terri said.

I gave Ryan a stern look to keep it PG, but I wasn't sure he interpreted it that way.

"Terri, truth or da—"

"Dare!"

Ryan chuckled at her enthusiasm. "Go make out with Ginger."

Terri hesitated.

"You said no rules," Ryan teased.

"I've kissed a girl before," she said. She glanced at Allen as she slowly waded over to me.

The first kiss was soft and tentative, but Terri didn't waste any time deepening the kiss and putting more enthusiasm into it—and into me. It was completely silent around us, and I knew the guys were focused on us as our kissing became more passionate. I didn't care if they stared. Terri was a wonderful kisser, and I was enjoying her more every second.

When we finally parted, and she moved back to where she was sitting, she had a look of euphoria tinged with guilt.

"That was great," she said, a little breathless.

Ryan grinned. "It looked great from this angle too."

Allen said, "Do it again."

"Allen, it's not your turn," I responded.

Then Ryan said, "Allen, truth or dare?"

"Dare. And no, I'm not doing anything outside of this hot tub."

"Go make out with Ginger."

I didn't mind being on the receiving end of everyone else's dares. I glanced at Terri, who seemed both hesitant and expectant.

She apparently wanted to see this too. Allen glided toward me through the water and put his arms around me, and we began kissing. Allen was a pretty good kisser, but I definitely enjoyed Terri's lips a little more. But I would never tell either of them that.

After a moment, he backed away with a smile.

Ryan broke up the silence again. "Ginger, truth or dare?"

"Since I know what you're capable of asking, I might just say truth."

"You'd better not," Terri blurted out.

I pinned Ryan with a look to tell him to tread lightly before I finally gave in. "Dare!"

He grinned and rubbed his hands together. I was suddenly regretting my choice. "Okay, Ginger, go over and suck on Terri's boobs."

Terri seemed nervous.

"Are you guys okay with this?" I asked.

"Oh yeah!" Allen replied hastily.

I drifted over by Terri, and she sat up a little higher in the water, fully exposing her breasts. I smiled and gave her a kiss on the lips as I cupped both breasts with my hands to ease her into it. I glided my lips down to her left nipple, circling my tongue around the firm peak. When I closed my lips around the nipple and sucked gently, she threw her head back. I didn't like too much pressure on my breasts and nipples, but I wasn't sure what Terri would like. I sucked a little bit harder, careful not to hurt her, and she grabbed the back of my hair.

I guess she likes that.

I moved to her right breast and sucked on that nipple in the same way. Again, there was an almost deafening silence as I knew the men were concentrating on us. I swirled my tongue around her nipple one last time before straightening to give her a passionate kiss. When I pulled away, Allen's mouth was hanging open.

"Allen, you can close your mouth now," I said with a chuckle.

That woke Terri out of her trance too.

"Wow, that was great. Are you bi?" she asked.

Ryan made a show of putting his hand up to his ear and turning to ensure he heard my response.

"I wouldn't say I'm bi, but there are some women I can really get into," I said, sliding back into my sitting spot.

"Oh, yeah she can," Ryan said. "She says she's bi from the waist up."

I reached over and slapped his shoulder playfully. I had to admit, this was getting fun.

"Okay, Ginger's turn," Terri said, bringing us back to the game.

I wasn't sure how far to take things, so I figured keeping the heat level where it was would be safer. "Allen, truth or dare?"

Allen, of course, said, "Dare!"

I didn't even know why we bothered asking. No one ever picked truth. I had to think for a minute. I was sure he wouldn't want to do anything with Terri, and it felt weird daring him to do something with me. *Oh, I know . . .*

"Allen, I want you to make out with both Terri and me at the same time."

That seemed to be a winner. He and Terri happily drifted to meet me in the middle of the spa. I kissed Allen first, then slightly tilted my head to invite Terri's mouth and tongue. Kissing was one of my favorite things, and kissing them both together turned me on even more.

We all backed away, and Allen said, "Wow, that was really hot."

Terri looked like she was staring into some other dimension with a goofy smile on her face.

"Terri?" I said. "Are you all right?"

She snapped out of it. "Oh, I'm great. Is this what y'all do with others?"

"The swinging lifestyle isn't all about people getting their clothes off and fucking other people. Everyone has their interests, limits, and fetishes. Some just enjoy the environment for enhanced electricity, and then they get together privately with their own partner without sharing the bedroom with another couple. Some go a lot further, and others are in-between. So, it's really whatever you and your spouse want it to be." I took a sip of wine. "But it is an absolute must that both spouses communicate and are on the same page. If not, it can be disastrous."

Both Allen and Terri nodded as they absorbed Everything I said. Then Terri said, "Okay, Ginger, it's still your turn."

"Ryan—"

"Dare!" he immediately shouted.

I rolled my eyes—*typical Ryan.* But I'd give him what I knew he wanted so badly. "Go over and suck on Terri's boobs."

Terri immediately positioned herself, exposing her breasts again.

"Wow, you don't have to appear too eager," Allen said.

"Oh, shut up." She turned to Ryan and lifted her breasts a little bit more. "Come and get it."

"Are you all right with this?" I asked Allen.

"Yeah, I'm fine."

He didn't look totally fine, so I decided to keep an eye on him. If he didn't take it well, I would interject.

Ryan stayed low in the water, his head just above the surface as he waded over to Terri. Her breathing increased, as did her look of anticipation. Ryan grabbed both of her breasts and sucked on one of her nipples.

A look of pure bliss came over Terri's face. While Ryan sucked on one nipple, he caressed and rubbed her other breast, slowly rolling her nipple between his thumb and finger, and then switched again. Terri's hands were in his hair, obviously enjoying every second of the experience.

Allen still looked uncomfortable, while Terri looked like she desperately wanted more.

"Okay, okay, time's up," I said. Ryan could have gone on forever if I hadn't said anything.

Ryan laughed as he backed up to his sitting spot. Terri, on the other hand, looked like she was about to have an orgasm, her mouth open as she watched Ryan leave her. She seemed desperate for more.

We all took a sip of our drinks.

"All right, Allen, it's your turn," I said.

Terri swam up to him, put her arms around him, and they whispered to each other for a minute. Ryan came over to me, gave me a kiss, and slid his hand between my legs, teasing me by rubbing my inner thigh.

Allen and Terri separated, and Terri tilted her head as if searching for the right words. "If we decided to split off with the other's spouse, how would we do it?"

"We would do just that, and stay within whatever limits you want," I said.

Terri went to whisper some more with Allen. Then he asked, "So, if we said no penetration, then there would be no intercourse?"

Ryan knew that was pretty much aimed at him and replied, "Absolutely. We keep to whatever limits everyone is comfortable with."

Allen looked at Terri. "I think we can spend time with each other's spouse in the hot tub for a while, but no penetration."

"But we can still use hands and kiss," Terri said.

"Is everyone okay with this?" I asked to be sure.

Allen nodded. "Yeah, I'm willing to try it."

I sensed he was either uneager to be with me or apprehensive of Ryan being with Terri.

I waded over to Allen, and Terri drifted over to Ryan. I put my arms around Allen's neck and kissed him. He kissed me back and felt up my breasts.

Perhaps he's into me after all.

I glanced over at Ryan and Terri; they were in hardcore make-out mode. I reached down to feel Allen's package, but he didn't seem very excited. I glanced up and saw he was intently watching Ryan and Terri.

I looked over at them again. Ryan was working her up with his fingers. She arched her back, about to have an orgasm.

Allen whispered in my ear, "I think they're fucking."

I looked again. "No, they're not. Ryan's just using his fingers.

"She's never reacted like that for me," he murmured.

I tried to smile without it looking fake. *He is so not into this.*

"Ryan won't break the rules," I whispered. "Come on over here for a little while."

I pulled him into a corner and kissed him again. After a moment, he reached down between my legs. *Now we're getting somewhere.* Our kisses grew more passionate, and he slipped a finger inside me. His other hand roamed over my breasts, and I used my hands to work him up.

Terri cried out with an incredible orgasm. Allen immediately forgot about me and turned around to Terri and Ryan.

Terri was quivering and laughing. Ryan was smiling, his hand still between her legs. Allen whispered at me, "I think they fucked."

"Allen! Ryan would not break that rule."

He called out to Terri, "Wow, you've never gotten off that hard with *my* fingers."

Well, I'm definitely not getting off now. I swam back to Ryan to take a sip of my drink, and then I gave Terri a hug. "Are you all right, girl?"

She put her arms around me and kissed me before responding, "That was fantastic!" She looked over my shoulder at Allen. "And no, he didn't fuck me. I could hear you whispering."

The tension was almost palpable. "Go kiss Allen," I whispered to her.

She waded over and kissed him passionately in the corner I'd just come from.

Ryan and I sat there, sipping on our drinks, watching. Ryan found my thigh again, and I reached over to find him quite aroused. Allen and Terri broke apart and sipped on their drinks.

"What do you think about your first experience?" Ryan asked.

"I loved it!" Terri responded gleefully.

Allen said, "I think it might take some time to get used to."

Terri rolled her eyes. "Pooh on that. When can we get together again?"

"Not sure when we're available next, but we'll let you know." I paused for a moment. "Just remember, it's not all about the sex. It's the understanding between like-minded adults who can relate to each other on a more passionate level from the rest of the world. That's what creates some of the electricity, regardless of where you're at."

I turned to Ryan. "I think it's getting late. We need to get going."

We got out of the pool, toweled off, and slipped into our dry clothes. We exchanged hugs and kisses goodbye, and Terri hugged Ryan for a long time. He made sure to get one last feel of her breasts.

"We need to do this again next Friday night," she said.

We laughed, and I replied, "We'll see. I'm not sure what's going on with the kids, but I'll let you know next week."

We thanked them for the drinks and hot-tub time as we walked to the car.

As we pulled out of the driveway, Ryan said, "Well, I think that went well."

I cocked my head and narrowed my eyes at him. "Really?"

"Okay, so Allen was a little apprehensive, but Terri sure liked it."

I shook my head. "If they're not on the same page, we will definitely not be playing with them anytime soon."

Ryan agreed. As beautiful and hungry as Terri appeared, and as fantastic as she would be to play with, Allen was nowhere near comfortable enough to go down this path. We'd rather keep them as friends than become home-wreckers. We would have to tread lightly with those two.

Later that week, I got a text from Terri:

"Allen and I have had more sex in the past few days than we've had in the past year! Thanks for being patient with us."

Well, that was a promising sign. Maybe we wouldn't be responsible for any marital troubles with them after all.

The following week, she texted again to see if we wanted to go see the Endeavors band again, this time at a different bar. We'd already made plans with Mercedes and Chet for that evening, since Mercedes would be back from her work trip. Terri suggested we ask if they'd like to come too.

I wasn't sure it was a good idea to mix the two sides of our lives together like that. I reluctantly texted Mercedes, told her about the band, and asked about Allen and Terri joining us. They typically didn't care for others to join us, so I hoped for a reason to decline Terri's invite. But Mercedes surprised me and said to count them in.

I stared at the phone for what seemed like an hour before I responded back to Terri and informed her we'd be glad to meet them there. I reminded her that Mercedes and Chet knew absolutely nothing about the lifestyle and asked her to please keep it discreet. Terri said she understood and agreed.

I was still nervous about it. Even more nervous than before we'd gone to the Hitching Post with Chet and Mercedes. Terri had been really excited in that hot tub, and she was definitely into Ryan. I just hoped she wouldn't flirt too much around Mercedes. With the way Mercedes had already asked prying questions, I was sure she'd catch on quickly.

CHAPTER 3

The Wonder of an Egg

Mercedes invited us over for dinner and a pregame drink before we went to see the band. I called Terri and asked if they were interested, but Terri said Allen was out doing something, and they would meet us at the bar.

We brought a couple of bottles of wine to drink with dinner. Mercedes had some homemade pizza in the oven, and it smelled great. Ryan opened the wine, and Chet held the glasses.

"Are Terri and Allen coming over to eat?" Mercedes asked.

"They had other plans," I said.

We toasted our glasses together, as we always did, and took our first sip of the Merlot.

"How do you know them again?" Mercedes asked.

Here we go again.

"We told you we met at the Hitching Post, remember?" I tried not to sound too exasperated. "Our daughter and their son dated, and the kids told Allen and Terri how much we would get along. Last weekend, we met them at the Boat House for some drinks, and they like to sing karaoke. That's about it."

I left out the part about the hot tub, of course.

"Oh, okay. So, your friendship is still new."

"Yes, but they seem pretty fun so far."

"They sound like it," Chet said. "I'm looking forward to hanging out with them tonight."

After dinner, we piled into their car, and Chet drove us to Cartwright's, another old biker bar like the Hitching Post, except the decor in this place had a football theme. The years had not been kind to it, but it didn't have to be a pretty place for us to enjoy the band.

We found a table with six seats not too close to the stage so we could chat. Allen and Terri arrived a couple of minutes later and joined us. We stood up to give each other hugs just as the waitress arrived to take our orders.

Since Terri and Allen hadn't eaten yet, they ordered appetizers, and we all ordered our drinks. Pretty soon, the band started up, and we were all out on the dance floor. There was no point in trying to talk, as the band was so loud we couldn't hear each other. About an hour passed, and the band took a break, so we returned to our table.

"So, Terri," Mercedes said. "Your kids dated for a while?"

"Oh yeah, for a few months, then I guess they parted ways. It was about a year ago?" She looked at Allen for confirmation.

"Yeah, about a year ago," he said. "But he still hangs out with the crowd, and I guess they're still friends."

Terri continued, "But he always said we would get along with

42

her parents, so here we are."

"I hear you guys like to sing karaoke at the Boat House?" Mercedes asked.

Terri looked at me like she didn't know how to respond, so I said, "I told Mercedes and Chet we went with you to karaoke last Friday, had some drinks and laughs, and watched you sing."

Allen exclaimed, "Yeah, but these guys wouldn't sing anything."

"You won't catch me with a microphone to my mouth either," Mercedes said. "And I also won't step foot in the Boat House."

"She might put other things to her mouth, but definitely not a microphone," Chet said with a sly grin.

We all looked at Chet in shock and busted out laughing. Mercedes blushed and slapped his arm.

What on earth? I'd never heard them talk like that.

The band started up again, and we went out to dance. We had a great time, and the music was fantastic as usual. Chet pretty much stood there, holding his beer, while Mercedes danced on him quite provocatively. It was hot to watch her. I danced with Mercedes, and then Terri came up to us, so all three of us girls danced up against each other.

When the band's next break came around, I realized it was 11:00 and suggested we go back to our house for a nightcap. Everyone agreed to the idea. The boys paid for the drinks, and I gave Terri our address. Then we got into our cars and off we went.

Fifteen minutes later, the six of us sat in the living room with fresh drinks and talked about all sorts of random things, all of which led to plenty of laughter.

Then Terri asked, "Have you ever gone to a toy party?"

Mercedes and I looked at each other and laughed.

"Oh yeah," I said. Mercedes acknowledged going too.

"I went to one for the first time last month," Terri said. "My sister hosted it, and I felt so naive. So many things were there, and I didn't have any idea what they were."

We all laughed. I reminisced about the first pamphlet I saw in the mall, which seemed like it had been ages ago.

At this point, the guys were in listen-only mode.

Terri went on, "I've never seen so many variations of a dick."

"Did you see a life-sized arm with a fist, by chance?"

Everyone looked at me with their eyes wide open. My face heated as I smiled. "What? I saw it in a magazine once."

Then Mercedes asked, "Were there any darker items for sale there?"

"You mean like a black dildo? Oh yeah, that was there, and there was no way that huge thing was going to fit inside me. They can't all be that big."

We laughed so hard I had tears in my eyes.

"I meant 'dark' as in whips or restraints. Or maybe ball gags?"

We all got quiet, and all eyes focused on Mercedes.

"What? I'm just curious."

"They had something called a cat-o'-nine-tails, a riding crop, handcuffs, not sure what else," Terri said.

Mercedes seemed intrigued, as though she might have some interests we may not know about.

"So, Mercedes, which of those items are you looking for?" Ryan asked eagerly.

Mercedes looked around at us with a flushed face. "I'm just curious."

Wow. She had never been good at lying. There was definitely something going on with her.

"They also had all types of vibrators," Terri continued. "Some even had remote controls. Not sure how that works."

I looked at Ryan, and he looked at me with slightly raised eyebrows, almost like he was daring me.

"I know how those work," I blurted out, then warmth immediately rushed over my face.

Ryan grinned. "Ginger has this vibrating egg that's pretty fun."

"No way! Go get it." Terri said as she leaned forward with the same intrigue I remembered from that night in the hot tub.

Ryan jumped up and quickly went upstairs.

"Is he really getting it?" Mercedes asked.

I nodded while taking a big gulp of my wine. *Of course, he is.*

Ryan came down with the egg and set it in Terri's open hand as he held the remote. He then switched it on. A look of amazement slowly formed on her face.

"Can I try it?" I nearly coughed up my wine, and the others almost fell over laughing at her request.

"You want to put that in your yoo-hoo and try it?" Mercedes asked. "Right now? Right here? Who's going to hold the remote?"

Ryan said, "How about Terri puts it in, and then she has to guess

45

who has the remote?"

"I like it!" Terri exclaimed as she got up and went to the bathroom.

I shook my head in disbelief. *First the hot tub, and now this.* Ryan gave the remote to Allen and explained how it worked. Chet sat next to Allen on the sofa, and Mercedes sat next to Chet.

Terri came back into the living room. "Okay, it's in." She sat down, got her drink, and looked around expectantly. "Okay, I'm waiting."

Apparently, she could be quite demanding when she wanted something.

Within seconds, she buckled over. We could faintly hear the vibrating noise. "Damn, that's pretty intense." Then it stopped. She looked around and said, "Ryan has it."

Ryan showed his empty hands, and then she buckled over again, setting down her drink. She held onto her knees.

Mercedes seemed mesmerized. "Damn, that looks incredible. I want to try it next."

Mercedes? Really?

After the noise let up, Terri sat back and looked around. She said, "Allen, you have it."

Allen showed his empty hands and said, "I had it the first time."

Chet showed his hand with the remote.

"Chet? You were doing this to me?"

Chet replied with a devilish grin. "You'd better believe it, and it looked pretty hot."

Mercedes stood up and grabbed Terri's hand. "Okay, Terri, my turn. Come with me to the bathroom."

I'm not sure what we'd started, but I would have really freaked out if the men wanted to try this too.

Chet came over and gave me the remote. "She would never suspect you."

Mercedes and Terri came back, and Mercedes was about to sit down next to Chet when I flipped the switch. She lost her balance and fell into Chet.

"Whoa!"

Chet caught her and helped her sit.

"Damn, that *is* intense!" A wide smile slowly spread across her face, and she giggled.

I turned it off.

"Hey, I was enjoying that."

Terri laughed. "I can't believe we're doing this. Have you guys done anything like this before?"

"Hell no," Chet replied.

Then, I flipped on the switch for the second time. Mercedes twitched again, but she didn't buckle over like Terri did. She just had a smile on her face. I could hear the faint buzzing of the egg inside of her.

Allen said, "Mercedes, you don't seem to have the same reaction as Terri. It seems like you've done this before."

Mercedes had her eyes closed and smiled. "This is fairly tame compared to what we've done, but I'm liking it."

I dropped my jaw and turned it off. What did she mean? I wasn't really sure who she was anymore.

Mercedes looked around and pointed. "It was Ryan, wasn't it?"

He showed his hands were empty. Then she reached for Chet's hands, which were empty.

"Allen?"

He raised his empty hands too. She slowly turned to look at me, and I pulled my hand out with the remote.

Mercedes grinned gleefully. "Ginger, you did this to me?"

She came over, placed her hands on my cheeks, and leaned down to give me a kiss. Just as she touched my lips with hers, I flipped the switch on again, causing her to fall into me, laughing.

"I need to get this out." She looked over at Chet. "Then you need to get me home and finish."

Terri looked at Allen. "I hope you're ready to finish me off too."

Mercedes went to the bathroom, and Ryan said, "Wow, this is definitely a big change from past nightcaps."

We laughed as Mercedes came back out. She said she had washed it and put it on the counter to dry. Everyone finished up their drinks and headed toward the door. We hugged and kissed goodbye, but this time, Mercedes gave me an unusually long kiss and rested her hand on my cheek.

"We had fun," she said. Then she grabbed Chet's hand. "Let's go, you have work to do."

Ryan and I laughed as they left. Then I looked at Ryan.

"I sure hope you have another thirty minutes of energy in you, because after this, I won't sleep until I get off."

"Baby, I'll take care of you all right," he said, practically chasing me back into the house.

On our way upstairs, we were already stripping down, and the moment I lay down on the bed, Ryan was on top of me and burying his cock deep inside me.

That little game had gotten me worked up. It didn't take more than five minutes of Ryan's fervent thrusting before the pleasure exploded through me. Ryan came soon after. He rolled over, and I cuddled into him. We lay there, staring at the ceiling.

"What did we just do tonight?" Ryan asked.

I shook my head. "I have no idea, but we definitely opened up something."

We cuddled, caressing each other until we drifted off to sleep.

The next morning, I woke up earlier than Ryan and went downstairs to have some coffee on the back porch and ponder over the previous night. I couldn't believe how comfortable Mercedes was with what we did. Some of the things she said made me question how conservative she was. Maybe I didn't know Mercedes as well as I thought I did.

Ryan came down a little later and joined me with his cup of coffee. "What a night."

I smiled. "I was just thinking about it. Do you think some of the things Mercedes said were a little strange?"

"She was strangely comfortable with the toys and seemed familiar with the BDSM gear she asked Terri about."

"I know! What was up with that?"

Ryan sipped his coffee and gazed into the water. "Maybe there's a side to Chet and Mercedes we don't know about."

While we sat there, I got a text from Mercedes: "We're moving a little slow this morning. How are you doing?"

"Sitting in our robes, drinking coffee and moving a little slow too. We had fun last night," I replied.

Mercedes asked if we were available for dinner. I told Ryan, "I think she wants to discuss last night."

He agreed.

It was almost noon when I got a call from Terri.

"Good morning, beautiful," I said. "How are you doing this morning?"

"We're just getting out of bed. I wanted to call and say we had fun last night."

"That's great, we did too."

Terri asked, "Do Mercedes and Chet play around with y'all?"

"Not at all. Last night was just a drunk fluke." I hadn't expected it last night, and I didn't expect a repeat.

"I guess so, but it was so much fun."

Then we discussed our plans for the rest of the weekend and our plans for next weekend. I told her we weren't sure yet, but we would let her know if we were available.

After a nice lazy day, we went to Mercedes and Chet's house for dinner. When we got there, Chet offered us a couple of beers.

"The steaks are on the grill," he said. "Ginger, you like medium-well, right? And Ryan, medium?"

That was right. I was surprised he remembered that.

Mercedes was working on a salad. She looked up with a bit of a sly grin. "Sooo, what happened last night?"

Ryan tilted his head with a grin that matched hers. "What do you think happened last night?"

"I think we took our friendship to a new level," she replied shyly.

I walked over and put my arm around her shoulder. "So, we had a little adult fun. It wasn't anything more than that."

"Yeah, you're right. It was just some adult novelty fun." After a pause, she laughed. "It was fun, wasn't it?"

Ryan went outside to help Chet get the steaks while I helped Mercedes set the table and put the rest of the dinner on the table. The guys came in, and we all sat down to eat.

Before any of us cut into our steak, Chet asked, "Just out of curiosity, have you ever done anything like that with Allen and Terri before?"

We both shook our heads no.

"We haven't done that with anybody before," Ryan said. "Terri started the subject, and it dawned on me that we had that egg, and based on how drunk we were, I figured what the hell."

"That was crazy, but we had fun," Mercedes said.

The rest of dinner was our simple, usual talk. After dinner, I helped Mercedes clean up, and Chet took Ryan outside to show him a project he was working on. Once the guys walked out the back door, Mercedes practically skewered me with a serious look.

"Last night was surprisingly fun, but are you sure you've never done anything like that with Allen and Terri? They seemed awfully comfortable with y'all."

I wondered if I should tell her the other things we'd done with them, but I still wasn't sure how she would take it, so I shook my head.

"No, we've never done anything like that before. It was just something Ryan came up with, and everyone went along with it," I said.

Mercedes stared at me, squinting her eyes like she was trying to see into my soul.

"Besides," I said, trying to cover up any guilt that might show on my face. "You seemed pretty comfortable with all of it too. And you did say it was tame . . ." I stopped short of actually accusing her of having a secret life of her own, but I let the implication hang there.

She burst into giggles, startling me. "I've got to order one of those eggs for me and Chet. That was really fun."

She hadn't addressed my non-question, but I didn't push it. Because then I might have to fess up about Ryan's and my secret. I hugged Mercedes, and we laughed some more.

When the guys returned, Ryan and I decided to head home. I was pretty tired since I'd woken up earlier than the other three. We gave hugs, and Mercedes kissed us both on the lips before we left.

Ryan and I began our walk home, holding hands.

"See? Everything went well," he said.

"Yeah, almost too well. Mercedes wants to buy one of those eggs."

"Maybe they are a bit more adventurous than we thought," Ryan said.

CHAPTER 4

Another Endeavors Trip

$\mathcal{T}$he next few weeks were more typical, filled with work and family. We searched on the Swing Lifestyle website, a dating site for swingers, to browse profiles and see what events or parties might be looming in the near future. We sent a few texts to some sexy friends with whom we wanted to stay in touch.

On Wednesday, I received a surprise call from Terri, who told me the Endeavors band was again playing at the Hitching Post on Friday night.

"Do you want to go? Chet and Mercedes can come along too."
"It looks good for us. I'll ask them," I said.

Before I called Mercedes, I remembered her birthday was this weekend.

Shoot. We hadn't made any plans, but we often liked celebrating birthdays together when we could. I called her up and told her about Terri's invite.

"I know it's your birthday weekend, but if you don't have

anything planned, it could be a fun way to celebrate," I said.

"That sounds great! I really didn't have any plans other than dinner on Saturday night. We had fun with Allen and Terri last time, so this will be perfect for my birthday."

"Great! I'll let her know and text you with the time."

I sent Terri a text that we were on, and she suggested meeting around eight to get a good seat and a few drinks during happy hour. I agreed and filled in Mercedes on the details. The next couple of days slipped by quickly, perhaps because I was anticipating the weekend. We hadn't been out with friends in a few weeks.

Ryan came home from work around six, and I had dinner ready. I told him our daughter would be at a friend's house for the weekend.

He looked at me with a puzzled expression. "We have the house to ourselves. Why aren't we inviting some of our lifestyle friends over for a little fun?"

"It's Mercedes's birthday weekend, so I thought we'd spend time with her."

Ryan cocked his head. "Okay, how about next week?"

I laughed. "We'll see."

I was the one who had wanted to take a break and spend more time with our vanilla friends. Ryan would have happily had a house party every weekend. I did miss a few of our lifestyle friends. And after what recently happened with Terri, Allen, Chet, and Mercedes, it was almost like our vanilla life wasn't so vanilla after all.

We made sure to arrive at the Hitching Post before eight to avoid the cover charge. Terri texted me that they were running late and asked us to get a table. We found a booth that fit six and ordered our drinks. Allen and Terri came in shortly afterward. We hugged, and I gave each of them a kiss.

Terri's desire for Ryan was quite obvious, as she gave him a kiss that looked as though they might throw themselves down right there on the table. I glanced at Allen, who seemed as perplexed by the kiss as I was.

He tapped Terri on the shoulder. "Okay, okay, come up for air and let's have a drink."

That was a good response. Maybe the jealousy he'd shown in the hot tub the first night was gone. We were in a corner booth, where the seat circled around so we could sit boy-girl-boy-girl. I informed Allen and Terri that it was Mercedes's birthday tomorrow, so we were celebrating.

Terri frowned. "I wish I'd known. I would have gotten a card, or something."

"Mercedes would just prefer a good time with some friends," Ryan assured her.

A few minutes later, Chet and Mercedes came in and walked to our booth. They sat down right away and didn't give us time to hug them hello. They were a little irritated, as it was a little past eight and they had to pay the cover charge.

As soon as we all had drinks, I raised my glass. "Happy birthday, Mercedes!"

Happy birthday sentiments echoed around the table, and everyone clinked glasses.

Terri was sitting next to Mercedes and gave her a nudge. "Did you buy one of those eggs yet?"

"Maybe." She blushed and gave her best expression of wide-eyed innocence.

"Actually, she found a few new things," Chet claimed with a grin. Mercedes just smiled, her face still flushed.

I stared at the two of them, confused again. I'd never seen them open up like this before.

"Terri, did you buy yours yet?" I asked.

"And then some," Allen said before Terri could respond.

"Shhhh." Terri slapped Allen's arm and blushed while smiling.

They were so cute. It was definitely a nice change from that first night in the hot tub.

Soon the band started to play, and we went out to the crowded dance floor. We all danced together, and most of us girls danced up close. And we made an effort to dance up against Mercedes as she danced against Chet. It was her birthday, after all.

I kept looking at Allen to make sure it was okay. I was a little apprehensive about what seemed like flashes of jealousy now and then. Fortunately, Terri and Mercedes switched it up and went to Allen, and then to Ryan too. It was a fun evening so far.

On our way back to the table, we came across some familiar faces: Craig and Theresa. They were lifestyle friends.

"Hi, guys!" Theresa said.

I tried not to go completely deer-in-headlights, as I briefly flashed back to my fortieth birthday party—the first lifestyle party we'd hosted.

We greeted them with hugs only and introduced them to everyone else.

Theresa looked as lovely as she had at the party. She reached over to put her hand on Ryan's arm. "We love this band. We try to see them as much as we can."

Mercedes responded, "I know, right? They're really good."

Craig looked at me, and I wondered if anyone else could see the hunger in his eyes, like he was looking through my clothing. He must have sensed we were a bit uncomfortable, because he quickly took Theresa's hand—the one she'd placed on Ryan's arm.

"Well, we saw you on the dance floor and thought we'd say hi," he said. "We're sitting at the other side of the tavern. Hope to see you guys again soon."

I went up to Theresa and gave her a hug. "It was really great seeing you. Let's get together soon."

"Yes, we'd like that."

We went back to our booth, and Mercedes asked, "How do you know them?"

Ryan jumped in. "They were at a birthday party we went to a while back, and we got along with them pretty well. I think I told you about it, remember?"

I didn't want Ryan to lie, but I was glad he could sound so convincing in this case.

Mercedes looked like she was trying to remember. "Oh yeah, I think so. They seem quite friendly for just meeting them one night."

I shrugged. "They like to hug. It's not like we kissed or anything."

Mercedes had a very suspicious look on her face.

Then Ryan whispered, "Look at the two eighties girls making

out over there."

Everyone's attention was immediately redirected to two girls in their twenties wearing flashy eighties outfits and big puffy hair, who were making out. *Really* making out.

"Now that's hot," Chet said.

Terri concurred, "That is very hot."

I was laughing inside. I looked at Ryan and gave him an appreciative smile for the way he'd managed to change the topic.

We got our second wind and went out on the dance floor again. The band was fantastic. I remembered many of the songs from my younger days. We danced our asses off, and then the band announced they were going on break.

We went back to our booth and plopped down in our seats.

"Damn, I haven't worked out like that in a long time. I'm going to be sore tomorrow," I said.

My laughter caught in my throat, and my heart almost stopped when Jack and Deedee walked up to our table.

"Hi, guys!"

Oh no. We'd already managed to explain away one set of lifestyle friends. *What are we supposed to do now?*

Ryan stood up. "Hey, Jack and Deedee! I'd like to introduce you to our friends Chet, Mercedes, Allen, and Terri. Friends, this is Jack and Deedee." He was on top of the rescue yet again. "We met Jack and Deedee here about a year ago. We were the only ones dancing to a really good band, so we sat in the same booth and talked for a bit. Then we went out a couple of times for drinks. They're a lot of fun."

Both Jack and Deedee picked up on Ryan's cue and reached out to shake hands with everyone.

"Would you like to join us for a drink?" Mercedes asked. "We can scoot over and make some room."

Deedee smiled. "Thanks, but we're sitting with some friends on the other side. We saw y'all and thought we'd stop by and say hi."

Ryan and I stepped out of the booth to say goodbye. I gave Jack and Deedee a hug. Ryan hugged Deedee and shook Jack's hand, and they walked off.

"You met them here at the Hitching Post?" Mercedes asked.

She might be my best friend, but I wanted to strangle her just then. Hadn't Ryan just said we'd met them here? What more was there to say?

"Yeah, it was when you were working long hours and weekends," I said, because I couldn't very well say, *We're allowed to know other people besides you.*

"You sure know a lot of people for only living here, what? Four years now?" Chet said.

"We're nearly empty nesters, so we've been getting out a bit more," Ryan said.

Mercedes shrugged. "I guess so."

Thankfully, the band started up again. We'd all had several drinks by then, and we couldn't help but get back out on the dance floor. When Mercedes wasn't interrogating us about our other friends, the night was fun as we danced and danced.

After a while, Jack and Deedee came out and joined us on the dance floor, and all eight of us danced in a little group. Deedee came over to me, put her hands on my shoulders, and danced with me. Then she went and danced around Mercedes, and then Chet. Chet didn't really dance. He swayed a little bit, and Mercedes danced around him. When Jack danced closer to Mercedes, Chet's face turned dark and serious. He didn't seem to like that very much, so I took Jack's hand and danced him over toward Deedee. I then danced my way back to Ryan. After seeing that little exchange, I thought it best to call it a night.

It was after midnight already, and I thought Mercedes might have had enough too.

"Do you guys mind going back home?" I asked her.

"Yeah, sure. The band is almost done anyhow."

Terri asked, "What are we doing next?"

"I think we're calling it a night and going home," I said.

"I'm not done yet," Terri whined. "Let's go and play with that egg again."

Mercedes and I laughed. As we headed out to our cars, Mercedes and Terri put their arms in mine.

"This was so much fun," Terri said. "Thanks for letting us come out with you tonight."

"It was your idea," I reminded her.

"Oh yeah!" Terri and Mercedes burst into more laughter, and I just shook my head.

"Hey, why don't we go back to our house and sit around the firepit?" Chet said from behind us.

"Oh, baby, that's a great idea," Mercedes said. "Are you guys up for a few more drinks?"

I supposed a few more drinks with just the six of us—without any lifestyle friends—would be okay. We all agreed to meet back at Mercedes and Chet's house.

CHAPTER 5

Playing With Fire

"What's going on tonight?" I asked Ryan as we drove to Mercedes and Chet's house.

"I have no idea. Why don't we just go with the flow?"

"Okay, but I'm not sure about this." The last couple of times when we'd just gone with the flow had been almost disastrous.

We all arrived at Chet and Mercedes's house at the same time. The guys went to get the firewood and prepare the firepit while Terri and I followed Mercedes into the house.

"If we're doing more drinking, I need something to eat," I said.

"We can cook some weenies on the fire," Mercedes said, chuckling over her own phrasing.

I wasn't a fan of hot dogs, but I was pretty hungry and open to anything.

I dug through the refrigerator for some hot dogs while Mercedes and Terri got out some beer and wine. When we went outside, the boys had an inferno of a fire roaring, maybe ten feet high. I was confident it was due to the lighter fluid Chet had in his hand.

Boys will be boys, but the parent in me believed we were so drunk we shouldn't be playing with fire. Chet had music playing through the outside speakers, and we all swayed to his 1980s selection.

As the flames died down, we moved up closer and sat around the firepit, watching the brilliant orange flames dancing on the wooden logs. I took out a hot dog from the bag and put it on the cooking stick, then reached out warm it in the flames, making sure I didn't burn the meat on my stick—or, more importantly, my hand.

I was confident I was drunk at this point, and I wasn't really sure why we were here, but that hot dog seemed surprisingly desirable to me. Mercedes had a hot dog on the fire too. Ryan and Chet just stood by the fire with beers in their hands, staring into the mesmerizing flames. Allen and Terri relaxed on the Adirondack chairs.

Mercedes interrupted our fixation on the fire. "So, how well do you know Jack and Deedee again?"

Again!

"Just like we told you, Mercedes," I snapped, my patience worn thin by alcohol. "We met about a year ago at the Hitching Post, and there was a good band playing, so we were dancing. They invited us to have a few drinks with them at their booth, and we hit it off. There isn't much more to it. Why do you keep asking?"

"I don't know, it just seemed . . . they were cozier than most friends, and then they danced pretty close to me. Maybe I'm just reading more into it, but it just seemed a little strange."

"They're a bit more personable than most," Ryan said.

"I'm sorry if it seems like I'm prying. They just seemed friendlier than most people you meet. I'm sorry, the alcohol is controlling my brain, and I'm not in total control, and I really need to eat this weenie."

We all burst out laughing as she took a big bite.

"Yeah, they are a bit friendlier than most, but that's okay by us."

"Okay, sorry for prying," Mercedes said again, this time with a mouth full of hot dog. "Who wants the first hot weenie?"

None of us said anything, since she had already taken a bite and continued eating it.

I glanced at Terri, who winked, putting a smile on my face.

After a few moments of silence, we all seemed to lose ourselves in the trance of the fire as we sipped drinks and ate hot dogs.

"Mercedes, are your boobs real?" Terri asked, breaking the silence.

Mercedes looked down, grabbed her breasts, and moved them up and down. "Yup, they're all mine."

Then Terri looked coyly to Chet, whose chest and shoulders resembled most NFL linebackers. "And Chet's?"

"You'd better believe it," he said with a grin.

"I wish I had natural boobs like that," Terri said. "I had mine augmented about two years ago, but I think the doc did a pretty good job."

"He sure did," Allen said. "I think we paid a little more than most, but they actually feel real."

Terri asked, "Do you want to see them?"

Chet and Ryan simultaneously yelled out, "Yes!"

Terri smiled shyly, but I was sure it was just an act.

"Go ahead, Terri," I encouraged. "Show us."

She stood up from her chair and took off her T-shirt, and then her bra, and showed off her boobs in the flickering light of the fire.

"They feel pretty good. Mercedes, come here and feel them."

"Terri, I'm not feeling your boobs in front of everyone," Mercedes whined.

"Go feel them," Chet said sternly.

Mercedes looked at Chet and smiled almost submissively. Then she went over to feel Terri's breasts.

What was that about?

Mercedes was quite extensive in her examination. "Wow, they do feel real. Not like some that are really hard."

Mercedes guided Terri over to Chet. "Can Chet feel them?"

"Of course he can."

Chet reached out and started feeling Terri's breasts.

"Anyone else want to feel my wife's boobs?" Allen said, but it was in a good-natured way, and as he asked, he looked directly at me.

I was glad Terri and Allen kept quiet about our experience in the hot tub, but this could get out of control rather quickly. Still, I stood up and joined the rest of them. Ryan was already by Chet, with one hand on a boob. *He's such a guy.*

Terri stared intently at Ryan as he massaged her boob, almost like she was starving for him. I needed to stop that gaze before Allen got upset about it.

I reached over and grabbed both of her boobs. "Terri, these feel really good."

Chet stepped back. "Okay, who's going to show their boobs next?"

Ryan held up one hand. "I could, but I don't think anyone would be impressed."

Everyone was looking between Mercedes and me.

"Go ahead, Ginger," Mercedes said to end the silent debate.

"Right after you, dear," I countered.

"Don't be a prude, Ginger," Ryan said. "Show them off."

Excuse me? Prude? I put every bit of irritation into my gaze as I stared him down. Then I figured I might as well show off the party trick everyone loved to see.

"Okay," I said proudly. "I'll show them."

I got up to where Terri had initially stood in the firelight, took my top and bra off, and exposed my breasts. I threw my bra to Ryan.

"Don't lose that."

I shook my breasts from side to side, then grabbed them for the real show.

"They may not be big, but I can still get to them with my tongue." I pulled one of them up toward my mouth and reached down with my tongue to lick my nipple.

Terri let out a delighted squeal, and both Ryan and Chet gave me a round of applause. I looked up and smiled. *Prude, my ass.*

Terri was laughing so hard that I thought she would pee her

pants. Chet looked at Mercedes.

"Okay, baby, your turn."

"You don't really want me to show my girls to everyone, do you?"

"I'm a proud man and want to show you off. So, pull them out, baby."

Mercedes walked up to where I was standing and took off her top, threw it over the fire at Chet, and then did the same with her bra. She put her hands up in the air as though reaching for the stars. I was impressed. They were beautiful, gigantic breasts.

"Can you reach your nipples like Ginger can?" Terri challenged.

She looked at Terri, then at Chet.

"Go ahead," Chet said.

Mercedes grabbed each of her breasts and heaved them up. It didn't take her much strain at all to lick her nipples. We all applauded.

Mercedes came back to her chair, blushing. "Is that all, sir?"

Sir? Ryan and I exchanged curious glances.

"That was great, baby. You can put your shirt back on," said Chet.

Terri and I put our shirts back on too. Then, there was a moment of silence as we all sipped our drinks.

It was, once again, Terri who broke the silence, exclaiming, "Damn! I like firepit time with you guys!"

"Yeah, I think a lot in our lives may be changing," Mercedes said. She looked at Ryan. "All these years, I bet you've wanted to see my titties, haven't you?"

Ryan blushed. "I'd be lying if I said no."

Mercedes smirked. "I hope they met your expectations."

"Well, partially."

"Partially?" Mercedes said as she snapped her head up, locking him in her crosshairs.

Ryan returned her smirk. "Well, I didn't feel them, so how do I know they're real?"

"Trust me, they *are* real," Chet said.

"I'm just kidding with you. They looked great. In fact, all the boobs tonight looked very delicious."

"Wow, after all of that, I need another weenie," I said, attempting to change the subject.

"That's a great idea," Mercedes agreed.

We cooked up our weenies, drank our beers, and talked. The conversation somehow revolved around Terri's last toy party again. I looked at my watch, and it was three in the morning. Those hot dogs were just what I needed, but after all the beer we drank, I needed to go to bed.

"Sorry to cut short this firepit party, but I need to get to my bed or I'm going to pass out," I said.

Terri finished her glass of white Zinfandel. "What are you guys doing tomorrow night?"

"We plan to go out for dinner," Mercedes said. "Y'all can join us if you like."

"We need to recover from tonight," Ryan said as he finished the last bite of his hot dog.

Mercedes stood up and gave me a hug. "I'm sorry if I was too nosy. I shouldn't be this way to a good friend."

"No worries," I said. "I love you, sweetie."

Ryan shook Chet's hand, and I gave him a hug. Ryan gave Mercedes a very long hug, and I could see him rub against her boobs, which made her laugh. She slapped his chest as he pulled away.

"Could you tell they were real? You're such a guy."

"Yes, he is," I said. "Come on, my man, time to walk me home and put me to bed."

As we walked, I said, "We need to keep these two lives separate. We can't afford another night like tonight. I don't want to lose Chet and Mercedes as friends."

I teared up, considering the possibility of losing our dearest friends to some lifestyle change revolving around sex.

"It really just played out, and we didn't push anything," he said, but he did agree that we needed to be more discreet.

I gripped his hand tighter, frustrated at myself for letting the evening go as far as it had.

"I know, I know. I can't think right now, but I just know we can't do this again."

"You're drunk, baby, and it's making you emotional. We can talk about it tomorrow," Ryan said as we arrived home.

We stumbled into the house, stripped down on the way to bed, and kissed each other good night.

The next morning was met with a pounding head, body aches,

and a layer of fogginess. We got our coffee and went on the back deck to just sit and stare at the water.

After ten long, silent minutes, Ryan said, "Wow. Mercedes and Chet are really close to figuring us out."

I continued staring out at the lake. "I know. We haven't been flaunting it, but maybe we need to take a step back for a while."

"Or perhaps they're curious but don't know how to ask us?" Ryan laughed softly. "We haven't done anything with our lifestyle friends in months for them to be suspicious.

"That would be something if they were curious, but I still doubt it. Let's just make sure not to cross any of those sexual lines with them again."

Ryan agreed. Our friendship was more important than this enhancement to our sex life.

CHAPTER 6

Wine Time

For several months, we spent time with our kids when they came home to visit and our *vanilla* friends. We enjoyed more time with Chet and Mercedes with no other incidents like that night around the firepit. Mercedes didn't ask any more questions about our lifestyle friends either.

We would occasionally text some of our lifestyle friends to stay in touch—something witty and flirty to let them know we were still around. Ryan and I were always very open with each other about who we were texting or talking to. We didn't keep secrets and believed that was what kept us healthy in the lifestyle. We didn't discuss the details of every text message—I was sure Ryan didn't want to see some of the pictures I'd received, and vice versa—but if he wanted to read anything, I would let him, and he would let me read his.

One day, I received a call from Maryann, one of our lifestyle friends. She wanted to know how I was doing and said she and Kurt hadn't seen us in a long time. I said we were focusing on family and our vanilla friends for a while, but we were still trying to keep in touch with our lifestyle friends.

"Lifestyle friends can be vanilla friends too," she said. "Our friendship doesn't always have to be about sex."

For some reason, that was a revelation to me—one that I was embarrassed not to have realized sooner.

"This is very true, and you two have been fabulous friends," I said.

Maryann told me about a wine festival at the Ole Clark Vineyard and asked if we wanted to go with them.

"There will be about ten other lifestyle couples there, so it should be fun," she said.

"I'll discuss it with Ryan and give you an answer tonight," I said.

We really liked Kurt and Maryann. They'd been good friends, with or without clothes on. In fact, we spent most of our time together in a public setting.

When Ryan and I sat down for dinner that evening, I told him about Maryann's phone call.

Ryan finished chewing and said, "Oh, the Ole Clark Vineyard is nice, and they have good wine. Why not? We haven't gone out with that crowd in a while."

I was happy he wanted to. I realized that I missed that part of our life. We had a wonderful life between friends and family, but the lifestyle had added a spice to our lives. The ability to flirt, tease, and socialize with others was something that needed to be experienced to be truly understood.

As soon as we finished eating, I called Maryann.

"Hey, sweetie, Ryan likes the idea of going to Ole Clark's. What should we bring?"

"Great! It starts at one. Just bring lawn chairs, sunscreen, and maybe some wine-pairing snacks. After a few tastings, we plan to hang out in our own little circle with some bottles for a while."

"That sounds fantastic. We look forward to seeing everyone again."

Ryan laughed as I ended the call. "Wow, you look like a kid who's just been told she's going to Disney World."

I simply did what any respectable wife would do in that situation. I stuck my tongue out at him and walked away. Then, grinning giddily to myself, I ran upstairs to plan what I was going to wear.

It was going to be sunny and warm, so I wanted my outfit to be cool, but I also wanted it to be sexy. After half an hour of searching, I realized that I didn't have a thing to wear and needed to go shopping.

I called my friend Lana. "Lana! Are you two going to the wine festival this Saturday?"

"Of course. We try to attend all of the socials and events."

"Do you want to go shopping with me tomorrow to find an outfit?"

"Of course I will. I wanted to pick something out myself."

"Great," I said, feeling like a teenager planning for her first date. "Let's meet at the mall at noon, and we can have lunch first and catch up."

"Sounds great. We've missed you, by the way."

I instantly teared up. "I've missed you guys too." More than I'd even realized. "See you tomorrow."

Ryan and I went to bed that evening, and I snuggled up to him with my head on his chest.

"I've really missed our lifestyle friends. I'm going shopping with Lana tomorrow to find an outfit for the wine festival."

He softly stroked my hair with his fingers. "Find something sexy, baby."

His encouragement and approval of me being sexy had been such a positive influence in my life. I found myself wanting to look sexy for others, but most of all, I wanted to look sexy for my man. I kissed him before he turned out the lights, and we went to sleep.

The next day, I arrived at the shopping mall just before noon. I did my normal window stalking and glanced at my favorite stores.

Lana was standing near the ATM just outside of the food court. We walked up to each other and hugged as though we hadn't seen each other in years.

"Wow, you're looking good," Lana said. "We've missed you guys."

"I know. We wanted to focus on family and our vanilla friends for a little while."

"I understand. This lifestyle is addicting, and sometimes it's hard to get out of it." We went to one of the food venders, bought some soup and a sandwich, and caught up on what we'd missed during the past several months. I liked Lana a lot. She made me feel so comfortable and was someone I could call on anytime.

After lunch, we strolled through the mall. We stopped at a few stores and tried on some outfits. Lana found a white miniskirt and a loose-fitting burgundy blouse that complemented her auburn hair and large breasts.

"What do you think?" she asked.

I motioned for her to turn around.

"Oh yes, your ass looks great! Keep turning."

She turned back and faced me. I glanced around quickly to make sure no one was watching, then reached up and pushed on her boobs.

"Yes, this outfit will do nicely, but you should shock the guys a bit and not wear a bra."

Lana laughed. "I wasn't planning to wear one."

We both laughed. *How fun is this?* I couldn't have this type of fun when shopping with my vanilla friends, or my kids.

I tried on a short gold-and-brown skirt and a loose-fitting top made of a slightly sheer material that felt really nice.

Lana approached me and said, "Bend over a little."

I bent over toward her, and she laughed.

"If you go braless too, you'll definitely give a show every time you bend down for something."

"Hmmm."

"Go for it."

I couldn't believe we were thinking so naughty and that I was devising a way to discreetly show myself off at a public event. Ryan was going to love this on me.

Lana and I walked around some more, window shopping, and

talking, and laughing. Hanging out with her was so rejuvenating. She brought out the teenager in me, something I was sure Ryan would like to come out of me more often. But after twenty years, "Mom" was all I knew how to be. This lifestyle slowly taught me how to live again, as when Ryan and I first dated. Okay, maybe we didn't do *all of this* back then, but we had a lot of fun together, and I really wanted to bring that back to our relationship.

Before Lana and I left the mall, I hugged her. "This was fun. We need to do this more often."

"We absolutely do. I'm glad you called me."

So was I, and I was sorry it had been so long since we'd talked or seen each other.

"See you Saturday," I said.

She winked. "Can't wait."

*****

On Saturday afternoon, I asked Ryan to make lunch so I could get ready for the wine festival. He teased me about needing an hour and a half to get ready for an outdoor festival in lawn chairs, but he did as I asked. *Men never understand these things.*

After an hour, I heard Ryan walking up the stairs.

"I don't want you to see me," I called out.

"Okay, baby. I have your lunch. I thought I'd bring it up since we need to leave in thirty minutes."

"Just leave it on the end table, and I'll get it. I want to surprise you."

I heard him set the plate down, and he said, "You need to be ready in twenty minutes."

For some reason, I was as nervous as a teenager heading to prom. I didn't know why. It was just a wine festival with some friends. I quickly finished getting ready while eating the sandwich Ryan had made me, and then decided I couldn't leave him to pick out his clothing. He probably wouldn't even change. I wanted him to wear something that complemented my outfit. I found his white linen shirt and some black dress shorts. He could wear his deck shoes. *Perfect.*

Finally, I called for Ryan to come upstairs.

I stood in the middle of the open area in front of the bed and waited. A moment later, the door opened, and Ryan walked in. He stopped when he saw me.

"Wow, I like!" He walked closer and zeroed in on my nipples protruding through the thin material of my blouse. He lifted his thumbs up to each one and began to slowly circle them while he leaned in to kiss my neck. Goosebumps rose on my entire body.

Giggling like a sixteen-year-old, I draped my arms around his neck, kissed him, and pressed my breasts against his chest. He pulled my hips against his, and I could feel how much he was already affected. I stepped back and tugged his shirt off, then dropped to my knees with my face right in front of his crotch. I unzipped his shorts and slowly pulled them down along with his underwear. He was aroused, all right. I looked up at him as I wrapped my hand around his cock. He gazed down at me with a look of surprise and anticipation. I opened my mouth and leaned forward oh-so-slowly, maintaining eye contact and prolonging the tease as long as I could. Just as the head of his cock reached my lips, I simply kissed the tip. Then I quickly stood and stepped away, leaving him wanting.

"You need to get dressed," I said. "We need to leave in two minutes."

"You just got me rock-hard, and now you won't finish?" He practically pouted. "Such a tease."

I laughed. "I want you to wear the clothes I set out for you on the bed. I'll be downstairs. We need to go. Love you, babe!" I loved teasing him just as much as he enjoyed teasing me.

The weather was perfect for the festival, around eighty degrees, partly cloudy, with a slight breeze. A great day to be outside. The line at the entrance seemed to go on forever. I sent a text to Maryann that we'd arrived, but it might be a little while before we made it inside.

Maryann immediately called me. "Meet us at the entrance. We have tickets for you, so you can walk right in."

That was the best thing I'd heard all day. We turned around from our trek to the end of the line and went to the entrance, where there was a checkpoint for those with pre-purchased tickets.

Maryann met us there. "Here you go. I look out for my friends."

"Thank you so much." I hugged her tight. "We've missed you." And then I gave her a small kiss on her lips.

"Mmm, I missed you too."

At the gate, we handed over our tickets. They checked our identification and gave us our green wristbands, and then we picked up our commemorative wine glasses.

"Okay, let's go have fun!" Maryann stood between us, placed her arms inside both of ours, and guided us toward the rest of the group.

"We got here early to ensure we got a nice spot in the shade," Maryann said.

There were quite a few people there, many of them good lifestyle friends of ours: Tony and Lana, Sherry and Darren, and Jackie. I recognized the rest from the parties but didn't remember their names.

Lana walked up and gave me a kiss and a hug, then reached down to rub my nipples with the palms of her hands. "Nice, but you need to *keep* them hard like this."

Tony came up to hug me also. "I agree, very nice."

Then Jackie came prancing up to me and cried out, "Ginger! I haven't seen you in so long." She wrapped her arms around me and kissed me—over and over again. We were pretty much making out right there. I enjoyed kissing Jackie. Something about her just turned me on so much.

"No bra?" She looked down and didn't just touch my nipples but fully grabbed my breasts. "You're such a naughty girl. We're going to have lots of fun."

"I really look forward to that," I said.

Ryan and I walked around to everyone, giving them hello hugs and kisses, and reintroducing ourselves to those we didn't quite remember. We realized they had formed an arc with their chairs, so we set ours down to continue the circle.

In the middle, everyone had their coolers pushed together to form a makeshift table, where we placed all of the food. There was hummus, fruit, cheese, crackers, bread, and seasoned olive oil. I stood in front of the coolers, amazed at the variety of appetizers everyone brought.

"This is amazing," I said.

"Yes, we go all out when we go to a wine festival," Maryann said. "Help yourself. We love to *share*." She put her arm around me and squeezed my shoulders on the word "share." A few others concurred with chuckles and nods.

One couple stood up and walked toward the event. "Time to get some wine. Who's coming with us?"

We all grabbed our wine glasses and followed.

There were twenty or so wineries there. We knew some, but there were others we'd never heard of. We started with the ones we knew and liked, so that when we got to the others, we wouldn't mind as much if they tasted poorly.

We were among the flirtiest, carefree groups of people imaginable. It's somewhat like a gang that's braver when surrounded by their own. The workers had no way of knowing we were swingers, but I was confident they had to suspect it. We didn't hide it very well at all.

Someone might drip some wine on their fingers, and a different wife would seductively take the hand and lick it off their fingers.

At one point, someone's wife was up at the counter, with Ryan standing behind her to wait his turn, and she reached back and said, "Get in here, Ryan!" She pulled him up to her ass and then pushed herself back into his groin.

He looked right at me with his hands up and attempted to look innocent. I put my glass up and gave him an approving nod and wink. I was confident he wanted to take her up on that request, literally.

After about an hour, we returned to our seats, this time with a few bottles of wine we liked. Each of us opened a bottle and put it on the community table to share.

Ryan slowed down on his drinking since he was going to drive us home, but I continued enjoying the different wines. I was feeling mighty fine. We ate some of the food, and then I realized two very important people were missing.

"Jack and Deedee didn't make it?" I asked.

"We haven't seen or heard from Jack and Deedee in a long time," Maryann said.

I hoped everything was okay with them. I hadn't seen or talked to them since we ran into them at the Hitching Post a couple of months ago. Maybe they just took a break like we did.

"So, Ginger, when are you hosting the next party?" Kurt asked, and then ducked behind Maryann.

Everyone immediately stopped talking to hear my response. All eyes were on me. My head swam in a haze of wine and unexpected attention. I glared daggers at Kurt for putting me on the spot like that.

"I don't know. I haven't given it any thought. Doesn't anyone else host them?" My birthday party had been fun, but it was a lot of work. And a lot of mess. Not to mention we had been nearly caught by Mercedes and Chet.

"Most of us have kids in the house," Sherry said. "And your house is so great for this type of party."

I looked at Ryan, hoping he would be the one to decline so I didn't look like a spoilsport. "Do you have anything to say?"

"No, sweetie, you're doing great."

I wanted to wipe that devilish grin off his face.

"Isn't there somewhere else we can host a party?"

"We can rent a vacation house for the weekend," Kurt offered. "Maybe get a bunch of us in there to help with the cost?"

I looked around the circle of friends, who didn't have much else to say in support of this dialogue.

"How many would be interested in renting a house for the weekend?"

Almost everyone raised their hand. Of course. Everyone wanted to go, but no one wanted to do the work. *Why did Kurt have to ask me like this in front of everyone? And when I'm drunk!*

"Okay," I said slowly, feeling trapped in the position to set it all up. I paused long enough to give someone—anyone—a chance to speak up and offer a place, or to help coordinate. When no one did, I stared harder at Kurt. I think he knew I wasn't happy with him.

Fine.

"I'll start looking for a place and let everyone know what I find. But when should we do this?"

Everyone pulled out their phones to look at their calendars and started throwing out weekends that worked for them.

Maryann spoke above everyone. "How about Halloween? And then maybe each of us can invite another two or three couples we know for a Halloween party on that Saturday night?"

It took my Chardonnay-saturated brain a little longer than usual to do the math. "That's like . . . forty couples!"

Everyone's eyes lit up.

"Yeah, that will be one hell of a party," Kurt said.

"I'm not sure I can handle something that big," I said hesitantly.

"It's not your house, and we'll all be hosts to help," Kurt said. "And sweetie, I'm sure you can handle *big*."

I smirked at his sly look and attempt at humor.

"Okay then," I said, looking around the group. "Will Halloween weekend work for everyone? And does everyone agree on the party?"

Everyone raised their glasses and concurred.

Did I just volunteer to organize and host a swingers' party for forty couples, most of whom I don't know?

I stared off into the distance, trying to figure out the first place to start. Maryann pulled me up from my chair and put her arms around me.

"Don't worry, sweetie, we'll all help," she said, then kissed me.

I felt a little relieved, but I was definitely out of my league. There were some small discussions on the party as we indulged in more wine and appetizers. The band stopped playing and an announcer thanked everyone for attending. We'd been having so much fun we didn't realize how much time had passed. The event was over.

We all said our farewells as we always do, with a lot of kissing and hugging. Ryan and I walked out to the parking lot with Kurt and Maryann.

Kurt put his arm around me. "I'm sorry, sweetie, I didn't mean to volunteer you like that. I'll help you with the planning."

"I hope you realize you owe me a lot of tongue for this."

"Oh, I'll help him with that!" Maryann exclaimed.

We laughed and gave parting hugs before we went different directions to get to our cars.

We got in the car, but the line to exit the parking area was long and slow.

"Are you sure you're up to planning this Halloween party?" asked Ryan.

"I don't know how it happened. I was drunk, and I just took the lead somehow. I'll look for a place, but maybe everyone will forget about it."

"Oh, I doubt it," Ryan replied with a chuckle.

It was a long drive home. I just stared out the window, wondering what I was going to do. Our first time back with lifestyle friends after our break, and I managed to volunteer myself to organize a large swingers' party. Maybe I liked this lifestyle more than I thought. One thing I was confident about, though, was that I had really enjoyed the day with these friends.

CHAPTER 7a

Back in the Swing

The following day, I woke up early after a restless sleep. I couldn't stop wondering how I got into planning this party. I went downstairs, poured myself some coffee, and sat on the back porch with my laptop to look for a place to hold the party.

We lived in the middle of a vacation area, where there were hundreds of vacation spots within an hour's drive. I found five potential locations, each with eight to ten bedrooms. All five locations had extra amenities we could enjoy. One had a theater, a few had pool tables, one was next door to a Putt-Putt golf course, and all of them had hot tubs.

One house that stood out was a nine-bedroom, three-story house with an indoor pool, but there wasn't much for parking. I emailed my findings to Kurt to see what he thought.

I heard Ryan stirring in the kitchen and called him out to take a look. The nine-bedroom house with the indoor pool was more expensive, but with extra people sharing the rent, it wasn't much more.

87

Ryan said that was the house he would vote for. Kurt emailed back within a few minutes, letting me know that was the house he preferred too.

That following Monday, I called the rental company and made the reservation. I told Kurt he was responsible for half the security deposit if things went sideways. I wasn't new to organizing large events like this, but for some reason, this one really stressed me out. It was far beyond anything I'd ever expected to do when we first got into this lifestyle. I did enjoy the friends we'd made by attending and hosting parties so far. So, maybe it wouldn't be so bad.

Kurt and Maryann coordinated with everyone who was cohosting to ensure they paid their share. Everything seemed like it was going well. Our friends really came through. Ryan and I didn't know anyone else to invite, so we just let it play out with our friends inviting others.

Those two months went by quickly. We attended a few meet and greets, which were gradually getting more popular as we approached Halloween. We had a couple of meetings among the hosts to coordinate food, decorations, and other things we needed in order to stay there for a few days. My experience organizing craft fairs came in handy, and I shifted into automatic mode, assigning tasks and ensuring everything was taken care of.

That Friday, when the first day of our rental arrived, Ryan and I went to the realtor's office at 3:00. As the manager went over the lease with us, all I could think of was the massive security deposit we'd paid and that we would have close to a hundred drunk, naked people there. *Bye-bye, security deposit.*

As soon as we got to the house, I realized the parking availability was even worse than I'd initially thought. If people showed up late, they would need to walk a long way to get to the house. But there was nothing to do about that now. We walked through the house to familiarize ourselves with the layout. There were bedrooms on every floor and a pool table on the bottom floor. The indoor swimming pool was in its own separate room with a wide, concrete floor surrounding it. The water was set to a perfect temperature. A small kitchenette was by the pool, but the main kitchen area featured a large dining table seated twenty.

"Wow," Ryan said as we finished our tour and ended up back in the middle of the living room, where we'd initially set our bags. "You really picked a great house, baby. This weekend is going to be amazing."

His praise boosted my ego and reassured me that everything would go well this weekend. I really had picked a great house. And just thinking of all the fun, attractive, naked people who would soon fill it with laughter and *other* sounds had me more excited for this weekend than I'd been when Kurt first roped me into planning this party.

I walked up to Ryan and put my hands on his zipper. "Maybe my favorite husband would like a quick blow job before the party starts?"

He didn't need to say anything. The immediate look of glee that spread over his face as I pulled the zipper down was my answer. I looked around the room, and then inwardly laughed at myself. We were the only ones there. *For now.* I sank to my knees and reached into his pants for his rapidly hardening dick.

"The others will be here soon, so you need to hurry."

I didn't waste any time wrapping my hand around his length and stroking him as I first licked the tip and then closed my mouth around it. His cock filled my mouth perfectly as I slid my lips down to the base and back up again, following with my hands. Between my mouth sucking him, and my fingers circling his girth, and moving up and down, there was always pressure and friction on his entire length.

Looking up into his eyes, I could tell he was enjoying himself. I could also tell he was close, so I helped him along. "Come in my mouth, baby. I want to drink you so badly."

That was all it took. He grabbed my hair as his cock pulsated against my tongue and shot his thick load down my throat. *Men can be so easy.* I was able to swallow most of it before I gagged and had to pull off.

"Wow, you were worked up a bit. Anticipating anything this weekend by chance, baby?" I grinned and wiped my chin.

Before he could answer, the front door opened.

Kurt, Maryann, Tony, and Lana came walking in.

"Umm, did we interrupt something?" Maryann said, raising her eyebrows.

"Nope, just finished," I said as I stood up. I looked down at Ryan's cock. "Put yourself away, honey, we have guests."

Over the next couple of hours, the rest of the cohosting couples arrived, and we challenged our organization skills as we figured out where to put the food and drinks, made the beds, and put up the decorations. Everyone was excited for the weekend. None of us had ever spent a weekend like this together.

As soon as people started arriving, there were TGIF shots and beer all around. The party had started. To make it simple, we ordered pizza for dinner. After dinner, Tony suggested everyone go for a swim. Everyone agreed and went to get towels, but there wasn't a single swimsuit in the pool area. We all just stripped down to our birthday suits and hopped in, then swam around, evaluating who we wanted to play with first.

An attractive lady named Megan swam up to Ryan. We'd met Megan several times in the past but had never played with her.

"Hello, you."

"Hi!" Ryan replied enthusiastically, and they were soon making out.

Tony swam up to me, put his arms around me, and we started kissing. Neither of us needed to say anything. I'd liked Tony and his wife for a long time, so it didn't take much making out to get my arousal flowing. He caressed my breasts, and I didn't waste any time as I reached down for his shaft, which was already hard.

A guy in a warm pool full of naked women? I would be surprised if he wasn't hard.

Tony leaned down to suck on my nipples, but I was too far in the water for him to do that without drowning. Tony is a big guy, so it didn't take him much to pick me up out of the water and sit me down on the edge of the pool.

He told me to lie back, so I did. As he parted my legs, I gladly assisted his effort. Being exposed to everyone, the tantalizing caress of the air across my open folds was exhilarating.

"Slide down here."

He helped me shift my ass down on the edge of the pool. I bent my knees and rested my feet on the edge. I peered down the length of my body and made eye contact with him as he lowered his mouth to me. The moment his lips touched my swollen flesh, I rested my head back down to enjoy the incredible sensation.

He was aggressive with his lips and tongue as he tasted every inch of me. Then he sucked on my clit with enthusiasm and determination. Every guy had their own technique, and I realized that I liked every one of them. The intensity began to build up in me. He backed off, and I let out a little moan as he slid his fingers into me. He started sucking on my clit again, found that hot button inside of me, and rubbed it with his fingers.

My god, this is incredible.

All my nerve endings were sensitized and sending a constant pulse of pleasure through my body. An orgasm wasn't far off, and the part of my brain that was still coherent told myself to remain quiet and not scream out and make a scene. But then he rubbed me just right, and all I could do was beg for him not to stop.

Within seconds, the dam burst, and my orgasm rushed through me with explosive force. I yelled out instinctively, then cut the sound short. I trembled as he slowly licked me and coaxed the last waves of pleasure from me.

When I sat up, everyone had stopped what they were doing to look at me and Tony. They all started clapping.

Sherry yelled out, "The first orgasm of the night! Yay, Ginger!"

Tony turned around and took a bow. I rolled my eyes and laughed. I was so embarrassed. Once everyone returned to what they'd been doing, I slid back into the water. Tony caught me in his strong arms, and I kissed him and thanked him.

"Your turn," I whispered.

"Everyone switch!" Megan yelled.

Well, bummer. "I'll pay you back this weekend," I told Tony.

"I'm going to hold you to that." We kissed, and Tony swam off.

Nathan swam up to me.

"Hi, Stranger, do I know you?" I teased. We'd met Nathan and Penny at a couple of the meet and greets, and again at the wine festival.

"You will by the end of the weekend," he said.

I laughed. He was very attractive, and I was excited when he and Penny had confirmed they'd attend this weekend. We flirted quite a bit during our preparation meetings as well.

I put my arms around his neck, and we started kissing. Tony had gotten me started off right, and Nathan's confidence was another turn-on. I wanted him. *Bad.* He guided us to a shallower section of the pool, where the water level was just below my hips.

He reached down between my legs, which I immediately parted for him. *He can have me any way he wants.* I didn't usually think that way about men, but there was something about him . . .

"I think you're somehow wetter than the pool water we're standing in."

I blushed. "What are you going to do about it?"

He immediately turned me around, placed his hand on my back, and pushed me until I bent over. It surprised me how much I liked being manhandled like that. I would comply with anything he wanted. I reached out and put my hands on the edge of the pool for support.

He nudged my legs apart and wasted no time sliding into me.

He was right, I was extremely wet. A confident man taking me was so thrilling. I whimpered out a small gasp as his balls slapped against my clit. He had one hand on my shoulder and fucked me vigorously. He reached down and grabbed my breasts with his other hand.

He kept slamming that rock-hard cock into me so fast. Electricity coursed throughout my body. I wanted to come again so badly, but I didn't want to make a scene again. I looked down through the water and saw his balls swaying between my legs each time he bottomed out in me. I reached one hand back, and as I engulfed them in my palm, he yelled out, "Whoa, I'm coming!"

I grabbed onto the pool edge again, and he gripped my hips, holding me in place. The sensation of his thick cock pulsating inside me sent the electricity shooting over the edge. My legs shook with my orgasm, and my body shuddered as he held himself deep inside me and finished unloading into me.

Once he pulled out, I turned around.

"What did you think you were doing?" he asked.

"What did I do?" I laughed and tried to look innocent.

"I had my rhythm all set to avoid coming too quickly, and then you grabbed my balls and I lost control. I'm really not a minute-man."

I started to laugh hysterically.

"It's not funny," he said, but then he laughed too.

"Everyone switch!" Megan called again.

"Great, I'm already spent," Nathan said.

I couldn't help but keep laughing. I hadn't meant to ruin his fun.

"If you want, I'll get out of the pool with you. I could use a drink."

"Sure, let's go."

I walked over to where Ryan was sitting. Lana was just leaving him.

"Did Ryan take care of you?" I asked.

She replied with a happy grin. "As always!"

"Good hubby, taking care of my friend." I giggled. "I'm going upstairs with Nathan to get a drink."

Ryan nodded. Then Nathan's wife, Penny, swam up to Ryan. She was tall and had very large breasts, which I knew Ryan loved, and a great smile. I leaned over and kissed them both.

"Enjoy each other, and don't let him get away without completely satisfying you!"

"Oh, then he's going to be here for a very long time," Penny said with a determined grin.

I smirked at Ryan and walked upstairs to the kitchen with Nathan.

Ryan

Megan waded up to me, and we were soon making out. At thirty-two years old, she was a bit younger than most of us, with long dark hair and a beautiful face. I could remember every time I'd kissed her hello or goodbye. Each time, I felt compelled to kiss her longer. She had a soft, slow, romantic kiss that could just melt you.

I was thrilled that I got to enjoy more of those kisses now. Her naked body pressed against mine had me firing on all cylinders already. I caressed her gorgeous breasts. The water was shallow enough that I could lean down to suck on her nipples. The moment my lips closed around one, she grabbed at my hair.

"Sorry," she said, letting go again. "I just have very sensitive nipples, but I do love it when you suck on them."

I smiled and continued gently. She reached down and stroked my rock-hard dick as I alternated between sucking the nipple on each of her soft, beautiful breasts. Eventually, she pressed herself against me, wrapping her legs around my waist and her arms around my neck.

She kissed me and then whispered, "Now what are you going to do?"

It didn't take a genius to know what she wanted. I reached down and guided my hard cock into her entrance. She stared into my eyes, her mouth open with pleasure as I pushed myself in farther. As I pushed all the way in, she arched her back so far that I thought she would hit her head on the edge of the pool.

I grabbed the back of her head and pulled her back up to me.

"I was hoping you would feel like this." Her voice was breathy and soft. "I've been waiting to feel you inside me since we first met."

Fuck, that's hot to hear. I thrust up into her and pulled her mouth to mine. We made out and fucked, but I quickly learned that having sex in a pool while standing was not as easy as it looked. I moved over and pushed Megan against the wall of the pool so I could fuck her harder. Her mouth and tongue were amazing. Ginger and I both loved great kissers.

After a few minutes, Ginger's orgasmic cry interrupted the action. We stopped and turned to look at her and Tony, then clapped and cheered for the first orgasm of the weekend.

"What would happen if I yelled switch?" Megan whispered into my ear. "There's a pool full of naked people. Why not take advantage of it?"

"Let's find out," I said.

"But later, I want to pick up where we left off." She kissed me, then yelled out, "Everyone switch!"

She drifted away, smiling.

Lana was the next woman to swim up to me, and just like with Megan, we jumped right into making out like teenagers. *How amazing is this?* How could anyone not enjoy this with good friends? So many people had no idea what they were missing.

Lana suggested we go to the corner of the pool, where I could sit on the steps. We waded over, and I sat down.

"This is good. I can slide down on you much easier here."

She stood above me and slowly lowered herself down, giving me an incredible view as her pussy lips parted and my cock disappeared inside her. As she began to ride me, I grabbed her ample breasts and brought my mouth to them. Her slick heat sheathed my cock over and over. She lifted my face away from her breasts and leaned down to kiss me again, our tongues sliding against each other in a dance. Her hips rose and fell as she fucked me faster. She was in control in this position, and I was just along for the ride. *Literally.*

Lana gripped my shoulders and shifted her feet onto a higher step behind me. I placed my hands on her back, supporting her so she wouldn't fall back into the water. She rode me so hard that the waves spread throughout the pool. After a minute, her face contorted with an intense expression, and she suddenly stopped as her inner walls pulsed around me. She was much quieter as she came than Ginger had been, but that look on her face said it all. She draped her arms around my neck and leaned toward me again, slowly kissing me as she relaxed. She gyrated her hips, keeping my cock deep inside her, making sure I hit every spot she wanted. I groaned into her mouth at the incredible sensation.

"Thanks," Lana whispered. "I've been looking forward to this for a couple of weeks now."

My ego puffed up slightly to think she'd been looking forward to being with me.

"Everyone switch!" Megan yelled out.

Lana laughed. "Again?"

After she swam away, Ginger came over and said she was going upstairs to the kitchen with Nathan. I was hesitant about her going alone, but then she said she wouldn't play until I was with her again.

Just as I was considering getting out of the pool myself, a tall, gorgeous woman with short blonde hair and fantastically large breasts—and I do mean fantastic—came up to me and said hello. I knew I'd seen her around, but I couldn't think of her name just then.

Ginger kissed her, and then me, and said, "Enjoy each other, and don't let him get away without completely satisfying you!"

"Oh, then he's going to be here for a very long time."

Ginger grinned as she left us.

This lovely lady put her arms around me and asked, "Remember my name?"

I was trying fervently to remember. We'd met at a couple of meet and greets, and she was definitely at the wine festival. But I still couldn't remember.

She kissed my neck before whispering, "It's Penny."

"I'm sorry I didn't remember your name, but I definitely remember you."

"Great recovery." Then her mouth descended on mine.

Kissing Penny was intense and aggressive, different from most women I'd been with before. It was more like a fight between our tongues along with some lip-biting. Several times, she ran her fingers through my hair and then pulled it. Ginger never pulled my hair. But I had to admit the sudden intensity of it was exciting and kept me rock hard beneath the water. I was beginning to like Penny's style of kissing very much.

I kissed her neck and then ran my upper teeth between her shoulder and earlobe. She pulled back and pinned me with an intense stare.

"Get up on the top step," she demanded, and I didn't think twice about complying.

I climbed backward up a couple of steps and sat down. She followed, grabbed my cock, and instantly put it to the back of her throat. The unexpected sensation of being fully enveloped in her mouth had me throwing my head back and then forward again like whiplash. I grabbed the back of her head, and she sucked me in an almost animalistic way that was incredibly erotic. *This woman might eat me alive, and I don't even mind.*

She didn't let me get too used to it before she told me to lie back as she stroked my cock. I reclined on the concrete floor, and she pushed my legs up. She licked and sucked my balls, but then her tongue moved lower and lower. I jumped when she licked my asshole. I'd never felt that before. As she continued to lick me there, I tried to figure out if I liked it or not. I never would've thought to ask anyone to do what she was doing, but I'd be lying if I said it wasn't getting a reaction out of me.

She set my legs back down and asked, "Do you like that?"

"I don't know, really. I've never experienced that before."

"Okay. I won't do it again unless you say you like it."

Damn, I'm worked up. I grinned at her. "Your turn."

We switched places. Penny lay on her back on the concrete floor, with her ass on the edge of the pool. I opened her legs and slowly leaned in, trailing my warm breath across her mound, and then drifted off to her thigh to lick, and kiss, and nibble there before blowing more air across her wet sex.

"Oh, don't tease me like that." She grabbed my hair and pulled my mouth against her pussy.

Inspired by the way she'd devoured my cock, I sucked hard on her clit, unleashing the raw desire she elicited. She moaned and writhed against me, but I didn't let up.

"Oh, Ryan, I'm coming. Don't stop!"

I continued sucking on her little pearl, even as she gripped my hair hard enough to hurt and pulled my face deeper between her thighs as she rode out her orgasm.

She sat up with a bit of a giggle and slipped back into the pool, guiding me down a couple of steps to where there was a little more water. She wrapped her legs around me and leaned back.

"Fuck me, Ryan." Her voice was a sultry whisper.

I may have only been with one other woman as direct and hungry as Penny. It was exhilarating. And all this time, I'd never approached Penny because I had the impression she was too shy and would never play. It was one time I was happy to be wrong about something.

I slid my rock-hard shaft into her, and after what had been an erotic pool experience with three women, I couldn't wait much longer. I let go and fucked her hard and fast, letting a little bit of my own animalistic side take over as I thrust into her. It didn't take long for the pleasure to build to a breaking point.

"I'm coming!" I exclaimed.

"Keep fucking me. Don't stop." She whimpered with each of my thrusts. "Come in me, Ryan. I want to feel your cum shoot in me."

Those words were like electricity through my core. I exploded in her and continued thrusting into her wet sex. She gripped me tight and grabbed the back of my hair. We were both panting, almost gasping for air as I kept pumping into her. Just when I was sure I couldn't stand the intensity of it anymore, Penny moaned, and I felt her body shudder as she came again.

I slowed my motion, and she leaned into me and kissed me again. This time, very softly, not aggressively. Our breathing slowly returned to normal.

"Thank you, Ryan," she said.

She was thanking *me*? I'd never had anyone thank me after having sex. I was feeling very proud. We looked around and realized we were the last ones in the pool.

I said, "Let's go join the others."

Penny agreed, and we went upstairs to the kitchen.

The rest of the evening passed in a blur of naked fun that included Ginger and some of the women licking whipped cream off one another's breasts before hopping up onto the counter to let the men enjoy their whipped-cream-topped "pies".

I saw Ginger take one of the men off toward the bedrooms after a little while, and I smiled to myself. She seemed to really be enjoying herself after worrying so much about setting things up. I thought back to when we first started exploring the lifestyle. She was always so nervous about everything. Since then, she'd come a long way—and we'd come a long way together.

Penny and I sat and talked for a while, both of us still completely naked. It was great to be so comfortable with friends like this, where we could go from sex to chatting—and back and forth between the two—in various states of undress for the whole night, and never be embarrassed or feel the need to cover up immediately. This kind of fun and companionship couldn't happen in the vanilla world.

By the time Ginger emerged again to tell me she was heading to bed, I was pretty worn out. I leaned over and kissed Penny.

"I think I'll join her," I said.

"I think I'll find Nathan and do the same. I'm beat." She gave me another quick kiss. "See you in the morning."

I joined Ginger in our bedroom, and we slid naked into bed together, drawing the covers up. She snuggled into my chest and didn't say anything.

"Is everything okay?" I asked.

"Yeah, it's fine." She let out a little sigh, telling me it wasn't *fine*. "Just frustrated about men who want to play but then can't get it up. Once we're alone, I'm not enough to keep them going."

"Of course you're enough, sweetie. Was it Nathan?"

She laughed. "Oh, no. He was too quick, but that was partially my fault. I want him again, though."

Well, that was a relief. I would love to be with Penny again, but if Nathan had disappointed Ginger so badly, that might land them both on our "no-play" list.

"It was Rob. He went down on me when Sherry started that whole pie-eating thing. Then we went downstairs, but he couldn't get it up. At least he had some good fingers. But considering how often it's happened to me, I can't help but feel like I'm doing something wrong. Is it me . . .?"

"Of course it isn't you," I said quickly, pulling her close and kissing the top of her head. "You're fun, and gorgeous, and very sexual. Some guys just have problems with that, especially as they get older. You would think if they're in the lifestyle, they would get something to help with that. Especially if they want to be welcome at parties."

"I guess you're right." She rolled over, and I snuggled in close behind her.

"I love you so much," I whispered.

She twisted and turned her face toward me. Tears glistened in her eyes, tugging at some caveman protective part of me that wanted to obliterate anyone or anything that made her feel bad about herself.

"Make love to me," she said.

That, I could do. I turned her over and immediately slid my body over hers. My cock twitched to life at the feel of her familiar soft curves beneath me. I couldn't fix someone else's performance issues, but I could make passionate love to my wife to remind her how desirable she was and how much she turned me on. It wasn't the quick play stuff we did with others, but the heartfelt, whole-body-and-mind kind of sex that only two people in love can experience.

We moved together with a practiced rhythm, arms and legs sliding, hands groping, mouths seeking. Ginger's slick heat wrapped around me, urging me toward climax, but I held back until her body tightened and trembled, and the quality of her moans changed, telling me she was close. Then I drove into her with deep, firm strokes until we both crashed over that edge together. Afterward, I rolled off her and twirled the ends of her hair between my fingers as we both caught our breath.

"I love you," she said. "And thanks. I needed that."

I kissed her before she rolled over again.

"Good night, honey," I whispered.

CHAPTER 7b

The Next Day

Ginger

R yan woke me up with a kiss and a cup of coffee.

"Good morning, sweetie," he said.

I wasn't great with mornings, but after an eventful night and his bringing me coffee in bed, I felt pretty good. I beckoned to him with a finger, and he came down and gave me another kiss.

"Is anyone else awake yet?" I asked, sipping my coffee.

"A few, but not many. Nathan and Penny are making breakfast, though. They want you to have some while it's still warm."

That was sweet of them. *I think we're really going to like Nathan and Penny.*

"Tell them I'll be right up," I said.

Ryan left, and I slid my legs off the edge of the bed. When I stood up, the muscles in my body tightened after working harder than usual. I grinned to myself, replaying the events of the night before.

I briefly thought of my disappointing encounter with Rob, then decided not to dwell on the negatives. Today was a new day, and we had a house full of fun, sexy friends. I cleaned up a bit and threw my hair into a scrunchie before heading upstairs to the kitchen.

Kurt, Nathan, Penny, Ryan, Darren, and Sherry were there. Nathan walked up to me and gave me a kiss.

"Good morning, sexy," he said.

That put a smile on my face.

"What a fun and crazy night," I said. Everyone turned to look at me with a smile, nodding in agreement. Nathan handed me a plate with a breakfast sandwich and some fruit, and asked if I wanted some more coffee.

"Yes, please." I held out my cup. "If you're trying to win me over to get down my pants later, it's working."

Everyone laughed, and Penny patted him on the back. "That's my good and thoughtful husband."

Everyone was dressed in pajamas or robes, and we relaxed with our breakfast and coffee, laughing about our adventures from the night before.

Later that morning, some of the women had gone out shopping, and everyone else was spread out, watching television or lounging by the pool. Ryan was in the pool with Maryann and a few others, but there wasn't anyone playing. It didn't really make sense to have a house full of sexually active swingers with no one playing.

I'll just have to do something about that.

I found Nathan. "Are you ready to work up an appetite?" I asked.

His mouth dropped open like he hadn't expected that question, but he quickly answered, "Yeah, let me tell Penny what I'm doing."

"Okay, I'll tell Ryan too. Meet in my room?"

"I'll be there in five minutes."

I went out to the pool to let Ryan know I was going to play with Nathan. He swam up to me and said, "Have fun."

"You'd better be ready after lunch." I kissed him and then walked off, smiling as he stared at me.

I went to my room and jumped in the shower to rinse off. I wanted to be good and fresh for Nathan. I toweled off and lay down on the bed, and a minute later, there was a knock on the door.

"Come in."

Nathan opened the door, then closed it behind him and gazed at me lying naked on the bed, waiting for him. He had this dark, hungry look in his eyes that heated me through. Just thinking about how much he wanted me was turning me on. He walked slowly over to the side of the bed and removed his T-shirt.

"You know, I have some payback for you," he said, removing his shorts.

His half-erect cock fell out of his shorts only a foot in front of my face. He was a little bigger than Ryan in length and girth, and I found his wide mushroom head fascinating. I couldn't help but bite my lip in anticipation.

"Oh, really? Why is that?" I asked.

He slowly moved the head of his cock closer to my mouth. He had to feel my breath on it.

"You got me off too quickly last night, but now I'm prepared for you. You'd better be ready."

His words sent a shiver down my back. *What does he have in store for me?* It didn't really matter. I liked him, and more importantly, I wanted him.

He walked to the foot of the bed, his fingers lightly gliding along the inside of my thigh and down toward my ankle. The light touch sent a shiver down my spine. He slowly crawled up onto the bed between my legs, trailing kisses up the inside of my leg all the way to his goal. He hovered over my sex, blowing his hot breath on me.

"What a tease," I said. "Shouldn't you come up here and kiss me first?"

"The way I figure it, you owe me, so you just take it any way I give it to you."

A thrill shot through me at his words. The way he was taking control excited me. "Nathan, I'm completely yours. Do whatever you want, and I'll do whatever you say."

I'd never even said those words to Ryan before, but it felt so natural to say them to Nathan.

He seemed quite excited about that as he lowered his mouth to my aching core and hungrily sought out every spot that made body twist in delight. When I was moaning and panting, he stood up, leaving me wanting. He moved to the side of the bed and pulled me so the back of my head was hanging off the edge.

"I hope your throat is loosened up."

My heart pounded. I could take Ryan down my throat, but Nathan was a little larger and had that wider head. *He's not even going to let me work up to this. He's just going to thrust himself into my throat.* But I'd told him I would do whatever he wanted.

I smiled. "Just let me have some air once in a while."

I looked up at him, tilted my head back along the edge of the bed, and opened my mouth to invite his large cock into my throat. The head of his cock floated all around my face as he reached down and grabbed my breasts. I tried to follow to capture him with my mouth, but he was still teasing me.

As soon as I relaxed and stopped trying to taste him, he grabbed the back of my neck and pushed his cock into my mouth. I immediately gagged.

And he's not even completely hard yet.

I pushed him back and let him enter my mouth again. That time I held my breath and relaxed. His tip touched the back of my throat, and then he pushed harder, forcing himself into my throat. I continued to hold my breath and concentrate as he began to fuck my throat.

I finally gagged and pushed him back. I sucked in a breath and opened my mouth again. This time, when he pushed himself into my mouth, I grabbed the back of his ass with my fingernails and pulled him all the way in and fucked his cock with my throat, constricting my muscles around him. I could only do it for a few seconds before I had to come up for air.

"Damn, that was hot," he exclaimed. "I could actually see your throat expand as my cock went in it."

I rolled over and dropped to my knees on the floor in front of him. I looked up at him through the tears in my eyes from gagging so much. I began sucking on him again, then sucking his balls, putting each entirely in my mouth one by one, grateful that he was groomed and fairly smooth down there. The way he moaned and threaded his fingers through my hair told me he was enjoying himself quite a bit, and it turned me on knowing how much I was pleasing him.

He picked me up and bent me over the dresser. He opened my legs and lifted one of my knees up on the dresser, leaving my wet sex completely exposed to the cool air. Then he was behind me, cock pressing against my entrance, and then sliding into me in torturously slow increments. It was exhilarating to feel his thick head stretch me open. I was so wet, and he slid easily inside me. I only had a moment to appreciate the fullness of his cock fully inside me before he pulled back and started to fuck me.

He started off slow, but soon he picked up his pace. The way he filled me felt more intense with every thrust. I had one hand on the dresser top and the other on the mirror as he pounded into me for several minutes. I just had to hang on for leverage. He was doing all the work. And it felt amazing the way he drove into me over and over, the tip of his cock stroking just the right spot.

He pulled out and spun me around, then picked me up and set my ass on the dresser before I could gasp in surprise. He opened my legs, pushed my knees up, and thrust into me again. This time, he grabbed the back of my hair and pulled.

"Not so hard!" I yelped out.

He eased up and leaned in to kiss me as he fucked me. I liked kissing a lot.

Nathan was really using my body, and I was enjoying every part of it. I never thought being taken and used this way could be so exciting. Then I got another exciting idea. Another way to be completely at his mercy.

"The swing is in the other room," I whispered with a smirk.

He grinned, and when he pulled out of me, I was almost sorry I'd suggested it because I immediately wanted him back inside me. He took my hand, and I followed him to the swing. He helped me into the seat, and then picked up my right leg and put my foot in the stirrup. He then slowly caressed my thigh all the way down to my slick heat. Then he picked up my left leg and did the same, then knelt and buried his mouth in my drenched slit.

I was on fire. I held on to the bar above me and threw my head back, enjoying every stroke of his tongue. Like before, he worked me up until I writhed and moaned, and then stopped. I glanced down to see his mouth coated in my sweet nectar. He stood up and moved himself between my legs. My entire body was nearly immobilized with my legs in the stirrups. I was completely exposed to him.

I looked into his eyes, my mouth open in anticipation. He stared back, then quickly thrust himself into me. It was like a bolt of lightning penetrating my core. I held on to the metal bar above me as well as I could. He grabbed the straps for leverage and pounded into me. With my legs spread and body supported by the swing, and the straps for him to hold onto, he could go deeper and harder than before, and my body threatened to erupt with pleasure.

I arched back and just gave myself to him. Each thrust had him bottoming out, but the hint of pain was overwhelmed by ecstasy. Soon, I felt the electricity swell and try to erupt within me, but I couldn't move while in the stirrups, and the orgasm stayed just beneath the surface, waiting for the right movement to set it free. Doubt and hope ran through my mind on whether I'd be able to come like this.

Nathan continued thrusting into me, and it was almost too much. I was having a sensory overload like I'd rarely had before. I let go of the bar and reached around to grab Nathan's ass, wanting him to give me everything he had. My fingernails dug into his skin. He pushed into me and held himself there as I quivered. When I felt his cock pulse inside me, it finally sent me over the edge, unleashing my pent-up orgasm. I cried out, my voice eclipsing Nathan's groans as we both trembled with the force of our orgasms.

After I relaxed, I asked him, "Did you come?"

"Oh my god, did I come. I'm afraid of pulling out, since there's no towel on the floor."

"It's a rental. We'll clean it up later."

Nathan kissed me. "I hope I made up for last night?"

"And then some."

As he slowly pulled out of me, we saw others walking down the stairs to see what was going on.

"Damn, I knew that was Ginger's voice," Sherry exclaimed. "But Nathan? Good job!"

As everyone started clapping, I climbed out of the swing, my face on fire. "Okay, I'll just find a rock to crawl under."

Sherry came up to me and gave me a big hug. "This is what the lifestyle is all about, sweetie. The ability to play as hard as you want, with who you want, and having friends who can understand and appreciate the experience."

I hugged her back.

"Now hurry up and take a shower," she said. "It's my turn with you next."

"I'll need to rest up for a little while after this," I chuckled. Then I looked around and realized someone was missing. "Where's Ryan?"

Penny replied, "We were sitting upstairs, and he said he's heard you get off before."

I rolled my eyes. "Oh, really. Sorry to bore him," I snarked.

I took a shower and dressed in some comfortable shorts and a tank top with no bra. Ryan loved seeing my nipples show through my shirt, and I was sure others would too.

I went upstairs, where I found Ryan sitting on the sofa, talking about fishing with a couple of the guys. I went to get another cup of coffee, and when I looked up again, I caught a few smiling faces aimed at me. I blushed but didn't say a word.

"Wow, you're becoming a legend," Ryan said as I sat down next to him.

The other guys laughed, and I just sipped my coffee. I didn't know what to say. He put his hand on my leg.

"I'm glad you're having a good time."

I squared my shoulders. "Actually, I'm having a great time."

He reached over to give me a kiss. The coffee was nice and warm, but Ryan's kiss warmed me up even more. We'd learned the importance of reconnecting with your spouse after you play with someone else. It's like a sense of comfort that everything is still good.

"Hopefully you didn't wear yourself out," Ryan said. "We still have a Halloween party tonight."

Wow, I almost forgot. So much had happened in the past

eighteen hours that I'd forgotten all about the Halloween party.

Ryan continued his guy talk, and I snuggled into him and stared off into space, daydreaming and reminiscing about that playtime with Nathan. I'd never given up that much control with Ryan. But I actually told Nathan he could do anything he wanted to me and just accepted whatever he did.

And I liked it.

Was I really in the submissive category? Would I do the same for Ryan? I was gaining so many new experiences with these friends, it was hard to imagine going back to a vanilla world. Then I thought about Chet and Mercedes. I would so want to talk about this experience with Mercedes, but I couldn't. She was my best friend, but she wouldn't understand. I had to keep this a secret.

When the ladies who'd gone shopping returned, I got up to see what kind of goodies they'd brought.

Megan showed me some of the Halloween decorations, wall hangings, streamers, some blacklights, and spiderweb material.

"This looks great," I said.

Megan yelled out, "Maybe if we can get the men off the couch to help, we can get this place decorated in time for the party!"

Nathan stood. "Maybe with the right incentive . . ."

"Excuse me," I said. "I think I gave you plenty of incentive a little while ago."

He blushed. "Ah, yup, you sure did. What should I hang first?"

Megan looked from Nathan to me. "Did I miss something?"

I just gave her a peck on the lips. "What do we work on first?"

114

Megan was great at directing and organizing. She had all the guys working on high stuff, such as streamers, or changing out light bulbs with different colors; and the girls decorating tables and hanging pictures.

As I laid out streamers on the pool table, I saw Sherry walk up to Ryan, who stood on a chair, holding one end of a streamer on the ceiling, while Nathan ran it across the room.

"Hmm, something looks like it's just the right height," she said, then pulled down Ryan's shorts and sucked his cock right there. He initially twitched, and I laughed.

"Don't drop the streamer, baby."

Nathan stood up on another chair, taped his end, and said, "Okay, Ryan, you can let go now."

Ryan pointed down at Sherry's head bobbing on him and shrugged like he was helpless.

Sherry put Ryan back in his shorts after a moment. "Back to work now."

There was Ryan, standing on the chair with his tented shorts and a pout on his face. Megan snapped her fingers at him.

"Snap out of it. We have work to do."

We decorated the house pretty quickly after that and finished everything around three. Four hours to go before party guests arrive.

"Wow, all that sucking—I mean decorating—and I'm ready for a drink," Sherry said.

She went upstairs and made a fruity drink for all the ladies. It was good, but wow! Too much of that, and we'd be drunk before the party even started.

Tony started up the music to get a fun mood going. Sherry's drink was doing the trick as she started some provocative dancing around the room, providing a short lap dance to everyone sitting in the living room.

Kurt came up with a set of DVDs. "I've got our visual entertainment for the night."

"What's that?" Penny asked. He handed her one of the DVDs, and she read the title out loud. " 'Swinger Orgies #12.' Well, this fits in with part of our theme."

He had a porn video for every bedroom.

Ryan and I had watched porn before, but I'd never thought of watching it during a party. Maybe it would help some of those guys who forgot to bring a pill. If they were going to a swinger's party, they shouldn't lead a woman on if they couldn't perform.

I shouldn't be so mean. Some of them probably couldn't help it, but still. It was embarrassing and frustrating for everyone involved. Even though I knew it couldn't be helped sometimes, it was difficult not to think there was something wrong with me personally every time it happened. And when they apologized over and over about it, it just made things worse. I was hopeful that tonight would be different from last night.

Ryan and I gave ourselves plenty of time to get ready for the party. Showering, grooming, and a little bit of frisky fondling.

I dressed up in my cute purple corset and a black mini skirt. I had a purple, green, and gold Mardi Gras mask to wear, and of course, my sexy black strappy heels that Ryan loved. After putting the finishing touches on my hair, I emerged from the bathroom to find Ryan in a Caesar costume, complete with gold wrist cuffs and headpiece. He looked me up and down with an appreciative grin.

I placed my hands on my breasts and slowly glided them down my waist, then pulled up my skirt to reveal my bareness underneath. Desire flashed in his eyes. He pulled up his toga, showing me he wasn't wearing anything either. We laughed and came together in a hug and flurry of heated kisses. When the doorbell rang, we pulled apart.

"Game on," we said at the same time, then laughed as we left the bedroom.

Several guests had arrived by the time we got upstairs, so Ryan fixed us both drinks, and we started mingling. We first chatted with Dan and Carrie, a couple we hadn't met before. Dan was a bit shorter than average, average build, late forties, with brown hair peppered with a little bit of silver. He was also in a toga. Carrie was gorgeous in her Cleopatra outfit. She was about the same age, had short, thick blonde hair, was over an inch taller than her husband, and had a massively healthy chest that I knew Ryan was appreciating as we talked.

Like most lifestyle conversations, we started out by learning SLS screen names, how long we'd been in the lifestyle, where they lived, kids, and interests. Dan was great at keeping the conversation going, and Carrie wasn't shy. She kept touching Ryan's arm whenever she laughed. We knew it was a clear indicator of interest after being in the lifestyle for a few years.

About twenty minutes into our conversation, Dan put his arm around me. Ryan glanced at me to see if I was okay, and I nodded. We'd been married long enough and had some practice in this lifestyle to be able to read expressions better now. That was a nice perk to keep things from getting awkward. Ryan didn't need any more encouragement than my nod. He leaned in to kiss Carrie, and they were making out in no time.

Dan looked at me. "Looks like a good idea."

I happened to agree. I angled my body closer to Dan and kissed him. He had a certain level of dominance and confidence in how he kissed, which I really enjoyed. He pulled back after a minute.

"We usually like to play in separate rooms," he said. "Is that okay with you guys?"

Ryan looked at me, and I shrugged my shoulders. "Sure, that's fine with us."

Carrie took Ryan's hand. "Great, let's go."

Dan took my hand and off we went.

Dan led me to one of the available private bedrooms. There were nine bedrooms. Two were for group play, where anyone could walk in. The others were for private play, where people could close the door behind them and not be disturbed. Dan closed the door behind us.

He stepped in front of me, looked down into my eyes, and said, "Hi."

I smiled. "Hi," I said in my best sultry voice. We began kissing again. We made out while standing for quite a while.

I was expecting him to take the lead, but it didn't seem like he was going to.

"Why don't we get more comfortable and lay on the bed?" I suggested.

"Sounds like a great idea."

He started undressing, so I took that as a hint to undress myself as well. He lay down on the bed first, and I crawled up alongside him, where we started making out again.

Dan began grabbing at my breasts, but he would just squeeze them and let go as though they were stress balls. I thought this was sort of strange. I reached down to grab his cock, and it wasn't even close to being hard yet, so I started to stroke him to further things along.

Seeming to take my cue, he reached down between my legs. I opened them to give him access, and he massaged his fingers between my folds. He pushed one finger into me and just massaged around inside. I was starting to think he didn't quite know what he was doing. Before I could say anything, he got on his hands and knees and moved down between my legs.

Now we're getting somewhere.

I spread myself open for him to enjoy. He put his head down between my legs and began licking me. I was hoping his oral skills would be better, but he simply licked up and down my slit and began humming.

I stared at him in disbelief. It wasn't a bad feeling, but his technique and the humming weren't really doing anything for me. He came back up, and we kissed a little more. I reached down to check out his progress, but he was still soft.

"I may need a little help," he said.

"Oh, I can do that," I said softly, even as I braced myself for disappointment.

I went down on him, and began sucking and stroking him. *I know what Ryan said last night, but can I really be that desirable if this keeps happening to me?* I licked his balls, sucking each one, and stroked his shaft. I looked up at him as I closed my lips around his shaft again and started sucking hard. His eyes closed and head back, like he was trying to concentrate. I crawled up to him and kissed him.

"Is there anything I can do to help?"

"Oh, keep going, I'm really enjoying your mouth."

I paused, but then went back down to continue my efforts. *How long am I supposed to keep trying? I could be with Nathan right now.* I continued to go down on him, trying everything I knew to get him hard.

I spent another five minutes trying to get him up, to no avail. I looked up at him again. "I'm trying."

"I know," he said. "Sometimes it just doesn't work when I want it to."

"What would you like to do?" I asked.

"Let's return to the party and maybe try again later."

"Okay." Thank goodness he didn't expect me to waste any more of my time.

I felt a little guilty about my thoughts as we got dressed, but after enough guys who couldn't get it up for me, it began to wear on my self-confidence. He kissed me after we left the room, and I said I was going to get a drink, and we parted ways.

Ryan

Carrie put her arm in mine, and we walked toward the bedrooms.

"Would you prefer an open room or a private room?" I asked.

"Either is fine with me. I actually enjoy being watched."

I grinned. "Let's go to an open room."

"Want to put on a show, do you?"

Laughing together, we went to the master bedroom, which was still unoccupied. We aggressively made out. I groped and gently squeezed her large breasts. I'd been dying to get my hands on them. I wasn't sure just from looking before, but now I knew they were definitely real.

"The zipper is in the back. Would you care to help me?"

Her wanting me to undress her was a huge turn-on. I reached back and unzipped her dress, took her costume headpiece off, and then reached around to unhook her bra. She had a wide bra with several hooks, but I was able to unhook the entire bra in a couple of pinches with one hand.

"You're good at this, aren't you?" she laughed. "Typically, it takes several attempts for most guys."

"You'll find out I'm pretty good at a few things," I mumbled as I continued kissing her, tossing her bra to the bed.

"I'm counting on it." She pulled my toga over my head and saw that I was wearing nothing else. "You were definitely prepared for this party."

It was great to laugh even as we built up the heat between us. Carrie was an aggressive kisser, which I liked. It was very sexy. I pulled her close and leaned in to kiss her neck, dragging my teeth along the sensitive skin there. She pushed me back and stared at me for a few seconds with fire in her eyes. Then she pushed me back on the bed. I was already rock hard, my cock standing at attention as if begging for her hands. She wrapped her hands around me and started stroking. Looking into my eyes the whole time, she opened her mouth and drooled some spit onto my shaft while she stroked it.

No one had ever done that with me before. I'd only ever seen it in porn. But I immediately learned the benefit of the natural lubricant. Her hand was so slippery against me now, creating a more intense feeling. Before I could enjoy the hand job much, she engulfed me in her mouth. She locked her lips around my cock and sucked really hard while stroking me at the same time. It felt incredible. Maybe too incredible, too fast. I sat up and dragged her up onto the bed beside me before I could embarrass myself by coming too quickly.

As we kissed, my hands couldn't get enough of her gorgeous breasts. I needed them in my mouth. I kissed down her neck and chest, and then all around her breasts. She had small nipples, which made it more difficult to suck on them, but she still seemed to enjoy it. I then glided my tongue down her belly and continued between her thighs.

She spread her legs and reached down to open her lips, showing me how very wet and pink she was. I immediately dove my mouth between her legs, needing to taste her. I slid my tongue along her slit, dipping between her folds to circle her clit. Her scent was intoxicating, and she tasted so sweet. I dipped my tongue into her, needing to taste more, she gripped my hair.

"Fuck me with your tongue!" she cried out.

I gladly obliged, pushing her legs up and sliding my tongue in and out of her delicious heat. Her hips rolled and bucked, and her moans of pleasure went straight to my dick, getting me harder than I thought possible. I slid my mouth up and surrounded her clit with my lips, sucking on that sensitive spot until she threw her head back with a cry and her body shuddered with her orgasm. I didn't stop until she tugged on my hair to bring me up. She kissed me and licked at her juices on my chin. I loved how aggressive she was.

"Have you had a vasectomy?" she asked.

"Uh . . . yes."

"Great. You can fuck me without a condom and come inside me . . . if you want."

Yes, I want!

When I got to my knees to position myself, I realized a few people were in the room watching. Carrie pulled her legs back, and I sank slowly into her pussy. I was transfixed by the sight of the head of my cock disappearing, then my shaft, inch by inch. I glanced up and saw that Carrie was enjoying the gradual penetration just as much, judging by the look on her face. I leaned down to kiss her as I started thrusting very slowly. Soon I sped up my pace and ensured I was going in as deep as I could each time. She gasped with every thrust.

"Damn, you're a great length," she said between breaths. "You fill me all the way without hurting."

My face flushed. "Glad to please."

"Oh, you definitely please. Now fuck me like you mean it!"

I started thrusting harder, but then I stopped and pulled out.

"Get on your hands and knees."

She gave me a wicked grin before she complied. She seemed to like me matching her aggression. As we transitioned, we realized four other couples were watching us. I worked behind Carrie, pushed her knees apart, and thrust myself into her again.

My aim was perfect, and I slid all the way into her in one push. I didn't hold back, fucking her hard and fast, my balls slapping into her clit with every thrust. I grabbed her hair, pulling her head back.

"Take that cock. Take it all."

"Oh, fuck, yes . . ." Her voice trailed off into a low moan that gradually grew until she was calling out with another orgasm.

I continued thrusting as her pussy gripped my cock with rhythmic spasms. She rested her head on a pillow, and her moans became louder and louder with every thrust. After a couple of minutes, she came again. She slid forward off my cock and rolled over.

"Lay down. I want to ride you."

One of the women who was watching—someone I'd never met before—came over as I went to lie down on my back.

"Can I suck your cock really quick?" she asked.

Carrie looked at her, then looked at me for approval. I was a little bit surprised, but who was I to say no to an offer like that? I nodded.

The new girl reached over and started sucking my cock. I reached down to grab her breasts through her dress, which felt really good.

Who am I kidding? All breasts feel great.

She lifted her mouth off my cock with a naughty slurp. She looked at Carrie and said, "Your pussy tastes really good."

That's really damn hot. She continued to sucked Carrie's cum off my cock and balls.

"Well thank you," Carrie said proudly.

Soon after, Carrie positioned herself over my erection as the other girl held me in place with her hand. Carrie lowered herself down, slowly filling herself with my shaft again.

"I love riding on top. I can get it everywhere I like with someone of your size." She began gyrating, and my cock pressed against her inner walls, hitting different spots as she shifted slightly in different directions. Like I was a plaything she was using to get herself off. And I didn't even care, because it felt incredible.

The other woman hadn't moved far away, and she approached Carrie again. "Do you mind if I suck on your breasts?"

"Only if you're naked and we can play with you too."

The woman quickly slipped out of her dress and panties.

"What's your name?" Carrie asked as the other woman climbed up on the bed.

"Jenny."

Carrie looked down at me. "You don't mind if Jenny joins us . . . do you?"

Jenny looked to be around thirty. She had a pretty, youthful face, long, curly red hair, a slender body, and small breasts. All I could think was that if I got any harder, I was going to rip my skin open. Jenny looked down at me too. She stuck her tongue out and licked Carrie's nipple, waiting for my response. I was nearly speechless.

"I'm in heaven. How could I mind?"

Jenny giggled and started making out with Carrie while groping her breasts. She was small and petite, barely more than a hundred pounds, and her hands couldn't contain Carrie's generous tits. I reached over to feel Jenny's ass. It might have been small, but it was well-shaped and firm.

As I was feeling Jenny's ass, she positioned herself so I could see her wet slit under her ass cheeks. I took this as an invitation and slowly worked one finger into her sex. She was really getting into Carrie, and then started riding my finger.

"Would you like to ride Ryan's face?" Carrie asked her.

Jenny gave me a coy look. "Would you like me to sit on your face?"

"Absolutely!" Forget Halloween. I was pretty sure it was Christmas for me.

Jenny moved around and lowered her completely bare pussy onto my mouth. I began licking and sucking her vigorously. I couldn't quite tell what she and Carrie were doing, but I suspected they were playing well together. It was hard to concentrate on Carrie riding my cock and Jenny riding my face at the same time. Jenny moved her hips more and more, and I knew I was hitting the right spots. After a minute, she started moving faster.

"I'm coming!" she exclaimed just as I felt her sweet liquid roll on my face and into my mouth.

She didn't squirt as much as some, but I'd never had anyone squirt on my face before. It actually tasted very good. I continued licking and sucking, hoping she would come again.

I heard the two of them talking, but Jenny's legs covered my ears, so I couldn't make out what they were whispering.

Jenny and Carrie both climbed off me.

"Jenny wants you to fuck her from behind while I lick her from underneath," Carrie said.

As they were getting into position, I noticed about ten people in the room just watching. We'd really drawn a crowd. I motioned to the empty areas on the massive bed.

"There's more room. It's a swinger's party, folks. Have fun!"

They all smiled, and some moved closer to their partners, or shifted to be able to grope each other better, but no one took me up on my offer. That was fine. I enjoyed being part of the entertainment.

I turned back to the ladies, who had positioned themselves in a sixty-nine configuration with Jenny on top. Carrie looked up at me from between Jenny's legs.

"Let me get you wet for her."

I lowered myself into Carrie's mouth. She swirled her tongue over me, getting my dick nice and wet. I pulled out of her mouth, and then slid myself into Jenny. She shrieked and pushed me back with her hand.

"Damn, you're big. You need to go slower."

I slowed down my motion, leaning back a bit to watch myself slide in and out of her tight little pussy.

Jenny had her face buried in Carrie's wetness, and after a moment, she lifted her head and looked back at me. "Okay, you can fuck me harder now."

I thrust hard and deep into her, and she shrieked again, but this time I didn't stop, and she didn't ask me to. I held onto her slim hips and slammed into her over and over, loving the way her inner walls gripped me.

After a few minutes, Jenny raised her head. "I'm coming again. Don't stop fucking me!"

I did as she requested, and this time when she squirted, there was much more liquid splashing between us. I thought about Carrie, whose face was right underneath her.

I slowed my motion as Jenny calmed down.

She rolled off to check on Carrie. "I'm sorry. I didn't drown you, did I?"

Carrie laughed. I could see her hair and face were wet.

"That was extremely hot, but I could use a towel." She glanced over at the crowd of voyeurs, and someone quickly brought her a towel.

Carrie dried off, and then kissed Jenny. "That was fun. Thank you for joining us."

"The pleasure was mine," Jenny said. "But I think one of us didn't get off yet."

They both turned to me with Cheshire grins. Carrie started stroking me again.

"If you could get off any way you wanted with two women, how would you like to do it?" she asked.

I'd always prided myself on having a great imagination and was always good at making decisions. I must have had a hundred different scenarios developed in my brain over the years, and now that one was playing out right in front of me with two very attractive women, I was stumped.

"Is he your husband?" Jenny asked.

"No, mine went off with his wife."

"Well, he definitely has a good cock."

Carrie giggled. "I know, not many are like that."

The more they stroked my ego—and other things—the less I could think straight. The only scenario I could bring to mind was one I'd seen plenty of times in porn. It wasn't very original, but it was still erotic.

"Carrie, I want you riding Jenny's face and pulling back her legs for me while I fuck her. And when I'm about to come, the both of you kneel down, and I come in your mouths. Then you make out."

The girls' eyes got wide, but they smiled.

"This must have been something he's wanted for a while," Carrie said to Jenny before turning to me. "Did you read this in a book somewhere?"

Jenny and I laughed, and she said, "I'm game."

The two women positioned themselves as I'd described. There were still voyeurs standing all around the room, simply watching. I was a bit turned on by so many people watching our show.

Carrie settled herself over Jenny's face and pulled her legs back for me. Jenny's mound was flushed pink and a little puffy from all the activity so far. Her wet slit glistened, calling to me. I placed the head of my cock at her entrance, slid it up and down through her slit a couple of times, and pushed myself deep into her.

This time, I didn't start slow. I went hard and fast right away. She let out a muffled whimper at first, her mouth full of Carrie's delicious pussy. But it quickly turned to pleasurable moans and slurps. I looked around at everyone who was watching as I fucked Jenny mercilessly, and the excitement of performing for an audience fueled my fervent thrusting.

"I'm coming again!" Jenny cried out.

The sensation and sound of water splashing against my groin and balls was all it took for me.

"I'm ready." I pulled out and stood up on the bed as Jenny and Carrie knelt on either side of me with their faces together. My cock pulsed, and I shot multiple waves of cum into their mouths and on their faces.

Carrie grabbed hold of my shaft, squeezing hard and licking my tip.

"We want to make sure we get it all."

Then she turned to Jenny and kissed her passionately. Their tongues collided and twined together, disappearing into the other's mouth, and then sliding back out again as they licked at each other's lips, lapping up my cum. It was hotter than any porn I'd ever seen.

I looked around the room. Everyone who'd been watching seemed as enthralled as I was by watching the two women make out with my cum in their mouths. Carrie looked at Jenny and wiped more from her cheek, then sucked it off her finger.

I dropped to my knees with them on the bed again and put one arm around each of them.

"Thank you, ladies, for the best experience of my entire time in the lifestyle."

"Our pleasure," Carrie replied. "I should find out if my husband is doing all right. He gets a little nervous at these parties."

"I came with another girlfriend of mine, but I don't think she's having nearly as much fun," Jenny said.

We climbed off the bed, grabbed our clothes, and navigated through the crowd of onlookers to the bathroom to clean up. I kissed them both, and then went out to find Ginger.

I found her in the kitchen, talking to Penny.

"Did you have a good time?" Ginger asked as I approached.

"No offense, baby, but it was one of the best experiences of my life."

Ginger's eyes lit up. "Oh, really?"

"A young lady was in there and asked if she could join us, and we had one hell of a threesome with a crowd watching. We definitely need to keep Dan and Carrie on our repeat list."

"Um, I don't think so," Ginger said.

Ginger

Penny had come over to chat with me after my disaster with Dan. She helped to cheer me up. It was great to have close friends to confide in, who understood the lifestyle issues and helped you bounce back again.

After a long while, Ryan came over and boasted about his wild threesome. I was happy he'd had a good time, but then he looked like I'd told him his dog had died when I shot down his suggestion to put Dan and Carrie on our repeat list.

"What happened?" he asked.

"Nothing happened." I shrugged. "He couldn't make it work, so I didn't have as much fun. I'm glad you had the experience you did with Carrie, because we aren't meeting them anytime soon."

I was a little bitter and perhaps jealous that he'd had a fantastic time when my night so far had been a bust. Ryan slinked away to chat and flirt with others.

I took a shot of peppermint schnapps and told Penny, "I'm going to get me some."

"You go, girl."

All of my girlfriends were so much fun and understanding. I did love that part of the lifestyle. I strolled through the living room and then toward the swimming pool to see what others were doing.

Rob came up to me. "I'd like to make up for last night."

"I'm sorry, I'm looking for someone at the moment." I smiled as sincerely as I could and kept walking. Perhaps it was slightly rude, but I didn't want to take the risk of poor performance again. I wanted my world rocked tonight and didn't want to potentially waste my time with someone who'd already shown me he may not work.

I wonder where Nathan is hiding.

I bumped into Tony and Lana.

"How's your night going?" Tony asked.

I loved Tony and Lana as friends, but at play parties, they weren't very forward. Most of the time, they waited for people to approach them.

"I'm doing well, but I'd be doing better if I found a guy who can perform."

"Oh no," Lana said with a chuckle. "Someone didn't quite work for you?"

"Yeah, it happens. It just sucks because I'm all worked up, and then it happens, and I don't know what to do next."

Lana smiled and leaned close to whisper to me. "Tony's package still works."

"Oh, really?" I reached down to cup my hand over his groin. "I'm not sure about that. He doesn't seem to be working yet."

Lana reached down and put her hand over mine to feel him. "We'll fix that in just one second."

She knelt and pulled her husband's semi-limp dick out of his pants and began sucking him. I watched as he started to get harder.

"Can I share?" I asked, kneeling beside her.

Lana pulled her mouth off him and held his cock for me to devour. There was something exciting about one spouse offering the other to you for your pleasure. I slid my mouth up and down his cock until he was fully hard and seemed like he'd stay that way. He had exactly what I wanted.

"Why don't the three of us find a room?" I looked up at Tony. "If that's okay with you."

He nodded gleefully like a kid being offered a massive ice cream sundae.

We approached one room, where we heard the sounds of ecstasy through the closed door. We went to another, and that was closed too. It was later in the evening, so everyone was getting their freak on. We found one room with an open door. There were two beds, one of which was occupied by a couple. We asked if we could use the other.

"Absolutely," they said.

We shut the door and quickly undressed. Lana and I started kissing. She was such a good friend, and we always had a good time together. She had such great breasts, and I enjoyed caressing and sucking on them as well.

I glanced over at Tony, who was standing there, watching, and thankfully still fully aroused.

"You can join us if you want," Lana teased.

Tony leaned in, and all three of us were kissing at the same time. Mostly tongues moving about, but it was fun and exciting, and my body tingled with arousal.

Tony directed me to lie on the bed, and I complied. He slowly spread my legs. "Time for some dessert." He buried his face between my legs.

While he worked his mouth down below, Lana worked hers higher up. She kissed me, and then moved down to kiss and lick my breasts. I reached up to caress hers too. She lifted up and brought her nipple to my mouth. I gladly accepted and wrapped my mouth around hers.

Tony asked Lana if she would go down between my legs. Lana was hesitant for a minute. I didn't think her bisexuality went that far.

"You don't have to," I said.

She grinned. "Tony and I talked about it, and I told him if there was any girl I'd go down on, it would be you. So, now he's calling me out on it."

"Well, then let's not let him down."

Lana stared into my eyes as she touched me ever so gently, then slowly lowered her mouth down between my legs. Her warm fingers massaged my folds, and then I felt her breath and tongue. *Wow.* She was very slow as she licked through my slit and slowly circled her tongue around my clit.

The sensations heightened at the fact that a friend was going down on me when she normally didn't do this. I relaxed back into the bed and enjoyed the way she paused over my clit to lick over and over. Tony alternated between massaging and sucking on my breasts, and the two of them were working me up into a frenzy of electric pleasure.

Suddenly, the door opened and a woman said, "I'm just looking for my purse. I think I left it in here."

What the fuck!

"Sorry for interrupting, but I'm pretty sure I left it in here." She started searching around.

We just stared at her in disbelief. A man's voice from outside the door said he'd found it. The lady stood up, apologized, and walked out.

"Well, that ruined the mood a bit," Lana said.

"And you almost had me there," I said.

"Well, let me get you there again." Lana grinned as she went back down on me.

I pulled Tony toward my face and took hold of his dick, bringing him to my lips. He happily slid himself into my mouth. I wanted to make sure he stayed hard. I didn't think I could take another disappointment. I closed my lips around him and sucked. I moaned with him in my mouth as Lana brought me to the verge again.

"I want Tony in me," I whispered down to Lana.

She backed out, and Tony stepped between my legs, grabbed them, and pulled my ass to the edge of the bed. Lana looked between

Tony and me, wanting to watch my expression as her husband penetrated me.

I felt his tip against my entrance. I looked at both of them and nodded. He filled my depth instantly. I was very wet, making his entrance inside me relatively easy.

"Yes!" I shouted. "This is what I've been looking for."

Lana leaned down and started kissing me. Tony had a steady rhythm, and he was hitting all the right spots. With him fucking me and Lana's soft mouth on mine, it didn't take long for the fire to rush through my veins. I arched my back and felt Tony stop his thrusting.

"Keep fucking me . . . don't stop!" I yelled out.

He resumed his movements just as I came, my inner walls squeezing around his hard cock inside me. My body shuddered with the force of the orgasm. Tony slowed down as my moans subsided. I put my legs down and rolled over onto my side.

"Let me return the favor while Tony fucks me from behind."

"Gladly!" Lana replied gleefully.

I hadn't yet gone down on a woman, but Lana was someone who I wanted for my first try. And since she'd done it for me, I wanted to return the favor. It was a shame Ryan wasn't there. He had wanted to watch me go down on a woman ever since we started this lifestyle.

Lana positioned herself in front of me and spread her legs. I bent over the bed with my feet on the floor, and spread my own legs for Tony to enter me. Before I could even kiss Lana's thigh, he slid himself in. I paused to accept the sensation, and then focused on Lana again.

I kissed one thigh, and then the other, and then ran my tongue up her slit. She was already wet, and the scent of her arousal was surprisingly nice. I'd sucked on a guy's cock after he'd been with a woman, and I liked that, but I never thought I'd go down on a woman. As Tony fucked me from behind, slowly building up the electricity in my body again, I used my tongue and fingers on Lana. I thought of what other people did that felt good to me, and then tried to do the same to her, noticing what made her moan or twist her body the most. And then I did more of that. I slid two fingers into her as I sucked on her clit. I wasn't sure if I really enjoyed going down on her for myself, but I did know I enjoyed pleasing my friend.

Tony was a champ, firm and steady with his thrusting behind me, and finally, I felt the tendrils of ecstasy shoot through my body. It wasn't as intense as most of my orgasms, but it was still a good one. I buried my face in a pillow next to Lana and moaned into it. I still had my fingers inside her, massaging her inner walls.

"Can Tony come inside me?" I whispered to her.

She smiled and moaned. "Yes."

"Good. I need a man to come in me."

Lana pulled away from me and went to Tony. I heard her whisper something, and then he fucked me even harder. I dropped my cheek to the mattress and reached for the edge of the blankets, gripping them firmly. Tony's intensity worked me up all over again.

Tony yelled out, "I'm coming!"

The feel of him pulsating inside me sent me over the edge, and the orgasm shook through me like an earthquake. He pulled out, and I slid down onto my stomach to let the aftershocks roll over me.

When I calmed down, I rolled over and stood up with wobbling legs. Tony looked exhausted. I gave him a short kiss.

"Thank you. I needed that so badly." I kissed Lana next. "You two are such great friends."

"I'm glad we could help," Lana said. She gave me another kiss. "Where's Ryan?"

I thought for a second, and then it hit me. "Oh wait, you didn't get off! I'm sorry. I was being selfish."

She hugged me. "It's okay. I wanted to see my friend pleased."

"Go find Ryan and rock his world," Tony said. "I'm good to go for the night." He gave me a devilish smile that made my face flush.

Lana kissed me one last time before leaving to search for Ryan. The other couple had left, and we were alone, so I collapsed on the bed again and asked Tony to lie with me for a little while.

"Why did you ask for me to come inside you?" he asked.

I thought for a second. I wasn't quite sure, myself. The sensation of a man coming inside me felt amazing and often helped me reach another orgasm, but other than my own husband, I'd never specifically asked for anyone to come inside me like that.

"I don't know. It was just something I wanted at that time."

"I have to admit, asking me to come inside of you is a trigger where I lose control, and it makes me come almost right away."

"I'm just thankful you're able to get it up," I said bluntly. "I don't think my self-confidence could have handled it if you didn't."

Tony rolled over to face me, sliding his hand along my arm in a comforting manner. "Why, what's wrong?"

"I've had some encounters where a guy would work me up, but

he couldn't get hard. I know it's not me, but a part of me feels like it is me. And on top of that, I don't get the satisfaction I was looking for."

"Just so you know, it's absolutely not you. You're a lot more fun than many women in the lifestyle. You have personality, you enjoy the friendship, you're not jealous, and you like to have fun. Don't think about those other encounters. Lana has had a few of them herself."

I basked in the glow of his compliments. It was nice to hear. "Thank you. That made me feel better."

Maybe that's why I wanted him to come inside me: so that I could feel like I was enough to satisfy him.

I sat up and grabbed Tony's hand. "It's after midnight. Let's go see how the party is doing."

We left the bedroom and saw another couple looking for a room. I felt a little bad that we'd kept the room occupied longer than necessary. I probably should have known that most people were looking to play toward the end of the night.

We checked out one of the group playrooms, where there was a small orgy happening on the bed while a small group of fully clothed voyeurs watched. The couples in the crowd had their hands in various places on their partners, but they were all transfixed by the action on the bed. It was a pile of bodies in various positions with more thrusting, sucking, and licking than I could have imagined. I'd rather be in the pile than just watching and groping, but that was just me. And thanks to Tony, I was too spent to join in this particular orgy, even though I could see Sherry enjoying a woman's pussy while an attractive—and hard—guy really gave it to her from behind. Maybe another time.

I thanked Tony with another kiss and told him I was going to check out the kitchen. As I passed through the living area, I saw that Lana had found Ryan. They were sitting in a large lounge chair, with Lana riding him. I watched for a moment, and she smiled when she noticed me. I was glad my husband was pleasing her.

I walked to the kitchen, where I saw some of the girls cleaning up, so I helped them. It was close to one in the morning. A few other hosts made their way to the kitchen as well. Kurt said many guests were leaving already, but a lot of private rooms were still closed.

The invite said the party ended at two. Hopefully everyone remembered that, because I was dead-tired and didn't want to awkwardly have to chase people out. Ryan and Lana finished, and he came over and kissed me.

"I see Lana found you," I said with a smile.

Lana walked up also. "Yes, I did, and he found his way into me too."

I patted Ryan on the back. "Good boy, taking care of my friend." I gave Lana a kiss and a hug. "I'm glad he satisfied you."

"He always satisfies me."

I lightly slapped her on the butt. "I said not to say things like that! He already tends to have a god complex, and we don't need his ego getting too big."

There was some laughter as Ryan blushed.

"Wow," Kurt said. "If you ask me, that sounds like free advertising for you."

We got most of the kitchen cleaned up. We left some of the food out as snacks for those driving home, and then we lounged in the living room with our own spouses, waiting for the last of the guests to finish. Both Ryan and I had enjoyed our evening, but his arm around me as I nestled into him seemed like the warmest feeling in the world.

We sat and talked quietly about the night so far, how there had been no drama, and how everyone seemed to have had a great time.

"What was up with the people who were just watching?" I said. "Some of them were groping their spouses, but there were many who just watched and didn't play."

"I noticed that too in the group room," Ryan said. "We asked them to join us, and they just smiled and watched."

"Some like the electricity of watching the action," Kurt said. "They work each other up, and then they just play as a couple. It's like live porn."

Penny said, "So, they never play with others? The couple just watches, goes home, and then has sex with each other?"

Maryann replied, "Yup. It's just their thing. Everyone has their own interest in the lifestyle. Some just want that energy for their own stimulation. Some enjoy the adult conversation, maybe some kissing. And then we have the people like Ryan, who loves to jump into a pile and put on a show."

There was laughter around the room as Ryan replied, "Hey, I . . . I . . . I have nothing to say."

"Guilty as charged!" Penny said.

It was amazing to be so open with friends like this. Whenever I brought up sex to Chet and Mercedes, Mercedes would get a little

141

panicky and change the subject. I would have loved for Chet and Mercedes to be in this lifestyle with us—I found Chet quite attractive—but I knew it couldn't happen.

A few couples came upstairs, looked at the snack table, grabbed bottled water, and thanked us for the party, exclaiming how much fun it was.

Sherry came upstairs with a happy glow on her face. She made me smile just seeing her. She sat down next to me and Ryan and laid her head on my lap. "Are we in heaven?"

I laughed and ran my hands through her long black hair. "Sweetie, you bring heaven wherever you are."

She smiled and nestled into my lap. "You're such a good friend."

Kurt went downstairs to check everything out and see if everyone was gone. He came back up a few minutes later and said, "The coast is clear, everyone is gone. The pool area is a mess, but we can clean that in the morning."

Maryann stood up and pointed one finger in the air. "Time to change the sheets," she announced emphatically, then deflated with a sigh. "And go to bed."

The sheets. How could I have forgotten that part? That was the last thing standing between me and sleep.

Ryan and I went to our bedroom to assess things. A few drinks sat on the nightstand, and the sheets were soaked. But that was all that seemed out of place. Thankfully, we'd thought to put the comforter in the closet before the party started. I pulled off the fitted sheet and realized the mattress pad was wet too.

Damn!

It wasn't waterproof. I removed the pad and felt the mattress. It was damp. I looked up at Ryan, and he suggested we flip it. Fortunately, it was one you could turn around.

We put our extra sheets on the bed, got the comforter from the closet, and laid that out. Ryan collected the cups and bottles to throw them away and brought a bottle of water back from the kitchen. We brushed our teeth without saying a word, climbed into bed, and I asked Ryan to hold me.

He wrapped his arms around me and whispered in my ear, "I love you, sweetie."

That was all I needed to hear, and we fell to sleep.

*****

When I woke the next morning around eight, Ryan was already awake and out of the room. I put on my bathrobe and went upstairs to the kitchen. Ryan, Penny, Nathan, Kurt, Maryann, and Sherry were up already drinking coffee in the living room. They all said good morning to me, but I was still in slumberland. I waved and stumbled over to the coffee maker. I poured a cup of coffee and joined them in the living area. Ryan was in a chair, so I sat down by Penny on the sofa.

She leaned over to give me a kiss. "Good morning, Ginger."

"Good morning," I mumbled. "Why is everyone so cheery? We didn't get a lot of sleep."

"But we did get our world rocked!" Sherry said. "That makes me happy."

I smiled. "Yes, it was a fun weekend."

The rest of the host group must have heard us talking, as they slowly walked into the kitchen and living room.

Kurt asked, "Is everyone besides Ginger awake enough to talk about last night?"

Jeez, I'm not that dead. Am I? "Hey, hey, I'm waking up."

Kurt organized an open discussion to recap the weekend. Everyone had positive things to say. The fact that no one brought any drama was appreciated by everyone. No one got overly drunk, and it seemed like everyone had a great time. Penny brought up the fact that we had to throw away a lot of food.

"You don't know what people will bring or what people will eat, so that's hard to guess at sometimes," Kurt said. "We can take home what we want, but most of it will get chucked."

"We need to remember to bring something waterproof to put over the bedding during the party," I said.

Kurt laughed. "You slept in the wet spot?"

"Nooo. We flipped the mattress."

Everyone laughed.

Maryann said, "I'm sorry, that's my fault. I forgot to tell you to bring a shower curtain to put under the fitted sheet during a party."

"Okay, we have one lesson learned," Kurt said. "Anything else?"

"How do we keep people from walking into a private room while we're in there?" I asked, remembering the unwelcome visitor last night. "We had one gal walk in frantically looking for her purse."

"Maybe we should have a *rules brief* at the beginning of the party that everyone should listen to," Kurt suggested. "But some people come later, so not sure how that would work. But we can try."

Overall, the discussion went really well. We learned a few things from the experience and had a great time. Kurt thanked everyone for making this happen and gave a special thanks to Megan for organizing the decorations.

"Well, I'm sad to say this," Kurt said, "but we have about two hours to clean everything up and check out, so we'll see everyone at the Hitching Post next week."

I patted Ryan on the leg. "I'll pack our stuff, and you help clean up the house."

After packing up our things and tidying the room a little more, I changed my clothes and fixed my hair so it didn't scream *just fucked*, and so I could go out in public without embarrassment. When I was done, Ryan came back into the room. I'd left him a change of clothes on the bed. I went to check out the rest of the house and see if anything else needed to be done.

The place looked just like it was when we walked in. Looking around, I could visualize all the fun we'd had in the pool, kitchen, bedrooms, and living room. I smiled to myself, knowing that whoever rented the house next would have no idea what had happened here—and they might even be the kind of people who would frown on such adult activities. Too bad for them. If more people in the world were having sex like we did this weekend, there would be a lot less tension out there.

Nathan and Penny came up to me and hugged me.

"The party's over," Penny said sadly.

"I know, but it was so much fun. We need to do this again," I said.

Nathan said, "We live so close, the four of us need to get together more often."

"Absolutely!" I exclaimed, then ducked my head sheepishly. "Damn, I shouldn't sound so eager. It might give you the wrong message."

"Oh, I think Nathan got the message loud and clear," Penny said, nudging her husband.

He grinned and nodded. *I definitely want to play with them again.* I hugged them both as Ryan came out, carrying our luggage to the car.

Other husbands were walking down with luggage, followed by their wives carrying other bags. They all said they needed to get going and kissed us goodbye. Penny and Nathan followed.

Kurt and Maryann were the last ones to walk out, besides us. I locked the door, and we walked to our cars. I stopped to look back at the house.

"If that house could talk," Maryann said.

We all laughed and said our final goodbyes.

When we got home, our daughter was eating a late breakfast.

"Did you guys have fun?" she asked.

Guilt ran through me, and I couldn't find an answer quickly enough.

"You're hungover, aren't you?" she said.

I smirked. "No, just tired."

She kept looking at me like she didn't believe me.

"I'm going to take a nap," I said. "I'll see you a little later."

"I'm going to the mall with my friends. I'll be back around six."

"Okay. Have fun," I said, then went up to our bedroom to take a much-needed nap.

CHAPTER 8

Back to Reality

I woke up a few hours later to the sound of a text message coming through my phone. It was Mercedes, wanting to know if we could come over for dinner tonight around six. I asked if she minded our daughter coming with us. Mercedes replied that would be great. I figured with my daughter there, Mercedes would be much less likely to ask questions about our weekend. I texted our daughter to let her know our dinner plans. She liked Mercedes, so she was glad to go.

Ryan and I showered without saying a word the whole time, then he made coffee for us to drink as we got dressed. We were moving pretty slow. *I guess a weekend of sex really takes it out of you.*

I made a salad to take to dinner, and Ryan ran out for a bottle of wine. When our daughter got home a little before six, the three of us walked over to Mercedes and Chet's house together. As we got closer, the aroma of grilled meat tantalized us. We arrived to find Chet was grilling some ribs, and Mercedes had made a baked sweet potato dish with cut baby red potatoes and basil, covered with cheese.

I put the salad on the counter and gave Mercedes a hug hello. We poured wine for everyone and sat down to talk. Their daughter, Bailey, came downstairs to join us.

We chatted about what we'd been up to since the last time we got together, what the kids had been up to, and what future trips they planned. We moved the conversation to the dinner table when Chet brought in the ribs. The food and company were fantastic, as always.

After dinner, we poured some more wine.

"We noticed your car was gone most of the weekend," Mercedes said. "Did you guys go somewhere?"

Uh-oh. Here we go.

"They got home this morning, and Mom was hungover," our daughter volunteered.

Mercedes sat up in her seat. "Oh, really? Details! I want details!"

I just sat there, dumbfounded. Perhaps bringing our daughter was a mistake. *Details?* What was I supposed to say? If I told her we and nine other couples rented a house for the weekend and had a party, she'd be insulted that I didn't tell her or invite her. And then she'd really be suspicious.

Ryan jumped in. "You know Jack and Deedee? They had a free weekend stay at the Queen's Court Resort and asked us if we wanted to join them. Dinners were included, and they had a hundred-dollar voucher for drinks, which didn't last long."

He sounded like he'd prepared that story ahead of time.

"We really need to get to know Jack and Deedee better," Chet said. "They sound like a lot of fun."

If only they knew.

"What did you do during the day?" Mercedes asked.

I looked at Ryan in anticipation of the continuation of his story.

"Jack and Deedee had to do the time-share ordeal. While they did that, we just drifted around the grounds, checking things out. We wanted to go to the lazy river, but there were too many kids, and they didn't allow alcohol."

Wow, he is good.

"Yeah, too many kids, I wouldn't like that either." Mercedes looked directly at me and continued, "So, you four slept in the same room?"

She was fishing for something. Fortunately, we both had daughters here, the inquisition couldn't get too bad.

"Yeah, they had a king suite, so Jack and Deedee had the bedroom, and we stayed on the fold-out sofa bed," Ryan said.

Mercedes still stared at me. "Ginger, were you even there? You're not saying much."

I laughed it off. "My brain is still running slow."

"Wow, I guess you really tied one on late last night," Mercedes said.

"We had a lot of wine and did some dancing," I said. That much I could ad-lib. "We were up until two or so."

Mercedes was looking at me with curiosity. "Bailey, honey, why don't you go up to your room?" she said, immediately making me suspicious.

"Can I head home then?" our daughter asked.

I wanted to say no, but I really didn't have an excuse except to use her as my shield. Before I answered, she started walking off, so it didn't really matter what I said at that point.

When the girls were gone, Mercedes said, "So . . . you guys seem to spend a lot of time having fun with Jack and Deedee."

Was that a question or a statement?

"We spend a lot of time having fun with you guys too," Ryan pointed out.

Chet remained silent with a little smile on his face. Obviously, he knew where Mercedes was going with this. They'd been talking about us. It was time to go on the offensive, since defense was no longer working.

Mercedes continued, "I was just wondering if you guys are a little closer to Jack and Deedee than you've let on?"

"Mercedes, honestly!" I let my exasperation slip into my voice. "What is with you lately? We might give a kiss hello and goodbye like we do with you, but that's it."

Mercedes put her hands up, apparently surprised by my reaction. "All right, all right, I just wanted to know. You spend a lot of time with new friends and . . . well . . . you just seem very close to them."

"We have a lot in common and have fun together, just like we do with you guys," Ryan said. "We'll set something up for all six of us to go out, and you'll see then."

Chet said, "Okay, sounds good. I'm looking forward to going out with them."

"I'm sorry for reading into things more than I should," Mercedes said sheepishly. "Yes, we would love to go out with Jack, Deedee, and you guys."

Whew. Dodged that bullet. I was pretty impressed with how we handled that.

"Don't forget," Mercedes said. "Birthday drinks for Chet next Saturday. Allen and Terri are coming out with us. It should be fun."

"We wouldn't miss it," I said.

We finished up our wine and helped Chet and Mercedes clean up. I said I needed to get to bed early, and then I hugged them both goodbye. Mercedes kissed me on the lips again. When Ryan hugged her goodbye, she kissed him on the lips too.

I tried not to show any expressions as we were leaving, because I was sure Mercedes was watching us from her window. I squeezed Ryan's hand and kept my face neutral as I said, "Oh! My! God!"

But before I could continue, Ryan said, "We will discuss it when we get home."

When we got in, we looked around for our daughter but didn't see her. She must have been in her bedroom. We went up to our room, where Ryan finally said, "Wow, that was close. She knows something."

I started pacing. Ryan sat on the bed.

"If they were disapproving, they wouldn't ask with such intrigue, would they?" Ryan pondered.

"Could they be asking because they're curious about the lifestyle too?" I asked.

We'd heard horror stories of lifestyle couples trying to introduce the concept to their vanilla friends, and in every case, it was met with disaster and a loss of friendship. We did not want to risk that. Chet and Mercedes were great friends. To lose them would be unimaginable.

"What if they were already in the lifestyle, and we didn't know it?" Ryan said.

Hmm . . . We'd been gone a lot on weekends lately, and I never thought to ask them what *they* were doing during that time. I'd been more worried about not letting them know about us.

"Would you play with Mercedes?" I asked.

Ryan laughed. "Would you play with Chet?"

I'd seen Chet many times at the pool with his shirt off. He was very stocky and had a lot of hair on his chest and back. The thought of running my hands through that hair or having his entire body on mine had always turned me on.

"Hello? What's going through your mind?" Ryan said. "You would play with him, wouldn't you?"

I smiled slyly. "I don't know, maybe. If they're already in the lifestyle, they may already be comfortable, and it wouldn't change our friendship."

I thought about Mercedes. I loved her as a friend, but now I was thinking about her large breasts, her dark hair, and how much I would love to spend more personal time with her.

"Hello again," Ryan said. "What was going through your mind that time?"

I shrugged. "Just thinking."

"Well, get those thoughts out of your mind. We're not going to risk it."

"Could you play with Mercedes?"

He pondered for a moment, then replied, "I don't know. Mercedes is like a best friend, and I don't want to say it would be like playing with my sister, but I'm not sure I could make 'it' work." He looked down toward his crotch, and I had to laugh.

"Oh, baby, you get hard when the wind blows."

"Ha-ha. I really don't think I could. I would feel way too awkward. Which is why we're going to stop talking about this and stay the course."

I'd always been the one to say 'no way' when it came to the idea of letting Mercedes and Chet in on our secret. But now that I have been thinking about it some more, . If they were so curious, they must already be in the lifestyle, right? And they were both very attractive. And we already had the friendship there that we liked to have with others we played with . . .

"If thinking about them is working you up, maybe you should focus your heat on me for a little bit," Ryan said, breaking into my wandering thoughts for a third time.

"I have no idea what you're talking about," I teased even as I went to close the bedroom door.

When I turned back to him, he dropped his pants.

"I don't know what I'm supposed to do with that." I climbed onto the bed and painted on my most innocent expression.

"No clue at all, hmm?" He covered my body with his and kissed me passionately, sending little sparks of pleasure all through me. Then he went for my neck. He knew all the spots on my neck that made my entire body shiver, and he knew I couldn't handle how it made me tingle when he kissed my neck and shoulders that way. So, of course, that was what he did.

It was too much. I moaned and squirmed and gasped almost all at the same time and tried to push him away. He took my hands in his, pinned them above my head, and darted for my neck again. He wouldn't let up. I started to laugh and tried to use my chin to push his head out of my neck.

"No marks!" I pleaded, and he finally let up.

He shifted to the side but still held my hands over my head. He slid his free hand up under my shirt, cupping my breast.

"Don't sass me again, or I'll have to punish you another time."

For some reason, that thought excited me. "Oh, this is supposed to be punishment? Maybe I need to sass you more often."

He leaned down, and I flinched, thinking he was going for my neck again. He chuckled against my mouth before kissing me deeply. With my hands pinned over my head, all I could do was relax into his kiss and arch my back, pushing my breast into his hand as he gently massaged it. He pressed his body alongside mine, and I could feel the evidence that I was in for a night of passionate sex rather than sleep. Ryan pulled back from the kiss.

"You know, after you have sex with others, it seems like your engine runs pretty hot for a few days afterward," he said.

I really hadn't thought about it, but he was right. The sexual electricity usually lasted a few days after parties like that.

"And you're not liking that benefit?"

He laughed. "Oh, I'm not complaining, just stating an observation. It's definitely a benefit I enjoy."

"You'd better get me naked and enjoy it, then," I said.

He narrowed his eyes like he was debating whether that sass required more "punishment" or not. Then he released my hands and pulled my shirt up and over my head.

We did have amazing sex that night. Slow and passionate, fully enjoying one another's bodies. When we snuggled together to watch some TV afterward, I marveled at how I'd evolved since we got into the lifestyle. Our first fifteen years of marriage, we had a lot of sex, but I would always need to have intercourse to have an orgasm, and I would only have one. Now, I could have one just by kissing, or being fingered, or with toys—and I could have multiple. I thought of how many women out there who hoped to just have one orgasm with a guy and relished the thought of how lucky I was before falling asleep.

*****

Later that week, we met with several lifestyle friends at the Hitching Post for drinks, dancing, and fun. While there, Megan got the idea for a bunch of us to go to the haunted houses in the park on Friday night. Mercedes texted me Friday afternoon to see if we wanted to go see a movie with her and Chet. I felt bad about telling her we already had plans, so I told her we should meet up next week. She never responded.

Ryan and I had a blast at the haunted houses with our friends, laughing, kissing, and an occasionally wardrobe malfunction. It was casual, but there was still that extra special bond between all of us.

*****

On Saturday morning, Ryan and I sat on the back porch, sipping coffee.

"This is what I want from the lifestyle," I said.

Ryan gave me a puzzled look.

"Last night, I mean. Did you see how our friends flirted, socialized, and had a great time together? The hugging, the kissing, the innuendos. I really enjoy that with trustworthy friends who are fun to be around."

"So, you don't want the sex part?"

I snorted in surprise. "Oh, I like the sex. But our friendship with these people makes the sex so much more fun. It's something you could never explain to the vanilla world. I'm not sure I can explain it at all."

"I know what you're saying. I feel the same way, but for me, all I need outside of the sex aspect is you."

He sure could lay it on thick, but I liked it. He got up to refill our coffee cups, and when he sat back down, he said, "If we get too engaged with this rapidly growing group of lifestyle friends, we're not going to have any time for our family or our vanilla friends we enjoy."

"I know. That's my fear." I thought about having to turn down Mercedes yesterday. Would we migrate away from our everyday life? "How many of the couples we're friends with could we call and easily set up a date?"

We went through some names and determined it were more than twenty couples. Wow. I hadn't even realized our circle had grown that much.

"Think about fifty-two weekends in a year," Ryan said. "Subtract holiday weekends, about fifteen to twenty family weekends and vacations, and you might have fifteen weekends left. Now you try to grow your friendships beyond twenty couples, and you need to get creative to see them all."

"I'm quite confident you could devise a plan to get five or six of those couples together at a time," I said.

We both laughed, but he still had a point. We couldn't let this take over our lives. It was initially a simple extension of our already great sex life. *What are we turning this into?*

"What should we do tonight?" I asked.

"Isn't it Chet's birthday?"

I nearly dropped my coffee. I completely forgot about Chet. *What kind of friend am I?*

"You forgot, didn't you? She just reminded us last Sunday at dinner."

"I know. I did forget. But it's been a busy week," I said, trying to justify my slip. "We need to get him something."

"A good bottle of single malt, and he'll be happy. I have a tee time in an hour, so could you run out and get that?"

"Sure."

"Thank you, sweetie." He stood and kissed me. "I'll see you this afternoon."

While Ryan was golfing, I went out shopping to get Chet a birthday card and a bottle of something good.

I stopped at the local liquor store and saw Terri as I turned down the whisky aisle.

"Hi, Terri. What are you up to?"

She gave me a hug. "Probably the same thing you are."

"Well, then it's a good thing we're here together so we don't get the same thing."

"You've known Chet longer. What does he like?"

I showed her a few things he would like, and we each picked a different single malt.

"Tonight should be pretty fun," Terri said. "We'll go out to eat, and then head back to our hot tub for a nightcap."

This was the first I was hearing about that plan.

"Chet and Mercedes don't know anything about our times in the hot tub, do they?" I asked.

"I never said anything."

Whew.

"Great. They don't know about us, and Mercedes can be a bit conservative, so I didn't want them to find out."

"She didn't seem too conservative," Terri said. She dropped her voice as we made our way to the front. "At least, not when you brought that egg out."

"Well . . . she always has been. That time with the egg was a bit of a fluke."

Terri shrugged.

We paid for the alcohol, hugged each other goodbye, and went on our ways.

That evening, we carpooled to the restaurant with Mercedes and Chet. Ryan had already had a few drinks while golfing, and I knew he'd have something with dinner, so this way he didn't have to drive.

I didn't say anything to him about the hot tub plan, because I wasn't even sure Mercedes would agree to it. Why would Terri invite all of us back to their hot tub anyway? I was getting nervous thinking about it, considering what happened the last time. The hot tub didn't come up over dinner either, because some of Mercedes and Chet's family had joined us. We ordered an assortment of tapas to share, along with some excellent wine that only helped me relax a little bit. Toward the end of the evening, everyone gave Chet gifts to open. There were some cool fishing-related items, and the rest was whiskey or bourbon.

Mercedes laughed. "I guess we won't run out for a while."

As we were finishing the last of the wine, Terri and Allen went up to Mercedes and told her about the hot tub plan. They left to get the towels and tub ready, and we could come over anytime.

I whispered to Ryan, "Did you know we were going to Allen and Terri's hot tub with Chet and Mercedes?"

"Uh, no." He looked as shocked as I'd been feeling all day. "Are we going?"

"I think Chet and Mercedes are expecting us to go."

"You know what? If it happens, it happens. Let's just go with it and find out."

I narrowed my eyes at him. "How much did you drink on the golf course today?"

He just shrugged.

Oh boy. We're going to have a crazy evening.

Everyone who was left said their goodbyes quickly. It was a much easier process with a vanilla crowd. Less kissing. Ryan helped

Chet carry his gifts to the car.

"You know Allen and Terri invited us to their hot tub for the evening, right?" Mercedes said.

"Terri told me earlier," I said.

"Good. I heard y'all have gone over there a few times and had fun. We'll stop by the house, get some beer and swimsuits, and head over."

Wait, Terri said what? I thought she'd said she had never said anything. *Oh my god, what else did she say?* But Mercedes had mentioned swimsuits, so maybe she really didn't know what happened last time. Maybe it would be fine.

When we got to Chet and Mercedes's house, we told them we'd be back in about ten minutes after we got our swimsuits and some towels.

"This is a bad idea," I whispered as we walked home.

Ryan put his arm around me. "You know what? It's probably meant to be."

I looked at him and asked again, "How much did you drink today? Or did someone whack you in the head with a golf club?"

He laughed and squeezed my shoulders. "We'll just let Allen, Terri, Chet, and Mercedes set the pace. And then we'll be innocent participants who will be shocked if anything happens."

I contemplated what he said, and it sounded reasonable. At least it made me feel a little better. We put on our swimsuits, put towels and a change of clothes in my beach bag, and walked back. Ryan and Chet loaded the cooler into the car, and then we were off to Allen and Terri's house. Luckily, Mercedes didn't have any prying questions on the short ride over.

When we arrived, the back gate was open, so we walked through the gate, along the walkway, and up to their deck with the spa. Terri was already in her swimsuit, bringing towels out to the table.

"Now the real party can start!" Terri said, hugging me and Mercedes.

Ryan set the cooler down alongside the spa and grabbed a beer for everyone. Allen came out in his swimsuit.

"Why are we all standing around?" he said. "Let's get in the water."

I stepped up first, then Terri and Mercedes, and then Ryan, Allen, and Chet. We all sat by our spouses with our drinks. So far, so good.

We spent a little while just talking and laughing about funny things in our lives. Then Terri said, "This is boring. Let's play a game."

Oh no. I knew where this was going.

"What kind of game?" Mercedes asked.

"Truth or dare."

Ryan didn't say anything, and neither did I.

"Aren't we a little old for truth or dare?" Mercedes asked.

Chet held up a hand. "Hey, it's my birthday, and I like the game."

"What are the rules?" Mercedes asked.

It really was déjà vu. I heard Terri's voice in my head even before she responded.

"No rules!"

Mercedes laughed nervously. "I'm not sure about no rules."

"Damn it, it's my birthday, and she said no rules," Chet said.

How many beers had he had? Mercedes took a sip of her drink and gulped it down. "Well, okay then."

"Maybe this isn't the right game to play this evening," I said, trying to put the brakes on the impending disaster.

Everyone looked at me like a party pooper.

"Why not?" Terri asked. "You were fine with it before."

I stared daggers at Terri, and her eyes widened when she realized her mistake. Mercedes didn't seem to catch it, thankfully.

"Okay, we're all adults, and Chet wants to play," Mercedes said. "So, let's play."

"I'll start," Terri said. "Ryan, truth or dare?"

I held my breath. If he said truth, she might out us as swingers. If he said dare, it could be innocent. Probably not.

"Dare!"

Of course. He's drunk.

"Stand up, drop your shorts, and dance for us."

Ryan slowly stood up and looked around at everyone.

"Go ahead, Ryan, drop them," Mercedes said with a smirk.

I stared at her in disbelief. She seemed very eager to see his package. *What's going on? Am I the only one with any sense left?*

He dropped his shorts, exposing himself to everyone's gaze, and danced around for about ten seconds before sitting again. I was still

164

trying to figure out how to get out of this. All I could think was that we would be found out for sure.

"How far do you guys usually take this?" Mercedes asked with a note of suspicion to her voice.

"I said no rules," Chet said sternly. "Okay, Terri, pick Mercedes next."

We all laughed at his enthusiasm in volunteering his wife.

"Okay, Mercedes, truth or dare."

Mercedes looked at Chet as she answered. "Truuu—"

"She picks dare," Chet cut in.

The laughter continued.

"Mercedes, take off your swimsuit," Terri said.

Mercedes looked at Chet again.

"Do what she said."

Mercedes stood up and started to slide the strap of her swimsuit off her shoulder. "Why don't we just save some time and all of us take our swimsuits off?"

Terri nodded enthusiastically. "I think that's a great idea."

Where was this coming from? *This isn't the Mercedes I know.* Ryan was drunk and in a compliant mode. *I'll comply . . . for a little while.* Everyone took off their swimsuits and threw them over the side of the spa.

"Okay, that dare doesn't count since everyone did it," Terri said. "So, it's a redo."

"Wait, wait! I did the dare."

Chet said, "Go ahead, Terri, she'll take another one."

I couldn't quite read Mercedes's expression: worry, but maybe a little bit of excitement too? Was that really my conservative friend?

"Truth or dare?" Terri asked again.

Mercedes looked at Chet and hesitantly said, "Dare?"

Chet hugged her with one arm. "That's my girl!"

Terri looked over at me, and I immediately knew what she was going to say. "Go make out with Ginger. For at least thirty seconds."

Mercedes waded over. "Are you okay with this?"

I just smiled and put my arms around her. The first kiss was tentative, but soon we were kissing passionately. I enjoyed making out with Mercedes immediately, but I wasn't sure how I felt about that. She reached up to grab my breasts, and I reciprocated. I didn't know how much time had elapsed, but there was dead silence except for our lips together.

Mercedes backed up slightly, opening a small gap between us, and motioned Terri over. Terri waded over, biting her lip with a look of anticipation. Mercedes put an arm around her and started kissing her too. Then switched back to me, and back to Terri. *Who is this woman? Was she putting on a conservative cover for all these years?*

Mercedes pulled both of us together and said, "I think we've moved our friendship to a new level."

I wasn't sure what level she was talking about, but I laughed along with them before we sat back along the spa wall.

"Who's next?" Chet said with his arms resting on the top of the spa and a drink in his hand. He was clearly enjoying this.

"Chet, truth or dare?" Terri said.

"Dare."

She thought for a minute until Ryan called out, "So that we know, there is one rule. No guy-on-guy stuff."

"Why not?" Mercedes interjected. "The girls made out."

"I agree with Ryan," Allen said. As did Terri.

Finally, Terri said, "Go suck on Ginger's boobs."

"Oh, he's going to like that." Mercedes grinned.

Why would Mercedes say that? What didn't we know about them?

Chet came over by me, and I lifted myself out of the water a little so he could have access without drowning. He grabbed on quite firmly and began sucking. *Hard.*

I winced. "Ease up a little."

He backed off and apologized.

"Wow, there are no problems with Chet's suction skills!"

Mercedes smiled proudly. "Yeah, baby, he knows just how to use those lips."

Chet went back to Mercedes and kissed her.

Terri seemed eager to continue the game. "Allen, truth or—"

"Okay, let's just get to the point here," Mercedes interrupted. She took my hand and dragged me to Allen, then took Terri's hand and pulled her to Chet. "Well, don't just stare at me, start kissing!"

Then Mercedes went over to Ryan.

Ryan

I wouldn't have started drinking during my golf game if I had known how the evening would play out. Things were a little blurry around me as Mercedes moved Ginger and Terri around, and now she was floating toward me with her large breasts at the top of the water.

"Hi, Ryan."

I just sat there, confused.

"Are you okay?"

"What are we doing?" I asked.

Mercedes straddled my lap and put her arms around me. She slid herself over me and maneuvered until my cock was nestled against her core.

"All these years, haven't you thought about me being naked on your lap?"

I couldn't help myself. I kissed her. We kissed like we were on fire. I reached up and felt her breasts. They were colossal and firm. Her pussy lips slid back and forth on my rock-hard shaft as she rubbed herself on me. I wasn't even sure when I got hard. I was still in shock. I didn't push for anything and seemed to slip into an automatic mode as I made out with one of my best friends.

What are we doing?

We stayed just like that for a few minutes until Allen came up behind Mercedes and kissed her shoulders. He reached around to feel her breasts while she and I continued kissing. Mercedes slowly moved her ass up, and Allen reached down between her legs.

I'd been to so many lifestyle parties, handled many different scenarios, some much more robust than this, and yet now . . . it didn't feel the same. I was uncomfortable for the first time since Ginger and I started swinging.

I looked over and saw Ginger and Chet making out. Terri drifted across the hot tub and stumbled over Allen's feet. She fell next to me and cheered that she hadn't spilled a drop of her wine.

"Terri, what are you doing?" Allen asked disdainfully.

Terri's apologetic look flashed to anger. "I want to be part of this too," she whimpered.

Mercedes reached over to stroke Terri's cheek, then slid her hand to the back of Terri's neck and lightly pulled her in for a kiss.

Okay, this part is hot.

I reached up and grabbed both women's breasts at the same time. Allen was fingering Mercedes now. He could be fucking her, but she wasn't giving me that impression. And I wouldn't think so, based on our past experience in the tub with Allen and Terry.

Mercedes pulled away from Terri and guided Terri's mouth to mine. Terri and I had great chemistry that instantly ignited when we kissed. Mercedes soon pushed her lips between ours, and we had a three-way make-out session. My discomfort quickly faded. Or was it the alcohol washing it away?

I looked over at Ginger again and saw Chet sucking on her breasts. I broke my lips from the ladies' and decided to suck on Mercedes's tits some more. I grabbed one and heaved her breast above the water, exposing her nipple. She had very small nipples, and I sucked on them softly.

"You need to suck harder than that. And use your teeth," she said.

169

I was a little surprised. I'd never had a woman tell me to use teeth on her nipples. I sucked harder and licked around her nipple, as I did with most women.

"You need to suck really hard and bite it. I can take it."

I was in some uncharted waters here, but I started biting on her nipple. She kept saying harder. I continued to suck and bite. I was biting so hard I felt as though my teeth would bite her nipple right off. I finally got to a point where she jumped and exclaimed, "Okay, that was it."

"Damn, I thought I was going to bite that thing off."

Terri quickly cupped her own breasts. "Stay away from mine!"

We laughed, and Mercedes said, "I have an extremely high pain tolerance, and I don't get excited easily without a lot of pressure, suction, or pain."

Ginger's shout interrupted us. "Okay, stop, I can't take anymore!"

"That's why Chet sucks so hard," Mercedes said with a grin.

Mercedes and Allen went off to another corner, and Terri sat on my lap and made out with me. She reached down and stroked my erection.

"I want this inside of me."

"Remember your rule about no penetration?" I said reluctantly. I wouldn't have minded sinking my cock into her over and over.

"I don't give a fuck. I need your dick in me right now."

I looked over at Allen, who was only making out with Mercedes. Terri moved to position herself to straddle me, grabbed my cock, and was about to slide herself down on it when I stopped her.

Is this real life? First, one of my best friends was all over me, and I wasn't sure how I felt about it. But now I had a beautiful woman I was attracted to begging for me to fuck her and trying to put my cock in her pussy . . . and I had to say no. A few years ago, I probably wouldn't have had this type of restraint.

"Terri, I gave my word, and don't want to cause any strife."

She pouted, but then I reached between her legs and slid two fingers into her instead of what she really wanted. She was so hot. Maybe hotter than the hot tub. I fucked her with my fingers and kissed her at the same time, whispering a little dirty talk in her ear between kisses.

"Just think of my cock in you like this, fucking you so deep and hard."

I kept kissing her and whispering about how my cock would feel where my fingers were. She soon she arched her back and stared into my eyes as she cried out and came around my fingers. I struggled to keep her head above water while she convulsed.

"Good one, Terri!" Mercedes called from the other corner.

Terri's face flushed red. "That was fantastic, but I still want your cock in me," she whispered.

"Trust me, I want to fuck your brains out." I kissed her long and slow. "But you need to convince Allen. In the meantime, get ready for orgasm number two."

I stared into her eyes as I slid two fingers back into her. I could see her expression change as my fingers entered, and then I vigorously finger-fucked her again. The way her face contorted with pleasure as I hit just the right spot got me even harder, if that was possible.

She seemed to enjoy me talking to her the first time, so I leaned closer and said quietly, "I know you want my cock."

Her eyes grew wide and her mouth dropped open, then she whispered, "I'm coming."

She closed her eyes and gripped me tightly as she arched her head back. Her body quivered, and her inner walls spasmed around my fingers again. Then she snapped her head back up to look at me and pulled me in for a kiss.

"Damn, how did you learn how to do that?"

We laughed, but I could see Allen looking at us with concern. Terri and I sat back with our drinks in our hands, watching the others.

Ginger

I got cozy with Allen and watched Mercedes guide Terri to Chet. I still couldn't believe it. Mercedes floated toward Ryan, and I simply shook my head.

"Is everything okay?" Allen asked.

"Just great," I said and kissed him.

He felt my breasts, and I reached down to feel his cock, but so far, there wasn't much more reaction than I'd gotten from him last time. Every once in a while, he glanced over at Terri and Chet. Finally, he reached down between my legs and slipped his fingers inside. I kissed him harder as he explored me below. It didn't feel bad, but the chemistry was lacking. We did that for a while, and then he asked if I wanted to join Ryan and Mercedes.

"Go ahead. I'll join you in a minute." I watched him float up behind Mercedes, who was making out with Ryan. I laughed to myself, thinking of how well Ryan would process this once he sobered up.

Chet and Terri separated from each other, and she went over to join the other three. I strolled over by Chet as he sat there, sipping his drink.

"Hi, stranger." I gave him a coy smile.

"Are you here to give me my real birthday present?"

I bit my lip. "Perhaps. What would you like?"

He slid his hands around my waist and pulled me close. As we kissed, his hands were all over my body, igniting something in me that Allen hadn't been able to. Chet was one of the hairiest men I'd ever known, which was a huge, if unexpected, turn-on for me. And I finally had my hands on him. I ran my hands through his chest hair, down his stomach, all the way down to his semi-erect dick. He got hard very quickly as I stroked him, which excited me further.

Suddenly, he lifted me onto the side of the hot tub and aggressively devoured my pussy. I gasped as I balanced myself, concentrating on what he was doing. He sucked my clit really mercilessly and then harder still, which turned into pain. I tapped the top of his head and laughed.

"Not so rough."

He apologized and sucked more softly. My sensitive area was quickly getting sore, however, so I slid back into the water, and he sucked on my nipples. I had to tap his head several times, as he was being especially rough with those too.

Finally, I winced and cried out, "Okay, stop! I can't take any more!"

He stopped and apologized again. We grabbed our drinks and took a moment to watch the other four trying to make something happen, but I couldn't figure out what it was. I absentmindedly stroked Chet's cock, which was still hard, and then realized this might be our first and last time with them like this. I might as well give him a birthday present to remember.

I set my drink in the holder on the edge of the spa and told him to sit up on the side of the spa. He complied, and I eagerly went down on him. He definitely had a lot of hair, but I didn't mind it so much with him for some reason. I liked it. I worked him with my mouth and my hands, sucking hard, stroking him, licking his balls. Then I pushed his cock to my throat. He didn't quite reach as far as Ryan, but I didn't feel like gagging tonight. His hand worked into my hair, and I felt him tense up. I sucked harder. He groaned and then gripped me tighter as he came in my mouth. I continued to slowly suck him as his cock pulsated his seed. When he finished and I was sure to get every drop, I pulled my mouth off him and swallowed. I grabbed my drink and took a couple of gulps before I leaned over to kiss him.

"Happy birthday, Chet."

"It was a very happy birthday indeed! Thank you for my fantastic present."

"What time is it?" Terri called out.

Chet checked his watch. "I think it's 2:00 a.m., but my eyes are still a little foggy from the present Ginger just gave me."

All eyes were on me as I blushed and sipped my drink, smiling.

It was late. We were all exhausted. My private parts had never been so sore. Mercedes's need for a lot of suction somehow meant

174

to Chet that all women needed a lot of suction, and I'd be lucky if my nipples didn't fall off by tomorrow. He latched on to my boobs and clit like a pitbull to a steak. Most of the time, I wasn't sure if it was pain or pleasure, but now realizing it was definitely more pain.

We sat in the hot tub for a while when Mercedes said, "Ryan, are you okay?"

He looked dumbfounded. "I wouldn't have expected this in a million years. I'm still not believing it. But I do know that I need to get out of this hot tub."

We all laughed and agreed. Many spa warnings stated not to exceed thirty to forty minutes, and we'd been in this one for a few hours.

We started climbing out of the tub in all of our nakedness, grabbing towels and drying off.

"I don't know about y'all, but I had a great time," Terri said. "We need to do this again!"

"I think we need to let Ryan digest what just happened," Mercedes said.

Ryan laughed a bit. "I know what just happened. I'm just trying to figure out *how* it happened."

We laughed some more, and I was glad we could do that instead of things getting weird. We changed into our dry clothes, gave Allen and Terri a kiss and hug goodnight—or, should I say, good morning—and got into the car to head home.

The first few minutes of the drive were so quiet I could hear each person breathing. It almost seemed like there was tension in the air. Or maybe I was just worrying and reading too much into it.

"I've got to ask, what just happened?" Ryan asked after a while.

Mercedes and Chet laughed.

"Like I said earlier, I think we just took our friendship to a whole new level," Mercedes replied.

"I got that, but you've always been more conservative," Ryan said. "Every time a sexual topic came up, you'd always roll your eyes and change the subject. Yet you seemed . . . almost comfortable in this setting. Have you done this before?"

Chet and Mercedes looked at each other, and then Mercedes turned back to us.

"What do you mean by *this*?" she said.

Damn it. She was still fishing for something. Ryan glanced at me, but we were both at a loss for words.

Mercedes continued, "We're a little more active than most, but we don't let anyone know. Not even our closest friends, because you never know what their reaction would be."

She could say that again. But I didn't know what she meant by "more active." What were they active in?

"How did you know we would go along with this hot-tub endeavor?" Ryan asked.

"We had some suspicions, and then when Terri said y'all have spent time in their hot tub, we figured you'd go along with it."

Ryan pondered for a second as we approached our house. "I've got to recover from this, but then let's get together for some wine and chat some more."

Chet and Mercedes agreed. We gave hugs and kisses, and waved as they drove off. When they disappeared around the corner, Ryan and I turned to each other. He still looked as confused as I felt.

"Let's go sleep this off and talk about it later," I said.

Ryan took some aspirin as soon as we got inside. Then we went to our room, stripped down, and climbed into bed. We gave each other a small kiss, and we were both out in a few minutes.

*****

I woke up around ten in the morning. Thoughts about the night before raced through my mind, keeping me from getting any more rest. I let Ryan sleep while I went downstairs to make some coffee. While it was brewing, I stared outside at the water in the backyard and tried to remember what we may have said or done to make them suspicious of us. Had they done that with Terri and Allen before? Were *we* the ones who were clueless about *them*?

As I poured a cup of coffee, Ryan entered the kitchen.

"Is it morning yet?"

I smirked, handed him the coffee, and got another cup.

"I had this strange dream that we played with Chet and Mercedes in Allen and Terri's hot tub last night," Ryan said.

I laughed. "I had the same dream."

Ryan narrowed his eyes at me as I went to sip my coffee.

"What?" I paused with the mug halfway to my mouth.

"What happened to your lips?"

I set down the coffee mug and touched my lips. *They are a little tender.* I went into the bathroom to check in the mirror. My lips were swollen and slightly discolored.

"Oh my god! What did he do to me?" I never thought kissing

could bruise.

Ryan stood in the doorway. "Was that from Chet?"

I nodded, pouting at my reflection. Ryan began to laugh, and I whirled around and swatted his arm.

"It's not funny. We're supposed to go to a meet and greet tonight."

"That's tonight?"

"Yes. What am I supposed to tell our friends?" If Chet had done this to my lips—*oh no*. I turned back to the mirror and pulled my robe open. When I'd gotten out of bed earlier, I was still groggy and had just slipped on my robe without a glance. Now I could clearly see the bruises on my breasts, especially around the nipples.

"Wow," Ryan said, staring at them in the mirror.

"I didn't think he sucked on me that hard. What are we going to do this evening? I can't see anyone while looking like this." I tested a few of the bruises, pressing gently with my fingers. They were tender too, but only with firm pressure.

"Just tell them you like to get rough every once in a while." He laughed.

"Not funny." I glared at him in the mirror as I tied my robe shut again.

"Sweetie, it will be all right. The lights are always dim, and we don't have to play with anyone tonight. Let's just go out and socialize with our friends."

I reluctantly agreed. We retrieved our coffee from the kitchen and went to sit out back.

As we stared out at the water, I got a text from Mercedes: "Are you two all right? We're a bit worried about you."

I showed it to Ryan and asked how he wanted me to respond. His forehead creased as he thought for a moment. Then he said, "Tell her everything's fine, but we're just exhausted from last night. And that we can get together tomorrow for some wine."

I sent the message while Ryan continued to brood. Mercedes responded that tomorrow would work for them.

"I thought we decided not to go down that path with them," Ryan said. "How did that happen?"

"I don't know, it just happened."

Ryan's reaction surprised me. He was disturbed by what had happened. We'd joked in the past that he was somewhat of a man-whore at swingers' parties. He would usually have no issue partying naked in a hot tub with three naked women and would probably please them all. But this had him out of sorts.

"What's going through your mind?" I asked.

"I don't want to say it was like making out with my sister . . . but we're so close to Mercedes and Chet in our vanilla world that it just feels weird."

I let the topic drop for the rest of the day, which mostly consisted of lounging around in our robes until we got ready for the meet and greet.

Even though I wasn't planning for us to play with anyone, I still shaved and did some extra grooming just in case. I'd hate to meet someone we really liked and not be prepared.

I brought up Mercedes and Chet again on the drive to the meet and greet. I wanted to know if Ryan was okay with everything, and if he'd thought about what we would say to them tomorrow night.

"I haven't thought much about it," he said. "Let's just enjoy tonight and not bring it up. We can't tell anyone about what happened, okay?"

If there was anyone who wouldn't bat an eye at last night's events, it was our lifestyle friends. But I agreed anyway, since it seemed important to him.

The parking lot was already half full when we arrived, and we could hear the music the moment we got out of the car. A bouncer was at the door checking names, and I realized the event had been organized as a private party. The only attendees were those who'd been approved through the website. That was great, because it could get awkward in public spaces with vanilla couples sitting along the bar or in the shadows, watching us.

Once checked in, we headed to the bar for a drink and immediately saw Kurt and Maryann, Tony and Lana, Darren and Sherry, Nathan and Penny, and some others we knew. Everyone was in sexy, provocative clothes. Even Penny was wearing a denim miniskirt and a very low-cut, loose-fitting top that exposed most everything except her nipples. That would probably change once she got on the dance floor. There was already so much positive energy and friendly adoration as we grabbed beers and sat down at a table near our friends. The organizers had done a great job.

I took a sip of beer and noticed Tony staring.

"Is there something wrong with your lips?" he asked.

I covered my mouth. Now, everyone was staring at me.

"Let's just say someone kissed her much harder than she thought last night," Ryan said.

"Let's see," Sherry said.

I took my hand away.

"Does it hurt when I do this?" She leaned over and started to kiss me softly. I kissed her back, and then she reached up and grabbed my tits too.

"Ouch."

Sherry backed away with a puzzled look. "What was ouch? Your lips or boobs?"

I halfway whimpered my response. "Both?"

Everyone turned wide-eyed and stared toward Ryan.

Sherry asked, "Ryan, did you do this to my girl?"

"Do you really think Ginger would let me get anywhere close to that point?" he said with a chuckle. "I'll let her answer how."

Great. He's the one who wanted to keep things secret, but he's making me answer.

"Let's just say we spent some time with a couple last night in a way we didn't expect, and we don't want to go into any details yet," I said. Thankfully, everyone seemed to accept that answer.

Sherry grabbed my hand. "Come on, girls, let's go dance."

All of us ladies danced together for a while as the men watched, no doubt entranced by the dozens of pairs of breasts all bouncing in unison. When the music switched from line dancing to pop music, Ryan and the other husbands came onto the dance floor with us. Ryan and I danced together while flirting and chatting with our friends. We couldn't have this same type of fun or energy in our vanilla world. Here, boobs constantly seemed to accidentally on purpose rub up against the closest person, and we could all smile and wink and laugh, or even kiss and grope a bit. And there was never any awkwardness or fear between this group of friends. Nothing like what we'd recently experienced with Terri and Allen, and then Chet and Mercedes.

Could it ever be like this with Chet and Mercedes? Did I *want* it to? It felt like Ryan was in my head now, worrying me about our friendship. I tried to push it out of my mind, to keep the vanilla and swinging parts of my life separate, and enjoyed the rest of the evening dancing and laughing with friends.

CHAPTER 9

A New Kind of Friendship

When I woke up the next morning around eight, Ryan was already up and out of bed. I went downstairs and found him on the back porch with a cup of coffee. I poured myself a cup and went to sit next to him.

"What time did you wake up?" I asked.

"Probably around six, and I couldn't go back to sleep. I kept thinking about Mercedes and Chet."

I could understand that. We sat quietly for a few minutes, staring out at the water and sipping our coffee.

"Remember my birthday party when Mercedes almost caught us?" I asked. That had been the first lifestyle party we hosted, and she'd called me in the middle of it because she'd seen the lights and the cars and thought our daughter was having a party, and offered to stop by to break it up. It still mortified me to think about what could've happened. But after what had happened last night, who knows?

"Chet and Mercedes are the best friends we've ever had," Ryan said. "We can't let what happened the other night get in the way of that."

"We're open to swinging, so maybe they're exploring too and decided to take the plunge."

"Would we play with them again?"

I thought briefly and said, "I don't know, maybe. But let's talk to them this evening and figure it out. She did text asking how we were doing yesterday, so that has to mean they're not upset by it."

Ryan stared off into the distance and just nodded.

*****

Ryan seemed stressed and preoccupied most of the day, so I let him play computer games to take his mind off things. But I did try to relieve some of that stress with a shower blow job as we got ready before dinner. It was strange to see him so worried about potentially losing this friendship. He was not my usually hot-blooded, easily aroused husband who would always tell me to relax and see what happens whenever it started to get heated with Chet and Mercedes. It felt like we'd almost switched places.

Ryan grabbed a good bottle of wine, and then we walked over to Mercedes and Chet's house. When we knocked on the door, we saw through the glass Mercedes motioning us to enter. Chet stood at their kitchen bar with a glass of wine, and Mercedes took the bottle from Ryan. None of us said much, and we didn't do our usual greeting hugs. It was a little more awkward start than our usually jovial get-togethers.

Mercedes poured us some wine. "Let's go sit down on the back deck."

Once we were all sitting, she looked back and forth between us. "Sooo, how are we doing?"

"Doing great!" Ryan said a bit too cheerfully.

"Are you sure?" Chet asked. "If we knew you two wouldn't be comfortable in that setting, we wouldn't have gone down that road."

"We kind of thought you were into it, so we didn't think there would be an issue," Mercedes added.

"Why did you think we were into that?" Ryan asked.

"Certain things you've said," Mercedes replied. "The egg party we had, the flirting and sexual talk over the years. The friends you've accumulated. We thought you . . . well, we were kind of thinking . . ."

"Just say it," Chet interrupted.

"Okay, we thought you two were swingers."

Aha! So, she really had been prying all those times because they suspected.

"We've been experiencing a new lifestyle for a while," I said. "But you've always been a bit conservative when any type of sexual discussion came up in the past, so we never said anything."

Mercedes got a devilish smile on her face. "Sooo, what type of lifestyle are you in?"

I looked at Ryan, and he looked at Mercedes.

"We have been swingers for about three years now." Ryan sounded like it pained him to finally say that to them.

Mercedes looked at Chet and exclaimed, "I knew it!"

"So, why were you two so comfortable in that situation?" Ryan asked. "It almost seems like it wasn't your first rodeo either."

Mercedes looked at Chet with a coy smile. "Well . . ."

"We have ventured out occasionally," Chet said, "but sort of in a different lifestyle."

Ryan looked from me to Mercedes and said, "There are quite a few different lifestyles out there. Which one would you say you're in?"

"Well, we're not swingers, but we have been naked around others," Mercedes said.

"So, you're nudists?" Ryan said.

Mercedes smiled. "Nooo, not nudists . . ."

For crying out loud. Was she going to make us guess every alternative lifestyle?

"Just tell them," Chet said, and I smiled gratefully.

"Okay, okay. We're into the BDSM lifestyle."

I almost dropped my wine. "You mean like whips and chains and stuff?"

Mercedes smiled sheepishly. "I like whips. And maybe other things."

"Is that why you nearly sucked my nipples off?" I asked Chet.

"I'm sorry, that's my fault," Mercedes said with a guilty grimace. "It takes a lot of pain for me to get excited, so over our thirty years of marriage, Chet just got used to, well, sucking hard." She strained to look at my lips and asked, "Is that why your lips are swollen? Oh my god, Chet, what did you do to her?"

"That's not the only place that's bruised. It's a good thing I'm not nursing a kid or they would starve."

We laughed a bit, and some of the tension dissipated.

"We consider you two to be the best friends we've ever had," Ryan said. "We've heard so many stories of people in the swinging lifestyle trying to bring their vanilla friends into the lifestyle, and they lost their friendship forever. We wanted to avoid that. We do know many are into both BDSM and swinging."

"We're not into the swinging part," Mercedes quickly interjected. "But we do get naked for certain things at events."

"So, if you're not into swinging, why did you go down that path the other night?" I asked.

Chet replied, "Because we're good friends, and we thought it would be okay. But if it will be uncomfortable, we won't do it anymore."

Ryan and I glanced at each other, and I said, "I don't think we will be uncomfortable, but—"

"But because we're so close to you, it might take a little while to get more comfortable," Ryan interrupted.

Chet and Mercedes looked at each other. Mercedes replied, "We don't have to do this again."

"We want to though," I said, almost without thinking. *Did I really say that? What am I thinking?*

Mercedes looked at Ryan. "Do you?"

"Sure," he said. "Let's do it. We can set up a date one evening."

Mercedes and Chet both replied, "Great!"

Chet continued, "What about next Saturday night?"

"Our daughter is off to school, so that works for us," I said, and Ryan nodded.

"We'll go out for dinner, and then back to your place for some playtime?" Mercedes suggested.

"Sounds good," I said.

Mercedes smiled. "So, Ryan, how well do you react to a riding crop?"

My eyes almost fell out of my head. Ryan laughed and said, "Perhaps we'll find out."

"Oh, yes we will." Her smile was downright devilish.

What did we just agree to? I just wanted sex. This was a very different side of my friend that I hadn't expected.

"Just so we understand, I'm not into the pain thing," I said.

"Don't worry, Ginger, it's just light and playful whipping."

"Umm. No, I don't think so," I insisted.

"Okay," she said. "Well, we'll bring a few things and play it by ear."

Ryan laughed and looked at me. "If you let Mercedes use a riding crop on you, and you won't even let me spank you, we will have words."

My face flushed hot as the rest of them laughed.

"Okay, so changing the subject," Mercedes said. "How are the kids?"

We shifted into our usual topics of conversation, with plenty of laughter and more wine. Before we knew it, it was 9:00 p.m., and we both had work the next morning, so we told them we had to go home. We got up and put the empty wine bottles and glasses in the kitchen. Chet and Mercedes walked us to the door, where we hugged and kissed each other goodnight. It had been a very joyous evening overall, and I thought we would have a whole new relationship with Chet and Mercedes.

Ryan and I started our short jaunt home.

"I don't know about this," Ryan said once we got out of their driveway.

Was he kidding? "You just said in there you were good to go."

"Well, it seemed the three of you were, so I didn't want to ruin it," he said. "I'll get over this issue I have."

He was quiet as we got ready for bed. Part of me wanted to let him sleep it off, but he was also leaving for a few days on a work trip in the morning. We climbed into bed, and I curled up against him.

"Do you think I'm being irrational?" he asked.

"I don't know." If an attractive woman showed any interest at a lifestyle party, he was usually all for it. I didn't know why this was different. "What do you think of Mercedes? Sexually, I mean."

"I never thought about it. Yes, she has *ginormous* tits, which I was finally able to touch. But I've always thought of her as a great friend and never developed a lust for her. Is that bad?"

I thought for a moment. We'd been friends with them for a long time, but that hadn't stopped me from recognizing Chet's sex appeal. I was surprised Ryan had never thought of Mercedes in that way.

Finally, I said, "No, it's not bad. But do you find her attractive?"

"Yes, of course she is."

"And you like her personality?"

"Absolutely."

"Well, then these next few days while you're out of town, just think about what it would be like to fuck her brains out." *I can't believe I just said that to my husband.*

"Do . . . what?"

I sighed and said it again. "While you're gone this week, just imagine what it would be like to fuck her brains out." I was glad we were in bed and the lights were out, because I was probably blushing.

Ryan laughed and kissed the top of my head. "Okay, I'll add that to my daydream list."

"I was really hesitant before, but now that the cat is out of the bag, I want to play with them," I said. "So, figure it out."

"Yes, ma'am."

"I'm serious."

There was a long pause, then Ryan said, "I'll open my imagination aperture a little wider."

"Thank you." I rolled over to my other side, and he put his arm around me and kissed my shoulder.

"I love you, sweetie," he said.

"I love you, too."

*****

Ryan didn't return until Thursday evening, and I made sure to have dinner and wine ready for him as soon as he walked through the door.

"Welcome home, honey." I held out the glass of wine, and he kissed me before taking it. "Did you have a good trip?"

"It was uneventful, which is always a good trip." He took a sip. "This wine is delicious."

"I'm glad you like it. I tried something new. Now, sit down and let's try this new pork chop recipe."

We sat down to eat. The pork chop was a winner too. After dinner, Ryan helped me with the dishes, and then we took our glasses and the bottle of wine out to the back porch to relax.

"Sooo, are you lustful for Mercedes yet?" I asked once we were settled.

He laughed. "Wow, how many wives want their husband to lust after their best friend?"

It did sound a little strange when he put it that way.

"Okay, we'll work on some flirting when we're at dinner on Saturday," he said. "I'm sure it will work out."

I sipped on my wine and didn't say any more. Ryan was definitely a player in the swinger lifestyle. He could captivate almost any woman and was an animal in the bedroom. What was the problem with Mercedes? We both agreed she was attractive, had a great personality, was playful, fun, and everything we wanted in a friend. There was that word again: friend. Could that really be the problem?

*****

I didn't mention our date on Friday or Saturday morning. Ryan said he was trying to psych himself up for that evening. I decided to lend a hand, among other things, and we had some incredible morning sex. Later that afternoon, we washed up and changed clothes. Ryan wore a linen shirt with jeans—no underwear. He looked very sharp. I put on a nice top that showed a little cleavage and a skirt, but no panties. Always ready for action.

Chet and Mercedes picked us up right at 5:00. Conversation was easy and relaxed on the drive to an Italian restaurant we'd been talking about trying for a while.

At the restaurant, when we got out of the car, I was a little surprised to see just how much cleavage Mercedes was showing. She usually dressed more conservatively than that. *But this is a date now, not our usual type of dinner.* It seemed she was really letting loose.

The restaurant's ambiance was rustic, reminiscent of Old Italy with water fountains, travertine flooring, plaster walls, and soft Italian music. The hostess sat us at our table and gave us the wine list and menus.

Ryan seemed to have noticed Mercedes's generous cleavage. He couldn't keep his eyes off her breasts. I kept looking too, but only because I was trying to figure out how her top was staying in place over her breasts. Mercedes noticed Ryan's attention and smiled slyly.

"Is there anything you like, by chance?"

Ryan didn't miss a beat. "I think that's a lovely necklace you're wearing."

Chet laughed, and Mercedes lightly touched the chain at her collarbone.

"This necklace?" She slowly ran her fingers down the chain and into her cleavage, then back up the other side.

"Yes, indeed. Very nice necklace."

The clear look of desire on his face made me happy. Maybe this would work out after all.

That interaction set the tone for the evening. We laughed and chatted about our usual subjects through wine, appetizers, and dinner. But unlike other times we'd gone out together, this time there was some playful innuendo here and there that slowly raised the heat level.

"Are we ready to go back to your place for some dessert?" Mercedes asked after we finished the last of our wine.

I looked at Ryan and said, "Absolutely!"

"Yes, let's go," he agreed.

We split the check and walked out to the car.

"Ginger, is it okay if I sit in the back seat with Ryan?" Mercedes asked.

"Go for it." I sat up front with Chet, and he started driving. I glanced to the back seat and saw that Mercedes already had Ryan unzipped and was working him up. I started talking to Chet about some random things while he drove, and when I looked back a few minutes later, Mercedes had her face in Ryan's lap, sucking on him. Ryan just smiled at me.

I think this will all work out.

Back at our place, Ryan brought out some bourbon and poured four glasses with an ice ball in each. Mercedes took a sip, then reached for her purse, which was much larger than she usually carried.

"I have something special for you, Ryan." She slowly pulled out a riding crop.

Ryan laughed. "Do you spank yourself to get going?"

She slowly slid the end of it up his leg, along his ass, up his side, and then down his arm. "So, Ryan, are you going to be naughty tonight?" she said coyly. Then she leaned in and dropped her voice to a whisper. "Say yes."

We laughed. I was curious how Ryan would respond.

"I already know you're not wearing any underwear, so why don't you take your jeans down?"

"No problem." Ryan dropped his pants and stepped out of them, exposing himself to all of us.

I quickly glanced up to make sure the blinds were closed on the windows. *Whew.* We definitely didn't need any other neighbors to know our little secret.

Mercedes slowly slid the crop up his leg. "Are you ready?"

Ryan stared at her almost like a dare. Mercedes quickly slapped his ass. That crack was louder than I expected. Ryan flinched a little but didn't say anything.

"Wow, so maybe you need a little more." She slid the crop up his leg, down his other leg, and then smacked his other butt cheek much harder. That time, Ryan jumped.

"Whoa, okay, that was a bit much," he said.

This wasn't going anywhere fun for me, so I said, "Why don't we take this party upstairs?"

Chet agreed. We grabbed our drinks and headed upstairs, pairing up with each other's spouses. I'd wanted to be with Chet for years, but I never really let on. When they were working on a project, Ryan caught me gawking at him once, and Chet had no shirt on. The way his sweaty body hair glistened in the sun was incredibly sexy to me. I didn't usually find that much hair attractive, so I couldn't explain why it was so different with him.

Once we got to the bedroom, Chet removed his shirt. I put my hands on his chest and moved my fingers through all that glorious hair as he leaned down to kiss me. We continued kissing as we lay down on one side of the bed, and he began removing my clothes. There was something truly erotic about a man removing your clothes, especially when you really want him to. Soon, he had me completely naked while he still had his jeans on. His lips traveled down toward my breasts, and I put my hand on his chin. He looked up at me, and I gave him a firm stare.

"No bruises," I said. "You get one warning, and then I snap."

"Don't you bruise her!" Mercedes exclaimed.

Chet sucked on one nipple while he groped my other breast. I could feel his body hair against the smooth skin of my thighs. It excited me even more than I thought it would. I glanced over and saw Mercedes sucking on Ryan quite aggressively. It appeared he was enjoying it, but I wanted to concentrate on my experience.

Chet slowly moved down to between my legs. Almost right away, he got aggressive with my clit. I put my hand on his head.

"Not so hard."

He lightened up a bit, and it was much more enjoyable after that.

I was getting into it when Mercedes said, "What am I doing wrong? Ginger, come over here and get your man up."

Chet stood up, and I rolled over to see what was happening. Ryan was sporting more of a willow tree than an oak.

What the fuck? He'd never gone limp on me, or anyone else as far as I knew. This was not going well. Mercedes's comment probably didn't help much.

"Let's switch for a bit," Mercedes said.

I crawled over to Ryan and began stroking him, and then I started sucking on him. I employed the things I knew he enjoyed, swirling my tongue around him and then taking him deeper into my mouth so the tip of his cock hit the back of my throat. He was going to get hard if I had to duct tape toothpicks to him. As soon as he was ready to go, I said to Mercedes, "Okay, he's hard. Passing the baton back to you."

Mercedes and I laughed as she took hold of Ryan from me. I was a little disappointed to see that Mercedes already had Chet's pants down. I enjoyed kneeling down and doing it.

Oh well. I had him lie down, and then I kissed his cock and ran my tongue around the head and shaft. He was just as hairy there as everywhere else. I usually preferred men be smooth in the groin, or at least trimmed, but it didn't bother me much with Chet. I looked up into his eyes as I took him into my mouth. He wasn't as large as Ryan, but there were so many differences that excited me in a new way. Sucking his cock while running my fingers over and through his body hair was erotic for me. Soon he told me to switch with him.

Now I lay on my back, and Chet spread my legs open, exposing my wet pussy. Mercedes was on her hands and knees next to me, with Ryan fucking her from behind.

I'm glad he's "working" now.

The hair on Chet's legs tickled my thighs as he positioned himself. I closed my eyes to enjoy the sensation as he slowly entered me. *It's finally happening.* I reached around to the back of his legs as he thrusted in and out of me. So much hair! I never thought it could be so sexy. With his rhythmic thrusting, I soon felt the beginning of my first orgasm start to build in my core.

I looked over at Ryan as he fucked Mercedes. Her massive breasts swayed back and forth with each of his thrusts. I reached out to hold one of them, and then Chet hit the right spot.

"Oh, fuck yes." I grabbed his hairy ass. "Fuck me harder!"

He complied, but I still wanted more. I dug my fingers into his flesh and pulled at him harder. His big, burly, hairy body against mine was everything I'd hoped it could be. He fucked me hard and fast until the pleasure couldn't be contained inside my body any longer, and the orgasm rolled through me.

"Yesssss!" I yelled out, then held my breath as he kept fucking me through the orgasm.

After what seemed like hours, Mercedes said, "Ginger, breathe!"

I took a breath as Chet pulled out, and we all laughed. Mercedes pulled away from Ryan, and I saw he was limp again. I couldn't believe it.

"I don't know what to do with that," Mercedes said.

Come on, Mercedes. You're not helping. I knew firsthand how frustrating it was when a man couldn't stay hard for me, but I knew better than to say things that would make them feel bad about it.

I crawled over to them. "Let's suck his cock at the same time."

"I'll try anything," Mercedes said.

We took turns servicing Ryan's cock. One of us sucked the tip while the other ran a tongue along his shaft or sucked on his balls, and then we'd switch. Chet positioned himself behind Mercedes and slowly fucked her. Pretty soon, Ryan was hard again.

Mercedes pulled away from Chet and asked Ryan, "How do you want me?"

"On your back." He grabbed her ass and pulled her to the edge of the bed where he stood, then opened her legs and buried his mostly hard dick in her pussy.

"Now we're talking!" Mercedes said.

Chet and I lay back together and watched. Ryan fucked her hard, but for some reason, it didn't seem like Mercedes was getting anywhere close to an orgasm. Ryan drove into her faster, and then he grabbed her ass and held her to him as he grunted his release. It was great that he'd gotten there, but Mercedes didn't seem like she'd gotten off, and Chet was still hard, so I didn't think he'd gotten off either. But neither of them made any move to continue the action.

We all lounged on the bed for a while and sipped on our bourbon, chatting like we were on the back deck and hadn't just had sex together for the first time.

After a little bit, Mercedes asked, "Do you guys feel better about taking our friendship to another level?"

"I do," I said.

All eyes turned to Ryan.

"Yeah, this was a good night," he said.

"Would you like to do this again?" she asked.

"Sure," Ryan said.

After a little more conversation and finishing our bourbon, Chet and Mercedes got dressed, and we walked them downstairs. Mercedes grabbed her purse and headed toward the door.

Ryan grabbed her riding crop from the top of the bar. "Were you wanting to leave this behind for me to practice?"

I took the riding crop from his hand and smacked him on the ass.

"Ginger!" Mercedes exclaimed. "You're showing promise."

"Nah, still not my thing," I said.

We hugged and kissed them goodbye, and they got into their car to drive home.

Ryan closed the door, and I said, "That worked out really well. And you seemed to get yourself working eventually."

"Not really. I couldn't get off."

"What do you mean? I saw you."

Ryan smiled. "Women aren't the only ones who can fake it."

What? Was he serious?

He started upstairs, and I followed.

"Wait, how can men fake it? Have you faked it with me?"

"I could never fake it with you, sweetie."

He's lying. Now I was getting mad.

"What happened?" I asked as we got to the bedroom.

Ryan finished his last drop of bourbon and said, "I don't know. I just couldn't get into the mood with Mercedes. She's attractive, but I don't have the lust for her that I've had with others." He sat down on the bed and looked really confused.

I sat down next to him. "You got hard when I went down on you, and I saw you fucking her, so it worked for a little while."

"I kept thinking it wasn't right, and I probably psyched myself out. That's the only thing I can think of. Besides, wasn't it you who didn't want to get involved with them?"

"Well, now that we are, I want to do this again, so you need to see about getting some pills next time."

Ryan gawked at me.

"I'm serious. Do you remember how upset I got when that happened to me with other men? You don't want to make Mercedes feel that way, do you? You're probably nervous because we're close friends with them and you can't tell me you haven't fantasized about fucking her."

He still didn't say anything.

"Besides, those pills might benefit us too." We'd never had an issue, but maybe some little blue pills could turn what was already great into something even more impressive. I leaned over and kissed him. "Get some sleep and make an appointment tomorrow."

Ryan got up to turn off the lights, and we went to sleep.

*****

The next morning, I woke up before Ryan and went downstairs to make coffee. I was still a bit worked up from last night. I poured Ryan a cup and brought it up to the bedroom. He rolled over, half awake, when I walked in.

"Good morning, honey." I set down our coffee on the dresser. "Since you didn't get off last night, perhaps I can help with that this morning."

When I pushed back the covers, I found he was already hard. I wrapped my hand around him and stroked slowly.

"What do you think, sweetie? Would you like me to take care of you?"

He reached over to take a sip of coffee and said, "I would love that."

I didn't waste any time taking him all the way into my throat, making him grunt. Making a man groan and grunt and lose control with my mouth is such a rush. Something animalistic took over as I bobbed my head up and down, vigorously sucking and stroking his cock. It didn't take long before he grabbed my hair and held me still as he unloaded in my mouth. It was quite a load, and I couldn't swallow all of it. A little bit dribbled down along his cock. I sat up and wiped my mouth with a laugh.

"Wow, you might not have gotten off last night, but you were definitely worked up." I got up and retrieved a towel, then returned to wipe him up as he sipped some more coffee.

"You need to wake me up that way every morning."

I laughed and kissed him. "Come downstairs, and I'll make some breakfast."

We sat on the back porch a short while later, eating and drinking our coffee.

"So, I take it you and Chet had a good time," Ryan said. "I heard you get off, but did Chet?"

"I don't know if he did. He was fucking Mercedes while she and I were going down on you, so I'm not sure if he came inside her. But he didn't with me." I paused to sip some coffee, then continued. "I do know he turned me on quite a bit, and if he got too rough, I just tapped him on the head."

Ryan reached into my robe to look at my breasts. "No new bruises?"

"I hope not."

We laughed and continued eating for a few minutes. He hadn't said much about his experience, or what we'd discussed the night before. I didn't want to seem insensitive to his issue, but I wanted to play more with them. Being with Chet was a lot of fun.

"We are going to try this again, right?" I asked after a minute or two.

He smiled. "Yes, sweetie, I'll get an appointment with the doc."

Just then, I got a text from Mercedes asking how we were doing this morning. I showed Ryan the text and responded that we were doing great and looking forward to the next time we get together.

"What if this becomes the expectation every time we get together now?" he asked.

I hadn't thought about that. We enjoyed being with them in what had been a vanilla relationship, but now, what should we expect? Would they want to have sex every time we get together?

Then, another text came in from Mercedes, asking if we wanted to get together again next weekend.

"You may be right," I said to Ryan. I told Mercedes that we had other plans next weekend but asked if she wanted to get together with me for lunch next week. She agreed.

Ryan went out of town for work again, and I set up my luncheon with Mercedes for Tuesday. Since my schedule was more flexible,

I picked a location near where she worked. We both pulled into the parking lot at the same time, and I waited to meet her close to the restaurant's door. She walked up and gave me a hug and a kiss. She seemed extraordinarily happy to see me.

Once inside, we grabbed some soup and a sandwich and found the table farthest away from any human life that could hear us. We talked about normal issues like work and kids.

Then she said, "So, how is Ryan feeling? Are you ready for another round?"

I smiled, searching for the words I wanted.

"What's the matter?" she asked.

"You know you're our best friends, and we enjoy every moment we get with you."

Her face fell, and she almost looked like she could cry. "But you don't want to get together with us again like that?"

"No, it isn't that," I said quickly. "But we don't think expecting to have sex every time we get together is healthy for a friendship."

She thought for a second and said, "You're probably right. It's not like we do this with just anyone. We get naked or wear sexy clothes at BDSM events, but we don't have sex with anyone. We've only had sex with you two."

Now I felt like a heel. "We will get together again, but let's let it happen naturally, not every time we get together."

She nodded. "We can live with that. Just let us know when."

I was touched that we were the only ones they'd had sex with. And now we were saying no . . . I felt bad. Well, not really saying no, just setting limits. I agreed with Ryan when he said expecting sex every time wasn't healthy for a friendship.

"What are you guys up to next weekend?" Mercedes asked.

"We're going to a birthday party for a friend."

"Is it a lifestyle party?"

"Yes, but it's at a public place, so there won't be any playing." *I just lied to my best friend.* We did actually plan to play with a few people, but I didn't want to tell her that right after I'd just set boundaries with her and Chet. *I'm such a bad friend.*

She sighed a little and asked, "When are you available for us to get together again?"

I thought for a second. "Let me talk to Ryan, and I'll let you know. But I'm sure we can get together in the next few weeks."

I have always enjoyed time with Mercedes, but this new relationship might be a little challenging. I knew we could never return to the way it was, but we needed to find balance. I changed the subject to talk about a cruise they were going on in a few months, which she seemed excited to talk about.

We both had to get back to work, so we finished up with lunch and walked out to the parking lot together.

"Sooo," Mercedes said cautiously. "What would you say to just you and I getting together to play?"

"No riding crop, right?" I said with a laugh.

She touched my arm with a look of surprise. "Would you be okay with it?"

She really seemed to want it. I didn't have much experience with women, and none of it was one-on-one, but Mercedes was my best friend. It could be fun.

"Sure, I'd play one-on-one with you."

Her face lit up with a huge grin. We hugged and kissed each other and went off on our way.

Over the next couple days, I still felt like I'd let Mercedes down, even though I'd agreed to have sex with just the two of us.

What did I just agree to? I've never done that before.

But it was with my best friend, so what the hell. It's not like I had to worry about getting it up. I laughed to myself about that. When I told Ryan over the phone about my lunch with Mercedes and what I'd agreed to, he was more concerned with reminding me of my previous "Strictly Dickly" stance when we'd first started. Oh, and he said he wanted *pics or it didn't happen*—typical guy.

It felt like the worry pendulum had swung back in my direction. We desperately wanted to maintain our friendship with Mercedes and Chet. But I'd be lying if I said I wasn't just as interested in playing with Chet again. And exploring with Mercedes could be a lot of fun.

I really hoped we hadn't made a mistake.

*****

Ryan returned from his work trip later that week and kept his promise to me about seeing his doctor. As soon as he got home with his prescription, I opened the bag and looked at the label.

"How many of these do you take?" I asked.

"Well, each is supposed to be good for five days, and since I don't want to fall into that 'over four hours, seek medical attention' category, I'll just take one."

I opened the bottle, tipped one out into my palm, and held it out to him. "Here you go."

Ryan just stared at me.

"Come on," I said, grinning. "I read about guys taking this and want to see if it makes a difference."

"I haven't had that problem with you."

"Well, since we've been together for over twenty years, how do I know if you could've been better this whole time? Now take the pill!"

He shook his head, but he got a glass of water and took it.

A few hours later, as we were eating dinner, Ryan's face had a bit more color than usual.

"How are you feeling?" I asked.

"A little flushed. My face is warm. I might not be up for you tonight."

"Don't even think that." His dry humor wasn't always funny.

He helped me clean up after dinner, and once we were done, he turned me around, pushed me against the refrigerator, and started kissing me. I wasn't expecting this. We made out just the way I like it. He was aggressive, but not too forceful, and his hands roamed all over my body. When I felt them sliding up my skirt, I said, "Let's take this upstairs."

"I have a better place."

He took my hand and walked me to the padded coffee table in the family room. There, he reached up and took my panties down, then set me down on the coffee table. When he took his pants off, he was already standing at full attention. I wrapped my hand around him. He was hard as a rock. I looked up into his eyes while stroking him.

"Wow, those pills work fabulously."

He laid me down on the coffee table and pushed my legs up. "Are you ready?"

I nodded, and he slid himself into me. I was already very wet.

Oh my . . .

I could have sworn he was longer than usual, and I could feel the difference in the firmness of his erection against my inner walls. He thrusted in and out, staring into my eyes the whole time. It was intense and erotic. He held me in a position that maximized penetration, so with each thrust, the tip of his cock tapped against my cervix. He was going to make me come in record time. My orgasm was building quickly, electricity sizzling through my veins with each thrust. Then he pulled out.

"W-why did you stop?" I asked in a panic.

He pulled me to my feet and walked me to the bar, where he bent me over the top and pushed my legs apart. I grabbed onto the bar railing as he entered me from behind. The sensation was incredible. Holding the railing for leverage, I pushed back against him and tried to bend over farther. But he was all the way in. Any deeper, and it would probably hurt. He continued his thrusting, harder and faster. There was a familiar pressure building along with my orgasm.

"My mind wanted to say stop, but my body demanded yes," He reached out to hold my hands in place as he kept fucking me, and I tried to hold back.

"I'm coming in you," he growled, and that sent me over the edge.

I came hard, crying out in ecstasy as I squirted all over Ryan and the floor. I was always a bit embarrassed when that happened, even though it felt amazing. However, this time, I knew it was exactly what Ryan was going for. My legs continued to shake as he pulled out of me.

"Let me grab a towel. Be right back," he said.

I just leaned against the bar, trying to catch my breath. When he returned a moment later, he dried my legs, his legs, and the floor.

"Wow, I guess those pills really do work," he said.

"Uh-huh." I couldn't form any other words just yet.

He kissed me. "Now we need to find out how long it takes to reload." He laughed, but I wasn't sure I could take another dose like that.

"You need to take one of those all the time," I said.

He'd never had a problem getting hard in the past, but this enhancement pill turned him into a piece of steel. I'd never felt anything like it. If only those other guys in the lifestyle took one of these pills. They would turn into rock stars within a couple of hours.

We picked up our clothes and went to our bedroom to watch television. While lying there, I stroked Ryan gently, almost as though it was a hobby of mine.

This is kind of fun. It was almost like being young again, sitting on our parents' couch watching TV at night with the blanket over us. After half an hour or so, his cock started to show some life again. Soon he was just as hard as before.

This time I straddled him. I gasped as his hard length filled me farther than usual, pressing against areas that didn't often get touched.

I had to move slowly, gyrating on him until it was more comfortable. Then I started moving up and down, and he stayed just as hard the whole time. He felt so good inside me. I leaned back to let him watch his cock slide in and out of me.

"Do you like watching yourself disappear into your slut wife's pussy?" I asked.

His eyes got wide, and he groaned. We didn't usually talk like that in the bedroom, but it felt naughty and right in that moment.

"Oh my god, yes," he said through gritted teeth. "This is a fantastic view."

I enjoyed pleasing him, and of course, I was enjoying the ride, so to speak. My body was on fire, and I kept riding his cock slowly, drawing out the pleasure. Suddenly, Ryan rolled us, so I was on my back and he was on top of me in missionary position, and he pounded into me. I barely had time to catch my breath. I pulled my legs back so he could go deeper, and his impossibly hard dick hit all the right spots again. It only took a few minutes before another orgasm burst through my body in tidal waves, and I squirted again.

Damn! I just changed these sheets.

Ryan didn't let up. He continued to fuck me ever so hard for a long time until I moaned and begged for him to come.

He finally rolled over. "I can't come."

"Why not?" I asked, panting like a rabbit that had just escaped a fox.

"Because I just did less than an hour ago. I could get it up, but I guess I'm not completely reloaded yet."

It sort of made sense to me. "Do you want to continue in a little bit?"

"I don't know, but if not, you'd better be ready in the morning."

I laughed, then sighed. I wasn't usually a fan of morning sex—mostly because I wasn't a fan of mornings—but if he was that hard again, I just might be. But for now, I was spent. That was amazing.

We ended up dozing off while watching television in bed. The next morning, Ryan woke me up with a gentle hand gliding along my body. Sleepily, I reached down to his groin, and he was impressively hard again. That woke me up almost instantly. Usually, our morning quickies are more for him, to get his day started in a good mood, but on that morning, I got off too. I really loved those pills. If I'd known what they could do, I would've told him to get them sooner.

*****

We enjoyed some alone time, just the two of us, no lifestyle dates or any other dates for a couple of weeks. Then Mercedes called to ask more about us playing one-on-one.

"I was wondering if you've given any thought to the two of us getting together for an evening," she said. "I can get a hotel room. We can go out, get some drinks, and I promise to take it slow."

Even though I was excited by the idea on the one hand, I was still a little apprehensive on the other. "I'm just nervous that I can't give you what you need. And I'm not into the pain part like you are."

"Ginger, we don't have to do all of that. I just want to experience being with a woman one-on-one, and I would really like it to be with you."

I paused for a few seconds, then asked, "Is this your first time with another woman?"

"We told you, we aren't swingers, and what we do doesn't involve sex. I have kissed other women, but you're the first one I've ever considered doing this with."

I was touched that she thought of me that way. "I'd love to," I said. "Let's do it. I'm free this Friday night."

"That's great, Ginger. We'll have a great time. I'll pick you up around seven, and we can go get some apps and wine."

We hung up, and I stared at my phone. *Am I really bi?*

Ryan came home from work, and I had a nice meal prepared. As we were eating, I said, "Remember when Mercedes asked me about the two of us getting together?"

He nodded.

"Well, it looks like we're going to do that this Friday night, if you don't mind?"

He grinned. "You're going to take pictures, right?"

I shook my head. "You're such a guy. I am not taking pictures. But I am nervous. I've never been into women like that, and I've seen what it takes to please Mercedes, and I'm not sure I can do that."

"It seems like you've gotten much more comfortable over the years, and, dare I say, you even enjoyed it with Jackie?"

I blushed, reminiscing about past experiences with Lana and Sherry, and how I recently enjoyed Jackie—*really* enjoyed Jackie. She was one of the first women I'd ever felt attracted to during our earliest days in the lifestyle.

"Mercedes said she's never been with a woman before, and I'll be her first time."

"Well, then it would seem like you have a little more experience than she does already."

I shook my head to clear all the confusing thoughts, then stood and gathered up the dishes from the table. "I'm not bi though!"

Ryan laughed and walked up behind me, placing his arms around my waist. "Baby, you don't have to put a name on it. You enjoy some of your friends sexually. Mercedes is your best friend, and she wants you for her first time. Just enjoy a fun evening with your friend."

I turned around, put my arms around him, and kissed him. "That is one of the wisest things you've ever said."

He grinned. "I have my moments."

*****

On Friday, Mercedes picked me up promptly at seven. We dropped off our bags at the hotel—there was a single king-sized bed, but I had naively expected two queens—and then walked a couple of blocks to a little jazz tapas bar. We ordered some fruity martinis and chatted for a little while. We talked about safe topics like work and kids, and laughed about fun things we'd done together in the past, which turned the conversation down a different path.

"Of all the times we've gotten together, have you ever thought about getting *together*?" Mercedes asked.

"I think I need another martini." We both laughed, and I waved down the waitress to order another one before I answered. "To be honest, we heard so many rumors about friendships breaking up after trying to introduce the lifestyle, and we love you two so much that we wanted to avoid that at all costs."

She grabbed my hands and held them like a lover would. "Aww, we love you two also. And I think we'll all be okay with this."

Our new drinks arrived, and I took a sip as Mercedes asked, "So . . . about the lifestyle I'm in . . . what is it that scares you?"

I took another gulp of my drink. "Oh, I don't know, the whole getting-beaten thing."

She smiled and held my hand again. "Oh, it's so much more than that."

I raised my eyebrows and she laughed.

"No, no, it's not like more pain and beating." She took a drink and continued laughing at my misunderstanding. "It's an exchange of power and will. It's an experience of giving yourself to someone completely, and without reservation, and having that person push your limits to new heights of ecstasy."

"What would be an example of this power exchange?"

She leaned forward in her chair. "Remember by the firepit that one night with Allen and Terri, and I didn't want to show my tits to everyone, but Chet was adamant that I did? Well, that was Chet exerting his dominance over me. Otherwise, I probably wouldn't have done it."

"Why didn't you just say no?"

She shrugged. "Because if I were to disobey him, he would have punished me for it."

I stared at her. "See, that's the part I can't take."

Mercedes laughed. "That's just our dynamic. But there are so many other areas of the lifestyle we're in. For instance, the psychological manipulation is fascinating."

"The . . . what?" I gulped down the last of my second martini and flagged the waitress down for a third. I was going to need it.

"You've been blindfolded while having sex, right?" Mercedes asked.

I nodded.

"What did you enjoy the most about it?"

I thought about it for a moment. "I guess not knowing what was going to happen next."

"Exactly," she said, her eyes shining with excitement. "The anticipation is what makes that so stimulating. Now, what if you were blindfolded and restrained and didn't know if you were going to be kissed or slapped with a riding crop?"

The waitress appeared at that moment with my drink. She handed it to me with a smile and a glance at Mercedes. We both giggled as she walked away.

"I just don't like pain. I hate it. I don't want it."

"Okay, okay, no pain. I get it." She took a sip of her martini. "What do you like about the lifestyle you and Ryan are in? How long have you been in it again?"

"We've been in this for a few years now. I enjoy the friendly atmosphere, the flirting, the laughing, the openness. But most of all, I love being lusted after. I like being complimented for dressing sexy. And. to be honest, Ryan and I are as happy together as when we first dated."

"I know what you mean about dressing sexy. Even though half the time I end up naked, it's nice to have people look at me like that while I'm dressed up," Mercedes said. "What's the strangest experience you've had?"

Oh boy. I told her about the first house party we went to, with the redneck basement and the host kissing his daughter-in-law as he introduced their son.

"We got out of there fast after that," I said.

Mercedes nearly spit out her drink. "Oh my god, they were having sex with their kids? Who was better, the father or son?"

It was my turn to nearly choke on my drink. "Mercedes, ew! We didn't stay long enough to find out. But the father was kissing his daughter-in-law and grabbing her ass, and she was enjoying it."

Mercedes was laughing so hard others were looking at us. I couldn't help but laugh too.

"It wasn't this funny then. We were horrified."

Our laughter died down, and we continued enjoying our drinks. After a few minutes, Mercedes asked our waitress for the check.

"Would you come to an event with us sometime?" she asked. "I promise you won't have to do anything you don't want to, but I think you'll realize it's not what you think it is."

The waitress dropped off the check, and Mercedes took it before I could.

"Thanks for the evening," I said. "And I promise I'll consider it."

We left the bar arm in arm, wobbled, and giggled the whole way back to the hotel.

Mercedes put her hands on my cheeks in the room and said, "You are such a dear friend."

And then she kissed me.

It was nice. Soft at first. I put my arms around her, and our kissing quickly turned passionate, our lips and tongues dancing together, my hands roaming through her long, thick hair. She slid one hand over my breast and fondled me. I followed her lead and did the same, cupping and gently squeezing her breast.

After a few minutes, Mercedes backed away. "Wow, umm . . . why don't we get more comfortable?"

We both shed our clothes and climbed onto the bed. Mercedes crawled up toward me and looked at my naked body up and down.

"We're going to have a very fun evening," she said, kissing me again. Her lips drifted down to my neck, and then my breasts, kissing and sucking.

I yelped at a sharp pain on my nipple. "Hey, hey, no biting those nipples. Ryan will be pissed if I come home without them."

She laughed and apologized, then kissed her way down my stomach.

She lay on her side with her legs toward my head and kissed her way down between my thighs. I laid my head back and enjoyed her fingers exploring my folds. I could feel her body move a little more, and then her warm, wet tongue slipped through my crevice and swirled around my clit. I opened my eyes and saw her legs open next to me. I reached over and began exploring her as well, exploring her pussy, and then pushing one finger inside of her. Her licking and sucking on me intensified, so I assumed she enjoyed what I was doing. I was enjoying it too.

"Mercedes, come up here and straddle my face."

I never thought I'd say that—to Mercedes, or any woman. She looked back at me with a smile and complied.

I never thought I'd sixty-nine another woman. I'd always been nervous and hesitant to reciprocate oral with other women—but it was different with Mercedes. We already had this connection that I didn't have with many others.

She shifted on top of me with her legs on either side of my head and continued her exploration of my pussy. Her scent was light but intoxicating. Thinking of the type of touch I enjoyed myself, I slid my tongue between her lips and focused on her clit, swirling my tongue around it and then licking it softly with gentle yet deliberate strokes, adding an occasional sucking with my lips. We continued pleasuring each other for perhaps ten minutes, learning each other's intimate places. There didn't seem to be a goal in mind, not even orgasm—yet. It was wonderful to just explore.

Mercedes rolled off and looked at me with a huge grin. "Oh, oh, I brought something! I promise no pain, but . . . can I blindfold you?"

I bit my lip as I thought about it.

"I promise, Ginger, no pain."

I blew out a breath, hopefully expelling my nervousness with it. "Okay, I trust you."

Mercedes reached into her overnight bag and pulled out a satin sleep mask that she placed over my eyes. "Now lay back and enjoy."

I laid my head back and listened to her dig around in her bag. Apparently, I hadn't gotten rid of my nervousness. It was still there, buzzing just under my skin.

Something soft touched my chest. It was light and ticklish.

Maybe a feather? It drifted down around my body. *This is nice.* I enjoyed the soft touch. Then something firm came to rest on my chest. It felt leathery, and my mind immediately conjured an image of her riding crop.

"I hope that isn't what I think it is," I said.

"Just relax and trust me," she said in an even, smooth, calming voice.

I was almost shaking with nervousness now. I didn't want her to hurt me. She said she wouldn't, but . . . part of me was still expecting it. She glided that object down my body, down my leg, and up my inner thigh. Then, I felt it against my mound. She tapped there lightly, and I jumped. It didn't hurt, but my body reacted on its own out of anticipation.

She slid her fingers over my mound and then between my folds. "That's what I was looking for," she murmured.

"What were you looking for?" I asked, realizing I was incredibly wet.

She continued to slide her fingers in and out of me, then up and down my slit. "You might think you don't like the anticipation of BDSM, but your body is saying otherwise. You are so very wet."

Heat flooded my face, and I was grateful for the blindfold at that moment so I couldn't *see her* see my reaction. I could hear her digging in her bag for something else. Something firm slid over my thigh and then pressed against my entrance. It lingered only a moment before she pushed it inside. I sucked in a breath at the sensation. It was . . . big. I jumped as she turned on the vibration.

"That's it, just enjoy." She handled the vibrator with one hand

and massaged my breasts with her free hand.

I tried to just relax and enjoy as she'd instructed. She worked the vibrator deeper into me, stretching me open. It was larger than any toy or man I'd had before. Once it was all the way in, the fullness actually felt amazing, and I couldn't stifle my wanton moan as she slid it out, then back in. She started slowly at first but soon thrusted it fully in and out of my drenched pussy. She was right about how wet I was after her teasing. My body was on fire from being worked up so much, and my hips had a mind of their own, gyrating and grinding against the beast of a vibrator. I wanted a body to grab on to and pull it in deeper. Instead, I pulled my legs back as she kept fucking me with it. It was breathtaking . . . The pleasure built up, and as I felt my climax approaching, I knew it would be intense.

I gasped and tried to push her away. "Pull it out, it's too much."

She whispered, "You're almost there, just let go." She kept going, and I couldn't hold back any longer. The orgasm crashed over me, and I let out a squeal that was probably heard in the adjacent rooms. I could feel myself squirt on the bed. Mercedes finally pulled the vibrator out, and I rolled over in the fetal position, letting my orgasm run its course.

Mercedes rubbed her hand along my back. "That's it," she said in that same soothing voice. "That was so good."

I rolled over and pushed up the mask to look at her. My face was hot and probably red.

"I wish I could have an orgasm like that," she said. "I've never been able to. That's why I started exploring BDSM, thinking I might be able to with that."

I touched her leg, and she leaned down to kiss me.

Once my breathing was back to normal, I said, "Okay, your turn!"

She relaxed on her back, and I knelt by her legs and slid the vibrator inside her. It didn't have the same immediate effect on her that it had on me, so I turned it up more and slid it in and out of her, trying to find a spot that made her moan, or move, or something. But it didn't seem like she was getting into it that much. I held the vibrator inside her and used my other hand to rub her clit. That seemed to get more of a response from her, but still not much. I turned the vibrator off and removed it.

"What can I do to make it better for you?" I asked.

"Will you bite my clit?"

I looked at her in disbelief. She wanted me to . . . bite . . . her clit?

"Keep the vibrator in me on high, and then suck my clit while biting down. I'll tap your head when you're there."

I gawked at her and started to shake my head.

She laughed. "I'm serious. Trust me, you can do it."

"Okay, if you're sure."

"I'm very sure."

I slid the vibrator back into her and turned it on high, then repositioned myself so I could suck her clit better. The vibration tickled my lips as I closed them around her little bud and started sucking. I sucked harder and harder until she put her hand on my head.

"That's it, now slowly bite me."

I was nervous about it, but I slowly applied my teeth to her clit

220

and bit down.

"Oh yes, harder, harder."

I complied, and she asked for it harder still until I thought I might break the skin. Finally, she yelled out and tapped on my head.

"That's it, now suck on it."

I kept the pressure on her clit and sucked. My entire face was nearly vibrating from the toy inside her. She gasped and then laughed.

"Okay, okay, that's enough."

I backed off her and pulled out the vibrator. Her clit swelled from my sucking, and the muscles in my face were fatigued.

Mercedes pulled me down to her and kissed me.

"Thank you, Ginger. This has been wonderful."

We lay there and caressed each other's skin. She slid her fingers across my nipples and said, "You have such perfect nipples. Mine are so small."

"Yeah, but your tits are huge!"

She laughed. "Yeah, Chet likes them."

I chuckled. "Ha, everyone likes them."

"So, how did you like your first BDSM experience?"

I turned my head to look at her. "What BDSM experience?"

She smiled, keeping my nipples hard with her fingertips. "Not all BDSM is whips, and chains, and pain. It can be as simple as giving your control to someone else so you can experience pleasure as the other person wants to deliver it. From how wet you got, your body said you liked it."

Heat crept into my face. "Well, I did enjoy it very much, but I was so nervous."

She kissed my lips softly. "That's what makes the experience so enjoyable, and why trust is so important."

"I think I could like this again."

"I'm glad to hear it, because I'd like to take you and Ryan to an event sometime."

"Umm. I don't know about all that." Doing this privately with her was one thing. Going to an event, though . . . I just didn't know.

"You can trust me," Mercedes said.

I leaned up to kiss her. "We'll see."

We caressed each other for a while until we drifted off to sleep. I woke up to my breast being caressed, and when I opened my eyes, Mercedes was smiling at me.

"Good morning," I said. "That feels nice."

"Good morning. I thought we would go down by the lakefront and get some breakfast. I know this little bistro that has a deck on the water."

I yawned and stretched my arms and legs wide. "That sounds great."

We rolled out of bed, took showers, and went off to breakfast. We never discussed the previous night or any of the lifestyles. It was just my best friend and me having breakfast at a fantastic restaurant on the water.

Mercedes drove me home. When she stopped in front of my house, she said, "Thank you for a fantastic evening."

I leaned over to kiss her. "Thank you. I enjoyed it as well."

I got my bag from the back seat and walked up to the house. Ryan opened the door for me. I walked through, gave him a hello kiss, and walked upstairs.

"Well, how was it?" he called after me.

I looked down at him from the top of the stairs. "I'm giving up men!"

"What?"

I laughed. "Just kidding. We had a great time together."

*****

The following Saturday night, Ryan and I had planned to stay in with a bottle of wine and watch a movie. I received a text from Mercedes asking if we wanted to have wine and watch a movie at their house. We said sure. Ryan got a couple of bottles of wine, and we walked over to their house. Chet saw us arriving at the door and waved us in.

Chet poured us wine from the bottle they'd already opened. Mercedes came downstairs and gave us hugs.

"I'm glad you could come over. We were going to watch a movie and thought of inviting you two."

I replied, "That's what we were planning to do tonight too."

We sat down on the sofa across from Chet and Mercedes. They set up a movie, and we talked a lot, as we always do. We reconnected with our friends the same way we did before our sexual encounters, and that's when I realized everything was good with us. It was a relief, and it made me happy and relaxed as I snuggled into Ryan and enjoyed the evening.

About an hour in, Mercedes asked, "So, Ginger, have you given any thought to that event I told you about last week?"

Ryan looked at me. We hadn't talked about it yet.

"Oops, you didn't tell Ryan yet?" Mercedes said.

"Umm, what event?" he asked.

"Mercedes asked me if we wanted to go to a BDSM event with them, and I said I would think about it."

Ryan immediately responded, "Hell yes!"

I rolled my eyes, having already known that would be his reaction. "Now you know why I didn't tell you."

We all laughed. Chet said, "The event is in two weeks, and it's mostly locals getting together at someone's large house. There's no pressure. You can watch. It's actually pretty fun."

I didn't say a word, but Ryan said, "We'll go and check it out."

I took a deep breath and sighed.

Mercedes laughed. "Ginger, it will be fine. Trust me."

Another hour passed, as did another couple of bottles of wine before Ryan and I said our goodbyes and walked home.

"I'm not sure about attending this event," I said.

"I know, baby, but have a little trust. Remember how often you *weren't sure* about going to our first swinger events? And now look at us."

That was true. But I doubted I would suddenly want to be whipped after going to one event. Did I even want to see other people experience that type of pain?

"Let's just check it out, and if you're truly upset by it, we can leave and never go again."

I sighed. "Okay, I can do that."

Over the next couple of weeks, I did some research on BDSM, thinking that maybe I was just naive about it. After my evening with Mercedes, which I really enjoyed, I wanted to understand it better.

According to my reading, BDSM stood for bondage and discipline, dominance and submission, sadism and masochism. That sounded intimidating, but I kept digging. There were so many new terms, facets, and perspectives to take in. Things started to click when I read something comparing BDSM to sports. I never thought a sports analogy would get through to me, but it did. The term "sports" was an umbrella term that applied to everything from badminton to mixed martial arts, swimming to baseball, and everything in between. You could enjoy a few sports, a lot of sports, or even just a single sport. And you couldn't judge or understand sports as a whole by just learning about figure skating. It was the same with BDSM. It encompassed so many different types of sexual play that fell outside of what was considered "vanilla." Being blindfolded and bound was a light form of BDSM. This made me realize that I'd been involved in some aspects of BDSM and didn't even realize it.

Perhaps it isn't as bad as I thought?

I read further, thinking about different aspects I might or might not like. Although I had a hard time with trust, I did enjoy being bound once in a while, and of course, blindfolded. The thought of being physically disciplined if I didn't obey an order was a huge turn-off, but there was a certain aspect of being forced and taken that aroused me. Reading about sadism and masochism made me nervous. I didn't think I would enjoy inflicting pain, and I definitely didn't want to be on the receiving end.

One article I read said that BDSM was 90 percent mental. That confused me, since most of the material I read seemed to give the most attention to the physical component. But I was intrigued by the idea of stimulating the mind.

I read a short story along that theme and was quickly drawn into the fantasy. The story was about a woman who enjoyed a confident and strong-willed man. A man who walked up to her and whispered how beautiful she was, building up her self-esteem with his words before adding in light touches. He would adjust based on her subtle movements or hesitations as the trust and attraction built. Then he leaned in to whisper in her ear, his warm breath against her neck, as he told her in detail what he was going to do to her. How he was going to take her to a room, remove her clothes, and use her like a goddess should be used. He would get more detailed and explicit as he took note of her heavy breathing, and other clues to her desire.

"Yes! This is what I want!" I exclaimed to the empty living room. Even though I was alone, my little outburst flooded my face with embarrassment. I read a little bit more, but I already knew what parts of BDSM I might be interested in exploring further.

I shared some of the things I'd researched with Ryan and let him know what I was interested in and, just as importantly, what I was not. I made sure those limits were clearly understood.

In the two weeks leading up to the BDSM event, Ryan was quite good at practicing the techniques that had interested me.

The Friday before the event, before Ryan went to work, he told me I couldn't wear panties all day, and that he was going to fuck me on the kitchen table when he got home. Throughout the day, he asked for proof that I wore no panties. I was reluctant to send him a picture like that, but then I found the arousal in it, and even a hint of empowerment, as I did what he asked. Especially seeing his text response about how much he enjoyed it. Before he left work that evening, he called me.

"Are you ready for me, baby? As soon as I get home, I'm setting down my briefcase and taking you on the kitchen table as I promised."

Hearing him say it excited me, as did the anticipation. I wasn't quite sure what to expect. All I said was, "Okay, baby."

When he arrived home a short while later, I found myself standing at the entryway to the kitchen. He walked up to me, dropped his briefcase, slowly pushed me back against the wall, and kissed me passionately. My heart raced. My body was so ready for this.

"I'm going to fuck you into tomorrow," he said in a low, deep tone.

Those words, combined with his touch, made me weak in the knees. He took my hand and led me over to the table, lifting my dress and hoisting me onto the edge. He dropped his pants. He was already hard, clearly as turned on by the anticipation of the day as I was. I barely had time to gasp as he spread my legs and pushed himself into me. No normal foreplay, just animalistic fucking.

I was already extremely wet from the anticipation of the day. He pushed my legs back and fucked me hard. All I could do was take him; it was all I wanted to do. I felt claimed and used, and . . . I *loved* it. He grunted with almost every thrust, and knowing that all of this was his attention toward me was a head rush all on its own.

"Tell me to come in you, baby," he said. "Tell me how much you want me to come in your pussy."

Those words sent electricity zinging through my body. I looked into his eyes and started to whisper, but he cut me off.

"Tell me to come in your pussy," he demanded, and that alone tore my orgasm from the shadows.

I yelled out as my inner walls clenched around him. "Come inside me, baby, fill that pussy up!"

He pushed in hard and held himself in place, grunting loudly as his cock pulsated inside me. I grabbed his arms to steady myself as intense waves of ecstasy rolled through my body. He leaned down to kiss me as we caught our breath and gathered our bearings, and then he pulled out.

All I could say was, "Wow!"

He helped my trembling frame down off the table and put his arms around me. "I love you, baby."

"Wow," I said again as I hugged him back. "That was incredible."

"It really was. I need to forbid you from wearing underwear more often."

I laughed and playfully pushed him away.

The next day, I woke up already nervous about going to the BDSM event. I got my coffee and texted Mercedes to ask what I should wear. She said she had "event clothes," which didn't mean anything to me, and then said I could wear something simple, perhaps a nice dress or skirt and a top. I had this miniskirt and brown silky top that Ryan liked, and I figured I could be a little free at the event and go braless. Ryan was going to wear some slacks and a button-down shirt. Mercedes gave us the address and said they would meet us there around seven. Ryan had suggested we drive ourselves so we'd be free to leave if I really didn't like it.

For the rest of the day, I tried to occupy my time to keep my mind off the event, but it wasn't working. So, I did what any self-respecting woman would do in that situation: I went shopping. It was much easier not to think about the event when I was trying on clothes, sampling perfumes, and ogling diamond jewelry I could never afford.

I returned home around five because Ryan wanted to take me out to dinner before the event. More than likely, he wanted to pour some wine in me to loosen me up, since there was no alcohol permitted at the event. And it worked, just like it did the first few times we'd attended swingers' events. I didn't get drunk at dinner, but had enough to feel loose and relaxed. I was grateful he knew me well enough and cared enough to make sure I felt good before we made our way to the address Mercedes had given me.

We arrived at the location, down a dark road with a private driveway. A man with a flashlight at the driveway's entrance stopped us and asked for our names. We told him who we were and that we were guests of Chet and Mercedes. He saw us on the list and told us where to park.

We drove up a snaking driveway to a large Spanish-style home. There were at least twenty cars there already. As we parked, we saw

Mercedes and Chet's car. I was already intimidated as we walked under an archway and up the steps to the sizeable double-door entrance. We rang the doorbell, and a woman with jet-black hair and a glossy black leather bodysuit opened the door.

"Welcome!" She stood aside as we entered. "I don't recognize you. Are you here with someone?"

Just as we were about to answer, Mercedes came running in.

"Mistress Tiffany, they're with us."

"Ah yes, you told me about these kink virgins," Mistress Tiffany said with a smile. "Welcome. Make yourself at home. You aren't required to participate in any play, or commit to a dom or sub role, but I do ask that you be respectful of the scenes going on."

Mercedes walked us into the main area of the house and explained there were different rooms with different things happening, and that lots of people were experimenting to see what kinky things they enjoyed.

"I'm in the middle of a flogging right now with a new guy, and he's waiting for his beating," Mercedes said. "But walk around and see what's going on. All the rooms are open. Just don't interrupt anything going on unless you're asked to be part of it."

She walked off, and Ryan and I looked at each other.

"Let's go check it out," he said.

We went to the kitchen and grabbed a couple of glasses of lemonade.

"I can't believe I'm here and there's no alcohol," I said. "Did you happen to bring a flask?"

Ryan laughed. "It's okay, baby, you'll be just fine. That's what the wine was for."

We walked up a short set of stairs and down a hall, where there were four rooms—one on one side of the hallway, two on the other, and an opening to a room at the end of the hall. We approached the first door on the right and saw it was empty. There were hooks with ropes hanging from the ceiling and multiple discipline instruments on the wall.

We continued to the next room, where one woman lay on what looked like a massage table while another woman dripped candle wax on her naked body.

"It's okay, you can come in and watch," said the woman on the table.

We walked in toward the table, and the woman who was standing smiled at us. She held a blue candle above the recipient's breasts. She tilted the candle so the melt dripped onto the other woman's skin. Her body looked like a work of abstract art with splatters and rivulets of now-dried wax in various colors from her breasts to her thighs.

"Wow, that is beautiful," I said.

The woman standing said, "Thank you. Would you like to be next?"

I smiled and pulled at Ryan's arm. "Perhaps another time."

We ventured to another room farther down and across the hall. There, a nude man stood with his legs spread wide and shackled to rings in the floor. His arms were lifted, forming a Y with his body, and suspended with ropes. A woman stood in front of him, placing clamps on his nipples. As we got closer, I noticed additional clamps on his balls with some type of weights hanging from them. He wore a collar around his neck that said, "Owned by Phibi." The woman—Phibi, I assumed—turned to look at us, and then continued with what she was doing. She opened a black box and removed some small clamps with wires attached.

This doesn't look like it's going to be fun. I tugged at Ryan's arm to go.

"I want to see what she does," he whispered, so I reluctantly stayed by his side.

Phibi placed the clips onto the clamps that were already on his nipples. She took two more clamps from the black box and put them on the chains hanging from his balls. She walked around to the other side of the black box and placed her hands inside. I couldn't see what she was doing, but the man's eyes widened, and he breathed heavily. It seemed like he was in pain for a moment, and then he relaxed again. Phibi walked up to him and whispered something in his ear that we couldn't hear.

He nodded excitedly. "Yes, Mistress!"

She returned to the box, and whatever she did had the man clenching the ropes tightly and quietly crying out. I pulled Ryan out into the hallway.

"I can't watch that."

"Okay, baby, let's see what's going on down this way."

As we approached the open doorway at the end of the hall, there were flickers of flame, or maybe candlelight. We stepped through the doorway into a large open area that looked like a medieval dungeon. Old wooden beams ran the length of the room above us,

LT Richards

torches adorned the walls, and there were old iron cages and many wooden contraptions like the torture devices you might see in a movie. Almost everyone else was in this room. They stood in a semicircle around a woman with red hair dressed in a maroon leather corset and black leather skirt.

If we ever come back, now I know to wear leather.

We walked up to the nearest couple. "What's happening here?"

They replied, "This is Mistress Tammy. She's demonstrating how to use the various instruments of pain, like the whip and flogger and stuff."

We walked to where we could see better just as Mistress Tammy was putting the flogger away. The table in front of her held so many various implements, half of which I couldn't even imagine how they'd be used.

"Tonight, I'm going to demonstrate the art of the mindfuck. Now, who wants to get fucked?"

A soft murmur ran through the group, and everyone looked around to see who would raise their hand. My pulse quickened as Mistress Tammy came up to me.

"How about you? You're new here. Would you like to take part in a demonstration?"

I held tight to Ryan's hand. "No, I'm just here to observe tonight."

She smiled and looked around. "Someone here has to want to get their mind fucked."

A young man nudged his female partner forward. She seemed timid.

233

"Do we have a volunteer?" Mistress Tammy asked, approaching the woman.

She looked over at her partner, then back to Mistress Tammy. It didn't seem like she really wanted to do it, as she bit her lower lip and gripped her partner as if he were the only tree saving her from a tornado about to whirl her away.

"If you aren't freely and enthusiastically consenting, then I'll find a volunteer who is." The dominatrix turned and pointed a finger, swinging it around to every person standing there. "And if any top ever tries to engage you in pick-up play like this without first gaining your consent, run."

Another murmur swept through the onlookers, and many people nodded. Mistress Tammy turned back to the woman.

"Now, use your words and tell me. Are you volunteering for this mindfuck?"

"Yes, Mistress," the woman said with a blushing grin, slowly releasing from her partner.

"Good girl."

The dominatrix leaned forward, and the two women whispered back and forth for a few moments. I couldn't tell what they were talking about.

Then Mistress Tammy stepped back again. "From here on, I will not stop until I'm finished, or you use the safe word we just discussed."

I remembered reading about safe words when I was researching. It was a specific word or phrase besides "no" or "stop" that would end whatever was happening.

"Now remove your clothes for all of us to see."

She stripped down and stood there nude. She was slim with full breasts and a shaved pubic area. Mistress Tammy led her to a wooden structure in the shape of an X. I also remembered that from my research. A Saint Andrew's cross. She secured the volunteer's wrists and ankles to four points.

"Something tells me you've been on one of these before."

The young woman blushed and didn't respond but looked to her partner and smiled.

Mistress Tammy turned to the audience. "A mindfuck is about leading the mind and how your body reacts to that mental stimulation."

She wheeled a small cloth-covered cart from behind the cross for everyone to see, then dramatically removed the cloth. There were a variety of knives and medieval-looking torture devices that I had no names for. Immediately, the woman on the cross looked panicked.

"I'm not sure about this," she said.

Mistress Tammy picked up a long, thick knife with a pointed tip along with a peach that randomly sat among the various blades. Holding up the peach for all to see, she lightly cut the knife into the fruit, causing juice to trickle out.

"Regardless of your preferred kink, always ensure all of your tools are in peak shape." She brought the fruit up to the girl and asked, "Would you like to taste it?"

She slowly shook her head. "No, thank you."

Mistress Tammy shrugged, took a bite, and then set the fruit on the table. The blade glinted in the light as she held it up to the woman's cheek. A reflection from the torchlight danced on her skin. Then the dominatrix placed the point of the knife on the woman's neck and slowly glided it down to her breast. The woman's chest heaved as she sucked in a breath. Mistress Tammy ran the knife tip over the woman's nipple.

"Please don't cut me," she pleaded. My anxiety flared up in solidarity. That knife was sharp . . . but it was arousing too.

Exciting? I had no idea where that thought came from.

Mistress Tammy kept the blade moving, guiding the tip of it down the woman's thigh and then flipping it to slide the hilt over her bare mound.

"I don't think this will work as well if you're watching. We can't have you twitching to sharp objects." She grabbed a blindfold from the cart and covered the woman's eyes. "Now, if you don't want to be cut, you should remain still."

She opened another compartment of the cart that held other adult toys. She turned to all of us watching and placed a finger to her lips in a signal to be quiet.

"Because this knife is so sharp, sometimes it does cut, so I'm simply wiping it with some alcohol." Instead of doing what she said, she picked up two other things and held them up for the audience to see: a small bottle of water and a metal device with a thin, spiky wheel at one end. "Now keep still, sweetie."

She held the roller by the handle and ran it down the woman's chest. The woman jumped and cried out, "Ow, you're cutting me!"

"I told you not to move." Mistress Tammy squeezed a little

water onto the spot, letting it run down the woman's chest.

"Oh my god! Am I bleeding?" She cried out.

Even though I could see it was water dripping down the woman's chest, not blood, I was still on that strange edge of anxiety and arousal. I wondered if that spiky wheel thing actually hurt or if that was part of the mindfuck. What would it be like to be in the volunteer's position? What types of things would I want someone to do to me? *Or just make me think they're doing to me . . .*

"Relax, it's not much of a cut." Then she took the roller to the woman's breast, and she jumped again.

"You cut my boob. You said you wouldn't—"

Mistress Tammy dripped more water on her breast, and it trickled down her body. The woman cried out and struggled against the restraints.

"Please don't!" She was breathing heavily and seemed slightly panicked.

I squeezed my thighs together as I stood there, simultaneously trying to ignore and stoke the flame of arousal that grew within me. *Why is this so hot?* I was waiting for the volunteer to use the safe word, but then Mistress Tammy set the instrument and the water on the table and removed the blindfold. The woman quickly looked down at herself and realized she was neither cut nor bleeding.

"Let's give our volunteer a hand." Mistress Tammy removed the restraints.

The woman swiped at the droplets of water on her skin. "I thought for sure you were cutting me. I could feel the blood run down my skin."

"That, my friends, is a mindfuck. I was able to get her mind to think one thing when something else was actually happening. You can apply this in many different ways, but when you can fuck the mind, you can bring so much more to your sexual experiences."

So much more . . . My imagination reeled.

"Okay, Ginger, do you want to go next?" a familiar voice said from behind me.

I turned, still stunned by what I'd just witnessed, to see Mercedes and Chet. Mercedes reached out and put a hand on my arm.

"Are you okay?" she asked.

I shook myself out of my daze. "I'm good. That demonstration was . . ."

"Amazing!" Ryan finished.

I looked over at him, then back to Mercedes. "Sure, we'll go with that."

I was still confused about my body's reaction and didn't want to let on. Ryan would probably embarrass me by trying to insist I go up for a demo right then and there, and I was definitely not ready for that, regardless of what was happening between my legs.

"We came by when she got blindfolded," Mercedes said. "We've seen that demonstration before, and it's hot every time."

"Where have you two been?" I asked.

I took a moment to admire Chet's outfit—leather pants, boots, and suspenders that crisscrossed his bare—and deliciously hairy—chest.

Wow. I've never seen him like this.

Mercedes looked up at him with a Cheshire-cat grin.

"Somewhere . . ." she said slowly. "Somewhere we know you wouldn't like."

I smiled, grateful they respected my boundaries and didn't invite me somewhere they knew I wouldn't care for.

A woman's scream sounded right behind us. I whipped around. Three men had put a cloth sack over some woman's head and lifted her. She kicked and tried to fight off her attackers, but they quickly bound her wrists and ankles with rope. She yelled for help, but no one did anything. I froze, and the men quickly took her away. Why wasn't anyone doing anything? I turned to Mercedes in a panic.

"What the hell?"

"Don't worry," she said, much too calmly. "That was just an abduction."

"What do you mean *just* an abduction?" I tried to keep my response to a whisper but Mercedes smiled, and her hand on my arm indicated I wasn't whispering.

"Relax. You're perfectly safe as an observer here."

Then I felt an arm around me, and I jabbed my elbow back and jumped out of the way, ready to fight if I needed to. I turned and saw Ryan, bent over and holding his stomach while trying not to laugh.

"I was just trying to hold you, baby."

"It's okay, Ginger, no one will touch you," Mercedes said soothingly. "That was just part of someone else's fantasy."

Abduction fantasy?

"Oh no, honey, I'm sorry." I took a deep breath, hugged Ryan, then looked at Chet and Mercedes. "Maybe I wasn't ready for this."

Chet replied, "It's your first experience. I'm sure you were nervous with your first swinger experience."

I thought back to our first swinging encounter and how nervous I was, compared to now when I almost got physically sick.

"You're right, but I think I need to go home and calm down."

Chet and Mercedes walked us to the door and gave hugs and kisses.

Ryan drove home, and I didn't say a word. Ryan glanced at me every few minutes, then finally said, "Are you okay?"

"Yeah, I'm okay." I rested my hand on his thigh to reassure him, but I continued staring into the darkness outside, going over everything we'd seen.

Especially the mindfuck. And then the abduction that terrified me. Terrified me, and yet . . . I didn't want anyone to throw a sack over my head and drag me away, but I had been excited by the idea of being at a man's mercy to use as he pleased. Like Ryan did the night before. I wondered if that could be part of a mindfuck scenario.

What am I even thinking? A few weeks ago, I was adamant that I wanted no part of BDSM, and now my mind wouldn't let go of certain images and feelings that were getting me very wet. What would Ryan think?

We arrived home a little while later and headed up to bed. We cuddled for a few minutes, he combed through my hair with his fingers, but my body refused to shift into sleep mode. I got up on my hands and knees, kissed him, and then yanked the sheets back and buried my face between his legs.

"Whoa, what's this all about?"

I didn't answer; just worked him with my mouth and hands until he was hard and ready for my purposes. Tonight had been a lot of mental stimulation, and I felt like I could come with just a few strokes. I straddled him, and his cock slid easily into my drenched pussy.

"Wow, someone is extremely wet. Your thighs are even wet already."

I smiled down at him. "Shut up and fuck me."

He thrusted into me as I rode him. Within a few short minutes, the pleasure tightened into a tiny ball of heat within me and then exploded out, flooding my mind and body with an intense orgasm. I cried out and continued to ride Ryan as my inner walls clenched around his cock. I could tell by the look in his eyes that he was close. A few more urgent strokes, and then he grabbed my ass and grunted as he came, his cock pulsing deep inside me. That was my favorite feeling. He let go of my ass, and we both sighed as I rolled off him. He put his arm around me and pulled me into his side.

"What brought that on?"

I stretched up to kiss him and said, "I just wanted to."

If I told him what had really turned me on so much, I'd never hear the end of it.

*****

The next morning, I woke up first and went downstairs to make some coffee and breakfast. Ryan came down just as the bacon had reached the chewy, but not crispy, point, and we took our coffee and plates and sat on the back porch.

"Thank you for breakfast, sweetie." He leaned over to kiss me. He kept looking at me and smiling while we ate.

Finally, I asked, "What's up with all of this smiling at me?"

He grinned some more. "It's because I love you so much, baby."

"Mm-hmm . . . Something tells me it's more than just you loving me."

He finished off his eggs and took a sip of coffee. "That mindfuck demo turned you on last night, didn't it?"

Busted. I stood up and took his plate.

"I'm not talking about that today." Then I smiled—a taste of his own medicine!—and walked away.

I stayed in the kitchen, loading the dishwasher. Ryan came in and pulled me into his arms.

"It's okay to be excited, baby."

I thumped him lightly on his chest. "No, it's not. That's not me." I broke away from his arms and grabbed my coffee to return to the porch.

"Swinging wasn't you a few years back, and now look at you," he said, following behind me.

I sat down and stared at the water. He was right about that. But still . . . there was so much out there that I really wasn't interested in. At all. So what if something excited me enough to immediately jump my husband? That didn't mean I was into BDSM, right? I sipped my coffee. Now I was just confusing myself.

I couldn't deny how much my body and, perhaps, my mind liked that mindfuck demonstration. It had been exhilarating to watch. I didn't know if I could go through that same kind of scenario myself, but the mental stimulation side of things was something I definitely wanted to research further.

CHAPTER 10

Boot Scootin' Booth Blow

We settled into our new friendship with Chet and Mercedes even more as the weeks and months passed. Ryan finally managed to get over the weirdness he felt with Mercedes, and now, on our occasional *adult* dates with them, he had no problem getting—and staying—up. I was glad our lifestyle crossover with them hadn't resulted in a big mess and ruined our friendship. Now we had best friends who we loved to hang out with and sometimes have amazing sex with. Mercedes occasionally mentioned other BDSM events, but that was still outside my comfort zone after the first one. I preferred keeping any experimentation private and fairly vanilla, compared to everything we'd seen at that event.

We also found a good balance with our lifestyle involvement. We saw lifestyle friends at meet and greets and occasional house parties—*not* ones that I was roped into planning, thank goodness—and sometimes one-on-one with another couple. All the things I'd ever feared—becoming addicted to swinging, letting it take over our lives or get in the way of family and vanilla relationships, ruining our friendship with Chet and Mercedes—were all in the rearview mirror now. This was a new, fun, fulfilling chapter in our lives, and I enjoyed every minute of it.

While we'd established a fairly large group of regular lifestyle friends, we still used the SwingLifestyle website to look for new and interesting people to meet. Ryan was usually the one to go online, and then he'd show me the messages and profiles to see what I thought. Sometimes we'd send messages and the response would be: "I'm sorry, we're not compatible." Other times, there was no response at all. When we first started out, these replies stung, but then we realized that if one couple already felt that way before meeting another, why spend a night trying to confirm it? There are many couples out there, so we learned to move on. Not everyone is compatible.

One day, we saw one local couple that had come up several times in our searches but who, for some reason, we'd never messaged. They only had pictures of the wife, mostly of her legs and backside, but none of the husband. That could be why we'd never reached out. But then we saw they had certifications from close to a dozen other couples, and we knew at least half of them. We were surprised to have so many friends in common, so Ryan went ahead and sent a message.

Hi, how is it that we have so many friends in common and we've never met? Let's fix that. Ryan and Ginger.

They responded the following day.

Hey there. Wow, we didn't notice that either. Yes, how could this have happened? What are you doing this Friday night? Doug and Lori.

I was hesitant, mostly because of one particular attempt to meet up with a new couple that had ended in disaster. Then again, those were newbies, and Doug and Lori clearly weren't newbies. We had a rule about that now. There was also the picture thing. Sometimes it could be a red flag when there were only pictures of one half of the couple. I wanted to at least see Doug before we met. It might seem vain or shallow, but if I was going to potentially have sex with someone, I at least needed to feel a spark of attraction. Without it, there was no point in meeting. Ryan opened our private pictures so they could see our faces and asked if we could see one or two of Doug.

We don't have Doug's picture online because of his job, but feel free to ask any of our mutual friends about us and let us know. We'd love to meet you two on Friday evening.

Well . . . many of our friends had already certified them on the site, so it wouldn't be a big leap of faith. I called around to a couple of the women I knew who were in Doug and Lori's certifications, and I got glowing reviews. They all said yes, he's very handsome and knows how to care for a woman's needs.

Okay, then!

Ryan wrote back to them to say we'd love to meet on Friday evening and suggested a new country- a western place. He gave them our phone number, and they confirmed via text message. It was all set. We were going on a date with a new couple!

On Friday evening, I wore a cute low-cut top with jeans, and Ryan went with a button-down and jeans. Nothing too fancy but still showing off the assets.

We arrived fifteen minutes early to get a seat and a starter drink.

The other failed first-date attempts were in the back of my mind, but I tried not to think about the potential for disappointment. Ryan texted Doug to let him know we were already inside, in a booth near the bar. A steady stream of people were filling up the seating quickly. It was good we came early.

A few minutes later, a couple approached our booth and asked, "Ryan and Ginger?"

I was astonished at how handsome Doug was. He was right around six feet tall with short gray hair and some silver in his beard and mustache too. He was broad-shouldered and had a smile I couldn't stop looking at as we stood up and gave hugs hello. When we sat down again, Lori pulled Ryan into the booth beside her. I was a little surprised to separate already since we'd just met, but my initial impression of Doug was good, so I sat next to him on the other side of the booth.

Doug and Lori got their drinks, and we ordered some appetizers and chatted for a while. We had quite a few friends and interests in common. Everything was going well so far. The band started up, and the girls who worked there got up on the bar and tables to do a choreographed dance routine. We all stopped to watch.

I looked across the booth and saw Lori watching the dancers, but her hand was reaching down and rubbing Ryan. He glanced at me and smiled with a shrug. He loved a little exhibitionism. As we talked and laughed, I rested my hand on Doug's leg, and he rubbed my shoulder. Judging by the hungry smile Lori kept giving to Ryan, she was really into him.

The band started playing another song, and Lori's head dipped toward Ryan's lap. Ryan put his hand on her head and just shrugged at me again. I was in complete shock that Lori was sucking his cock in this very public place. Her head was just under the table, and I could see it bob up and down, but I didn't think it would be as obvious to others around us. Then I caught sight of a group of women at the bar who could definitely see what was going on. Doug cleared his throat and Lori came up for air.

"Oh, I'm sorry, I must have gotten carried away," she said with a grin.

I leaned over the table to whisper, "You had an audience behind you."

She slowly turned around, and the young ladies at the bar raised their classes and cheered.

Lori blushed when she turned around again. "They're just jealous."

We laughed, and Lori pulled Ryan out of the booth to dance. As she walked by, the girls at the bar yelled out and held their hands up for Lori to high-five. She smiled and slapped each of their hands.

"I apologize for Lori," Doug said. "Sometimes she doesn't think about where she is."

"Are you kidding? She's exactly the kind of woman Ryan has been looking for."

Doug laughed. "Well, perhaps we're a great match after all."

I stared into his blue eyes and instinctively wet my lips. "Maybe we are."

Fortunately, he picked up on my hint and leaned down to kiss me. And what a kisser he was. I closed my eyes and got lost in the feel of his lips on mine, his tongue sliding against mine, the soft tickle of his mustache. He pulled away, and I reluctantly opened my eyes.

I blinked slowly and then looked down at my drink. "Okay . . . what were we talking about?"

We both laughed.

"Hey, we saw that kissing," Lori said as she and Ryan returned to the booth. "We haven't even kissed yet."

"Oh, kissing a cock doesn't count?" Doug quipped.

She blushed and sipped her drink. Then she grabbed the back of Ryan's neck and seemed to shove her tongue back to his tonsils. She was downright insatiable.

When a slow song started a few minutes later, we all got up to dance. I don't think Ryan and Lori were even on the dance floor before they started making out. Doug was more conservative in his approach, which was exactly what I enjoyed in a man. He held me and put one hand in my hair as we danced. I loved having my hair played with. Then he pulled my lips toward his. I hadn't expected this kind of chemistry when we agreed to meet them tonight. As we embraced, the music faded away. Our tongues danced, and I lost myself in his exceptional kissing.

Doug pulled back, and I realized the music had stopped and everyone was leaving the dance floor.

"Wow," I said. "That was some kiss—I mean dance." I felt myself blush as he chuckled.

We went back to our booth and ordered another round of drinks. Ryan kept shooting me looks across the table as the four of us sat and talked. There were plenty of suggestive caresses and touches the whole time. He was clearly thinking the same thing I was, and he finally spoke up.

"I think we're getting along very well," he said. "Maybe we should take our little party somewhere else for the evening?"

Lori and Doug exchanged concerned glances.

Uh-oh. That couldn't be a good sign.

"We would love to—we want to, but I had a procedure done a few weeks ago," Lori said. "I can't have sex for another few weeks."

I could practically feel the wave of disappointment shedding off Ryan. I was a little disappointed too, but Doug and Lori seemed like a couple we'd definitely want to meet again, and probably many times in the future. It wouldn't have been a total loss if nothing had happened tonight. We finished our drinks, paid the tab, and walked out to our cars.

We were on the same level of the parking garage. When we got to Doug and Lori's car, we traded off to kiss each other's spouse. Then Lori pulled Ryan over toward me and Doug.

"My lower half may be out of commission, but do you mind if I give Ryan a blow job? We can go to your car, and the two of you can play in our car."

I looked at Doug, and he said, "It's up to you."

I already knew Ryan's answer, but I looked at him anyway.

"Sure, why not," he said with a huge grin.

Lori walked up to me and gave me a lengthy kiss, then said, "Thank you." She took Ryan's hand and walked toward our car.

Doug held his arms around me. "We don't have to do anything

if you're not ready."

He was such a gentleman. I liked that. I kissed him and asked, "Do you have a condom?"

"In my center console."

If Ryan was going to get off, I wanted to as well since he'd surely be too spent to help me out with that later.

"My lower half is just fine. Let's go crawl in your back seat."

Doug opened the back door, and we looked around to ensure the coast was clear. I cursed myself for wearing jeans as I crawled into the back seat. I got my shoes off and quickly shimmied out of my jeans and panties.

Doug took one last look around the parking garage and then looked at me lying in the back seat, my legs spread wide open for him. I grinned and hooked my finger in a come-hither motion. That got him moving. He climbed in and shut the door. He fumbled while removing his shoes and jeans, all the while glancing out into the parking garage in case anyone came by. Ryan and I had done this a few times as teenagers, and I didn't remember it being so complicated.

Doug finally got his pants off, and I could see he was already hard.

That's what I like to see.

He reached into the center console and pulled out a condom, opened it, and rolled it over his erection. I only had a moment to admire the sight of his fingers encircling his shaft before he pulled me down toward him. He pushed one of my legs wider and slipped between my thighs. I gasped and moaned as he entered me.

The entire evening had been foreplay, and I was already incredibly aroused as he started thrusting. There wasn't room for much more than what he was doing, but he was doing it very well. The confined space did make it easier to pull him down to kiss me. His mouth on mine as he fucked me instantly cranked up the pleasure. I moaned against his lips as my orgasm started its slow build.

"Yes, just like that," I said.

He fucked me harder, his moans becoming deeper and louder. Hearing his noises and pleasure sent an electric thrill through me.

"Yes, keep fucking me, I'm so close."

He went hard and deep once, twice, and then he cried out with his own climax. The sound of his orgasm did it for me, and I gripped his arms and cried out as I came. He pushed in deeper, and I felt his cock pulsating in me. My favorite feeling. I continued to clench his arms until he pulled out of me.

"Oh shit!" he exclaimed as he sat up, nearly giving me a heart attack. Then he let out a sigh. "Oh, it's just Lori."

We both laughed at our shared momentary panic. Lori opened the door.

"I hope you took care of my new friend," she said.

"Oh, he took care of me very well."

I didn't even mess with my panties. I pulled on my jeans and picked up my shoes before climbing out of the car. Lori gave me a hug and a kiss.

"We had a great time meeting you two," she said. "I hope we can see each other as soon as I'm recovered."

I agreed and kissed Doug goodbye before slipping on my shoes and walking over to our car. Ryan already had it running as I got in.

"Did Lori take care of you, baby?"

His smile said it all. "We so need to add them to our speed-dial list."

I laughed. "I agree. I think we'll be seeing them a lot more in the future."

Later that night, we cuddled in bed, my head on his chest and his arms wrapped around me.

"Why couldn't we have gotten involved in this lifestyle twenty years ago?" Ryan murmured.

"I know I would have been a much happier mommy if I had these friends to keep me satisfied while you were deployed all the time."

He laughed. "With all that attention, are you sure you would even remember me?"

I reached down and rubbed his cock. "Trust me, baby, I will always remember this thing."

He laughed, and I snuggled in closer.

CHAPTER 11

A Very Special Birthday Surprise

Nearly a year had passed since the "hot tub incident" that changed our relationship with Mercedes and Chet, and her birthday was coming around again.

"What are you doing on the Saturday before your birthday?" I asked her over lunch one day, thinking we could go out somewhere or have one of our special date nights if she didn't have plans yet.

"Chet is taking me to a kink event," she said with a mischievous smile. "Oh! You and Ryan should come with us. It's only thirty minutes away. And this one has a theme."

She'd been asking us about going to another event ever since the first one, and I kept sidestepping it. It might not be so easy this time.

"What kind of theme?"

"It's a lords and ladies role-playing theme. That won't be the only thing happening, of course, but people are encouraged to dress up and role-play like kinky medieval lords and ladies, and masters and mistresses." Her eyes sparkled as she talked about it.

That actually sounded like it might be fun . . . to watch. Like maybe in porn. But participating?

"I don't know yet. I'm still a little nervous about all of it," I said. "How can I be assured that no one will hurt me?"

She took my hand. "Were you hurt at the first one?"

"Well, no . . ."

"Consent is really important in kink. Besides, you would be with me. No one would touch you. Well, not without my permission, anyway." She winked.

I tried to laugh that off, but it came out more like a cough.

"I'm teasing," she said. "It'll be fun."

"I don't know. But I promise I'll think about it."

We finished our lunch and went back to work.

That night, Ryan and I sat on the back porch, enjoying a Chinese takeout and wine dinner. I told him about having lunch with Mercedes and the event she'd asked me about.

"Let's go," he said. Just like that. Didn't even have to think about it.

"I'm just too nervous."

"Remember how nervous you were at our very first lifestyle event?"

"Oh jeez." I laughed at just how nervous I was before that event—and before a whole bunch after that one too. "Well, yeah, but that was different."

He just cocked his head, and I could hear the unspoken question:

Was it? But I couldn't think of a solid explanation for why it was different.

"It's her birthday, right?" he asked.

"Yeah, a few days after the event."

Ryan's eyes lit up. I didn't like that look one bit.

"You should go as her present," he said.

"What do you mean by 'her present?' " Did he mean that my attending this event would be a gift to her? That didn't seem like a very good gift.

"I mean, you should give yourself to her for her birthday. She said she wouldn't let you be harmed, so trust her and show up at the event with a collar and leash." He grinned wickedly. "Every mistress needs an obedient lady."

"Are you insane? There's no way I can do that." I gulped the last half of my wine and poured another glass.

"Come on, think about it. You know you can trust her, and she knows what you fear. It's perfect. We can coordinate with Chet so he knows what we're doing." He was getting more animated as he described the scenario. "And then, when we get there, I'll hand over your leash to her, and you can say, 'Happy birthday, Mistress.' Oh my God, she would eat that up. It would be the best birthday present ever for her."

I was aghast. "What have you been watching to get these ideas?"

He smiled and went back to eating his dinner.

It *would* be funny to see her expression in that situation. After all our time together, she understood my perspective and knew what I liked and didn't like. A small smile tugged at the corner of my mouth.

"You're thinking about it, aren't you?" Ryan said.

I stuck out my tongue at him and took the dirty dishes to the kitchen.

When I came back, I said, "Okay, so if we do this, you'd stay by my side the whole time, right?"

"Of course, sweetie. It's just some fun role-playing, and I'll be there to keep an eye on things so I can whisk you away if anything gets out of hand."

With fear running through my veins, I said, "Okay, I'll do it."

Over the next few weeks, I tried not to think too much about the event, or how much I didn't even like role-playing, but it wasn't easy considering the planning we needed to do. Not to mention Ryan being so excited about it himself that he often reminded me. He coordinated with Chet, who said Mercedes would absolutely love the gift. I texted her an apology and declined the offer to attend so it would be a complete surprise.

Then, there was an outfit to consider. What do you wear to give yourself to your best friend for her birthday? Ryan had suggested the collar and leash, and Chet agreed that those would be good. But I needed to wear more than that. I didn't have much time to put together something that would look historical, so I figured "submissive" as a general look would be fine.

After some questionable Internet searches about kinky clothing and what submissive women should wear, I still hadn't narrowed it down much. There were so many options. Leather, lace, sexy club wear, corset, skirt, latex . . . I thought back to some of the outfits we'd seen at the first event. Then I thought about what I wanted out of the outfit and what Mercedes might like best for me. I needed to be comfortable enough to walk around the party, where people could see me. I did enjoy dressing up in sexy and provocative outfits for swinger events, and having people look at me. Maybe this would be an opportunity to try out something a little more outrageous than I would normally go for. Since I didn't know of any stores nearby that sold things like that, I did my shopping online.

What will Mercedes want to do with me? Or to me?

No panties would probably be good. And no bra, of course. So then, something with easy access to everything Mercedes might want to touch . . . but still a little bit of coverage in the right places. I scoured sexy fetish dresses and lingerie, and finally decided on a fairly simple but still very sexy lace chemise.

The chemise was waiting for me when I arrived home a few days before the event. I immediately opened the package and ran upstairs to try it on before Ryan got home. The lace was stretchy and soft as I slid it on. I had worried the material would be flimsy and cheap, but it wasn't. It had a deep V-neck that was cut all the way down to below my belly button with a short chain of rhinestones at the chest to keep it from falling entirely off my breasts. The back scooped down low on my hips. It was just long enough to cover my butt— barely. The deep-purple color looked nice against my skin.

"Wow, all you need now is a collar and leash."

I nearly jumped out of my skin at Ryan's voice. I turned to see him standing in the bedroom doorway, holding—of course—a collar and leash.

"You scared me," I said. "What do you think?"

He looked me up and down, a familiar hunger growing in his eyes. "I think you need one in every color."

My face warmed at his appreciative stare.

"Now, let's see how this collar looks." He started to lift it to my neck, but I put a hand over his and stopped him.

"I don't know about this," I said. "When I was looking for an outfit, I read some other things about collars and what they mean in BDSM. Mercedes will know this isn't *that*, right?"

"What do you mean?"

"I mean stuff like actually having ownership over someone, or a collar being a significant part of a BDSM relationship. I just thought I was going to have some fun for one night."

Ryan squeezed my hand reassuringly. "Well, people have their own meanings and ways they do things. Think of it more like you're her pet for the night. Just not the animal kind."

Except I'd learned that pets were a thing in BDSM too. Complete with bowls and kennels in addition to collars and leashes. I was finding that I was way, way more naive about BDSM than I'd suspected. There was so much to it.

"I don't want to do it wrong," I said. "Or give anyone the wrong idea."

"The only person you need to care about is Mercedes, baby. And she's going to love it."

I turned to face the mirror again and let him fasten the collar around my neck. It was plain black leather with a silver buckle at the back and one silver ring in the front for the leash to attach. I couldn't believe I was wearing a collar. But at the same time, something about it made me feel giddy. It completed the outfit, and I knew Ryan was right. Mercedes would love it.

I touched the metal ring at the base of my throat. "Okay, you can take it off now."

I watched Ryan in the mirror as he unbuckled it, grinning the whole time. He clearly loved it.

"I'm still nervous. I don't want to go there and then say no to everything she wants to do."

"She won't torture you, baby. She knows you better than that. Just go and have fun. If you're that nervous, think of it as role-playing."

Role-playing. That didn't seem so bad.

I sighed. "I guess you're right."

"I know I am." He reached under the hem of my chemise and pinched my butt cheek.

"Ow!" I jumped away and swatted his shoulder. "Do that again and I'll be leading you around by the leash!"

"Hey, that could be fun," he said, wiggling his eyebrows.

I rolled my eyes, but then I laughed. He always knew how to make me laugh, and I loved him for it.

On the night of the event, I got dressed in my chemise, no panties, and put on a simple wrap dress over it so I could go out to the car without giving the neighbors an eyeful. I wore black ballet flats and figured I might take them off once I was at the event.

"Ahem, aren't you forgetting something?" Ryan said as we were getting ready to go out to the car. He dangled the collar and leash in front of my face.

"I'm not wearing that until I get there, so just put it in your pocket for now, or up your ass for all I care." I stuck out my tongue at him, and he laughed at me.

Half an hour later, we arrived at what looked like a private home. It was set back off a long driveway without neighbors in sight, similar to the first event we'd attended. As we exited the car, I saw a few people making their way to the door in various states of undress, so I figured I could do the same. Ryan texted Chet that we'd arrived as I untied my wrap dress and tossed it in the back seat. I kept the flats on for now.

"Okay," I said to Ryan. "This is probably the only time you'll ever hear me ask this: Can you put the collar on me, please?"

He grinned and happily complied.

We walked up to the door with Ryan holding my leash and told the security guy our names and that Chet and Mercedes were sponsoring us. He found our name, put wristbands on us, and welcomed us to the event without so much as a glance at the collar and leash, or the fact that I wasn't wearing much. Of course, most people coming in had racy outfits. But I was glad he didn't seem to think anything was wrong about the collar like I'd feared.

Either the house was normally decorated like a BDSM dungeon all the time or the owners had gone to a lot of trouble to transform it for the night. Portraits of nearly nude people tied in intricate ropework or in provocative poses adorned the walls, highlighted by flickering sconces jutting out from the walls. Some female voices were crying out from somewhere we couldn't see, and everywhere I looked, people dressed up in cloaks, or leather, or fishnets, or even nothing. *These people really get into this lifestyle.*

Chet approached us, carefully leading Mercedes by the hand because she was blindfolded.

I took a deep breath. *This is it.*

"Baby, we have a present for you," Chet said as he removed the blindfold.

As soon as she saw me, her eyes grew large and her mouth dropped open in shock and, hopefully, awe. Then she clasped her hands together and let out a screech of excitement.

"Happy birthday, Mistress," I said.

Ryan handed her the leash, and she took it gingerly as if it were the most precious thing in the world.

Then I whimpered, "Go easy on me, please."

Everyone laughed.

"I can't believe you would do this for me. This is the best present I could ever ask for. I love it." Her smile turned devious, and her voice became more sinister. "So very much. Now let's talk about rules."

I gulped. To say I was nervous was an understatement.

Once we started, I was to kneel when we stopped to talk to anyone, and when she tugged on the leash, I was to stand and walk with her. Don't say a word unless spoken to, and touch nothing and no one without her permission. I would refer to her as Mistress. Yes, Mistress and no, Mistress. Then she told me that any time I was too fearful, or if something hurt and I couldn't take it, I just had to say the word "red" and she would take me aside to discuss it. That helped put me at ease a little bit. But not much.

Mercedes grinned. "Here we go, my pretty little slut."

She tugged on my leash, and I followed.

As we walked through the house, I saw people on tables, people on crosses, things right out of the torture chambers you see in movies. I glanced behind us at Ryan; of course, he was grinning like a fool. We stopped to watch a naked woman lying face down on a table with wires connected to her back.

Mercedes looked at me and cleared her throat. I dropped to my knees and said, "Sorry, Mistress."

She ran her fingers through my hair. "Good girl. You'll learn."

I focused on what was happening in front of us. The wires were connected to a rope and pulley, and two men slowly pulled on the rope, lifting the woman up and off the table. I gasped when I realized she was being lifted by small hooks in her skin along her arms and the back of her legs. The skin around each hook stretched under her body weight. She was panting from the obvious pain.

She was suspended approximately three feet above the table. I wanted to look away, but I couldn't. Mercedes continued combing my hair with her fingers. Her gentleness with me was a strange contrast to the pain I was sure the suspended woman felt.

Mercedes looked down at me. "That is impressive, isn't it?"

"Yes, Mistress."

Thankfully, she tugged on my leash then, and I stood to walk alongside her.

I felt a tug on my leash and stood up to walk along with my Mistress.

We made our way down a dimly lit hallway. A tall man dressed in all black passed us, leading an attractive blonde woman on a leash. I was thankful I wasn't the only one on a leash.

We entered a room with many people standing along the wall,

watching the scene. I knelt and Mercedes put her hand in my hair again, combing it with her fingers. I actually really liked that part. In the center of the room, a woman was restrained on a cross that was tilted back at a forty-five-degree angle. A man stood next to her in front of a table that held various bowls, jars of clear liquid, and other items that were difficult to identify.

Mercedes leaned down to whisper in my ear, "Fire is always fun to watch."

My head whipped up in shock. "He's going to burn her?"

That's when I noticed the fire extinguisher sitting on the floor next to the cross. Panic consumed me.

"It's all safe, just watch."

The restrained woman didn't seem even a little bit afraid. I had to remind myself to breathe as I kept watching.

The man took what looked like a small sponge on the end of a stick and dipped it in some of the clear liquid. He wiped the sponge down her leg and ignited the liquid trail with his other hand. I gasped as the flame licked over her skin, but then he quickly wiped the fire away.

Nope. No way. I could never do that. I looked up at Mercedes, who seemed awed by the display.

The man did the same thing to the woman's other leg, then her stomach, and then her arms. Each time was the same: swipe, ignite, wipe to extinguish. To my surprise, the woman wasn't hurt. She never cried out like she was in pain, and her skin wasn't burned or blistered.

I felt a tug on my collar and stood up to follow my mistress. We walked up a set of stairs to a large room set up like a royal court. Groups of people conversed in many different areas around torches and firepits that were gas, not actually woodburning, but nevertheless impressive. I looked back at Ryan, who was walking with Chet, and he mouthed, "Wow."

Mercedes leaned close and whispered, "When I introduce you to anyone, look down, never directly at them."

"Yes, Mistress."

She leaned in closer, giggling. "You have no idea how much fun I'm having with this."

I couldn't help the proud grin that sprouted my face. That's all I wanted. To give her a good gift and be able to take part in her lifestyle. Well, to an extent. A lot still made me nervous, and I wasn't interested in getting into the lifestyle for myself. But taking part with my best friend? I could handle that in moderation.

She led me toward what looked like a small set of stairs to a throne. On this throne sat a man with long, dark hair who wore leather pants, a crown, and leather belts running crossways on his chest. He was talking to some others as we approached.

The others moved aside as we walked up the stairs. When Mercedes stopped, I followed her direction and looked down at the floor as I knelt beside her.

"Lord Ramirez, this is Ginger, my plaything for the evening."

I stifled a chuckle at being called her plaything. I heard him move, and his feet came into view before me.

Now what do I do? I didn't have to wonder too long, because he reached down and lifted my chin so I could look at him.

Do I smile? Not smile? I tried to go for a small smile as my eyes met his.

Holy shit! His eyes were a striking cobalt blue, contrasting with his tanned skin and black hair. That couldn't be his natural eye color. He was a very handsome man. More handsome than I had expected to meet in a place I found so unnerving.

"Welcome to my home, Ginger." His voice was smooth and deep. He could say anything and it would sound calming. My smile shifted from the careful facade to a genuine one that was maybe—*maybe*—a little lusty. Heat flooded my cheeks when I realized my sudden desire was probably written all over my face.

A sudden tug on my hair pulled my head back. Mercedes looked down at me.

"How do you greet a master, slut?" she said, then let go of my hair.

I was almost too shocked to respond. But beneath the shock, there was an undercurrent of excitement. I composed myself and said, "Thank you, Master."

He smiled down at me, and I looked at the ground again. I couldn't hide my desire for him very well. I could only imagine what Ryan was thinking behind us.

Lord Ramirez asked, "Who are these men behind you?"

Mercedes said, "This is Chet, and this is Ginger's actual husband, Ryan, who's watching from the shadows."

"Sir Ryan, what exactly are you hoping to watch?" Lord Ramirez asked.

My heart thumped wildly. I went to look back at Ryan, but

Mercedes quickly turned my head forward again.

"I enjoy watching her get used and pleasured. I like to see her expression when she gets off," Ryan said.

Lord Ramirez lifted my chin again and gazed into my eyes.

"Do you enjoy your husband watching another man having your body for his pleasure?" he asked in that seductive, smooth voice of his. A voice that sent electricity to my core.

My face was on fire. Other places, too. I nodded and replied, "Yes, Master."

His thumb brushed over my cheek, and he continued to stare into my eyes. I was so nervous, and the eye contact was so intense that I wanted to look down, but his hold on my chin prevented it.

I had no idea where this was going. Lord Ramirez was sexy. But what if he wanted more than just sex? What if he wanted to do things that were beyond my limits?

Role-play. Ryan said it was just role-play for me.

And I could use the safe word like Mercedes told me. I tried to embrace the role of a submissive slut with her Mistress, but I trembled with anticipation.

Lord Ramirez looked to Mercedes. "This is a fine plaything, indeed. Look at her innocence and fear of the unknown. I am envious of your find." He then went back to sit upon his throne.

Mercedes leaned down to whisper in my ear, "Do you want to fuck him?"

My heart rate doubled again. My body was screaming *yes*, but my brain was waving caution flags.

I looked up at her and nodded.

266

"Lord Ramirez, I would like to offer my plaything for your pleasure for a short while. She is very new and lacks discipline. I offer to attend and ensure she is obedient."

Why did that sound so erotic? I began to shiver.

"Come up before me," Lord Ramirez said.

I felt a tug on my collar, and I walked up to the throne and knelt before him. He picked up my chin again and looked into my eyes.

"Your mistress wants to give you to me for my pleasure. Would you like to provide me pleasure?"

I slowly nodded. He reached around, gently ran his fingers through my hair, then gripped a handful, pulling my head to the side.

"I asked you a question. I expect an answer."

"Yes, Master," I yelped. The electricity in my body hit every nerve and then converged at my core. My pussy was on fire, and I needed to be fucked by someone . . . anyone, but I needed it soon.

He smiled. "You're right, she does lack discipline. But I think when I'm done fucking her, she'll be more manageable."

My sex spasmed at his words.

Is this real life? I never imagined that giving myself, and all control, to Mercedes for her birthday would result in me getting to have sex with a hot, mysterious man. It was exciting, but I was still nervous about being pushed past my limits.

"I think a good fuck is just what she needs, Lord Ramirez." Mercedes pushed my head forward. "Pull out the Master's cock and show him how much you appreciate his interest in you."

With trembling hands, I unfastened his belt buckle. He assisted as I tried to pull off his tight leather pants. I pulled them to his knees and tried not to gape at the large, gorgeous dick before me. It was still limp, but it was already impressive. I couldn't wait to see how big it would get.

I grabbed hold of his cock, stroked it, and swirled my tongue around the tip to bring him to life. A hand slipped into my hair and gripped it. When he was hard enough, I wrapped my lips around his shaft and slowly fucked his cock with my mouth.

"Suck that cock like you mean it," Mercedes said.

I then knew it was her hand in my hair as she pushed my head down farther. She pushed my mouth onto his cock until the tip hit the back of my throat and I started to gag. She let me up to breathe, and then pushed me back down again.

As Mercedes guided my mouth up and down his shaft, he continued to harden and grow even larger than I expected. Other than some porn movies, I had never seen a cock as big as his. Soon he was stretching my mouth, and I couldn't take it all anymore. My lips stretched around his girth. I pulled off my mouth, suddenly overcome with a rush of girlish glee and a sense of the role I could get into playing with him.

I stroked him and put on my best innocent pout as I looked up through half-lowered lashes. "Master, I have never seen such a large cock. I fear it will stretch my tight pussy so much that it might hurt."

The muscles in his stomach flinched, and he clenched his teeth at my words. I'd learned a thing or two about what men liked to hear.

He pushed my hands away and stood, yanking his pants back up. "Come," he said to Mercedes. "Bring your slut."

We followed him behind the throne to a small room with a bed and other dungeon devices. Chet and Ryan followed but stopped just inside the doorway.

Lord Ramirez stopped near a padded table with stirrups like you'd see at a gynecologist's office, only this was leather, wood, and iron. "I want her here."

"Oh, this will be fun." Mercedes giggled and led me over. "Up you go."

When I was up on the table, I scooted down so my butt was at the edge and then set my feet into the stirrups. Mercedes fastened a strap around each of my ankles, then lifted my arms over my head and restrained my wrists. Since my chemise was so short and I wasn't wearing panties, everything was on display. Lord Ramirez—and everyone else—would be able to see how aroused I already was.

Lord Ramirez stood by my feet. "I want to see the rest of her."

Mercedes reached behind my neck, untied the halter top of the chemise, and pulled it down around my waist, exposing my breasts. All I could do was lie there, naked except for the lace bunched around my waist, legs spread wide open for him. Now he was stripped down too, with only his impressive half-erect cock dangling before him. He looked at Mercedes.

"Mistress Mercedes, would you do the honor of preparing me to enter your slut?"

"Of course, Lord Ramirez."

I couldn't miss the glint of excitement in her eyes as she dropped to her knees in front of him. She sucked and stroked him hungrily, bringing him back to his full size. When she was finished, he stood between my legs. My heart pounded in my ears. The tip of his cock slid up and down my slit, pushing slightly between my folds, but he didn't enter me yet.

"I'm going to fuck you hard, and you're going to take it. Aren't you, slut?"

I bit my lip and nodded. Mercedes gave me a stern look, and I said, "Yes, Master."

He pushed the head of his cock into me, and it felt even bigger than I was anticipating. I couldn't move except to lift my ass. I cried out, "It's going to hurt."

Lord Ramirez smiled, and it was equal parts devious and sexy. "Yes, it is."

And then he thrust himself completely into me in one swift motion. I cried out with a mix of pleasure and pain as he stretched me open and bumped my cervix. It was unlike anything I'd ever felt before. He didn't start with any slow warm-up strokes to let me get used to his size. He immediately began fucking me hard and fast, and I cried out with each thrust.

He was massive. I soon began to feel more pleasure and less pain, and I settled down on the leather padding. He reached down to grab my tits as he continued pounding my soaked cunt. He hit every electric spot inside me just from his sheer size. I was almost delirious with pleasure, but I still wanted to play my role. I was really starting to get into it.

"Please, Master," I whimpered, which caused him to grunt through clenched teeth. "Give me everything. I can take it. I want to please you."

Sweat beaded on his brow. Somehow, he managed to fuck me

harder still. My orgasm was starting to bubble just below the surface, waiting to break free.

"You're pleasing me very well," he huffed out between punishing thrusts. "And soon you'll take all my seed too."

I cried out, "Yes, give me your seed, Master. Use this pussy and fill it with your cum."

He grabbed my ass, breathing heavily, and let out a loud, rumbling moan as he pushed in deep. I cried out with the sensation of being so thoroughly filled. His cock pulsed as he unloaded inside me, and I could feel it more than usual because of how big he was. As usual for me, that feeling and hearing him come was all I needed to hit that climax. My muscles tightened, and I instinctively struggled against my restraints as I came. My pussy clenched around his cock while the rest of me shuddered. He held himself inside me until we were both spent.

When he pulled out, I felt as though I was gaping open for all to see. I could only slightly lift my head to glance toward the doorway, where Chet and Ryan were grinning from ear to ear. And I was pretty sure they'd been affected in other ways too. I rested my head back. Lord Ramirez came around to the side of the table and leaned down, his long hair brushing across my chest as he put his lips close to my ear.

"I appreciate a woman who really gets into the role-playing. Thank you." He smiled and winked at me, and in that moment, I got a hint of what he might be like outside of putting on a show as Lord Ramirez. He quickly put on the serious persona again though. "I'm finished with your plaything, Mistress Mercedes. You can take her away now."

Mercedes asked, "I hope she was pleasing to you, Lord Ramirez."

"She pleased me very well," he said, giving me another genuine smile.

Some silly part of me was proud to be complimented as he had, proud of serving him so well.

Mercedes unfastened my restraints, and I let out a little sigh of pleasure.

"You were a very good girl. Now let's get you cleaned up."

I followed her to the restroom, where she burst into giggles.

"Oh my god! You have no idea how much fun this is for me. I thought you might like Lord Ramirez."

I smiled and said, "Yes, Mistress."

She laughed. "We aren't mistress and slut in the bathroom. Let's just be Mercedes and Ginger again for a minute."

She wet some paper towels and handed them to me so I could clean up.

"I know he likes to have sex at events, so I figured it would be perfect to introduce you to him. So, how was he?"

"He's huge! At first, I thought he was going to rip me open. If I wasn't restrained, I would have run away."

We both laughed.

"But . . . he was still amazing," I said. I retied the chemise behind my neck and smoothed it out over my body again. "It felt so good once I got used to him. Thank you for sharing me."

"No, thank *you*!" She hugged me, and then kissed me. "Are you ready to go back?"

I nodded and followed her lead.

We found Chet and Ryan back in the throne room. When we stopped, I knelt before Ryan, and he placed his hand in my hair.

"A wonderful pet you have indeed, Mistress Mercedes."

I stuck out my tongue at him, and he raised his eyebrows.

"Mistress Mercedes, do you see this insubordination?" he said with mock disdain. "Sticking out her tongue at us. I demand retribution!"

Mercedes grabbed my hair. "Did you show disrespect to these masters?"

I tried not to laugh as I pointed at Ryan and said, "Only to this one, Mistress."

"Oh, you must be punished, woman."

I gulped. *She means pretend punishment, right?*

"Might I borrow your whip?" she asked Chet. He had one coiled on his belt, and he unclipped it and handed it to her.

I shook my head. *She wasn't serious.*

"You will either pull out both of their cocks and suck them well, and hope they forgive you, or you will see the end of this whip across your bare back."

Chet and Ryan pulled out their cocks without any hesitation and stood in front of me. I reached up, grabbed both cocks, and looked up into their smug faces. Two could play at this game. I started sucking Ryan, using a little more teeth than usual as my own private retribution.

"Did you teach your slut to use her teeth while sucking a cock?" he said. "I don't think she's asking for forgiveness very well."

Chet laughed, and then I heard a crack of the whip. It was so loud I thought for sure I would feel pain a second later, but I didn't. She'd only snapped it in the air.

"Suck that cock well, or feel this leather."

"Yes, Mistress," I said.

I could see a few other people standing nearby, watching as I sucked Ryan's cock and then moved over to Chet. I alternated between them for several minutes, really giving it my all. Chet tensed up as I had my mouth around him, and his hips started to move. I could tell he was close.

"Do you want me to swallow his cum, Mistress?" I asked Mercedes.

"Of course. Drink both of them."

With that permission given, Chet grabbed my head and fucked my mouth as I kept stroking Ryan with one hand. After a few thrusts, Chet pushed himself as far in as he could and held my head there as he came, shooting several waves of cum into my mouth. I swallowed it all until he was finished. Then it was Ryan's turn.

I knew exactly what would get Ryan going, and how to get him off quickly after being married so long. I massaged his balls while sucking his cock, taking him far back into my throat. Then I opened my mouth and stuck out my tongue as I looked up at him so he could see his cock in my mouth. I flicked my tongue against him, then said, "I want to drink your cum, baby."

That was all it took. He grabbed my head and pushed himself

into my mouth. I clamped my lips around him as he came, pulsing against my tongue. I loved that sensation in my mouth just as much as I loved feeling it in my pussy.

After he was done and I'd swallowed everything, I wiped my mouth and said, "Am I forgiven, Masters?"

They smiled at each other and then high-fived. I rolled my eyes and caught Mercedes doing the same when I looked over at her. We both laughed.

"Good girl," she said to me. "You've redeemed yourself."

She tugged on my collar, and I stood. The four of us walked around for a few minutes, but it seemed many people had finished up their scenes and were starting to leave. When we returned to the large foyer where I'd first been presented to her, she turned to face me.

"Thank you so much for this present, Ginger." She pulled me into a hug. "You have no idea how much it meant to me."

"You are so very welcome."

We kissed, and then she handed my leash to Ryan. "She's all yours again."

I quickly grabbed the leash away from him. "Oh, no I'm not. I had my fill of being anyone's plaything tonight."

"Well, it was really good that you came out to check our lifestyle and give Mercedes a great birthday present," Chet said. "And just a reminder, my birthday is coming up too."

We all laughed, and I gave Chet a hug and kiss.

"Perhaps we can work something out," I said.

Ryan and I walked out the door and toward the car. I stopped to turn around and take in the grandness of the house one last time. I would remember this night for a long time.

Ryan asked, "What's the matter?"

I linked my arm with his. "Nothing. Just wondering if Lord Ramirez would consider our lifestyle."

He laughed. "That was very impressive."

"What was?" I retrieved my wrap dress from the back seat and slipped it on before entering the car.

"All of it. How much you got into your role, and then how big he was." He started the car, and we got on our way. "I watched as he pushed into you and how much he stretched you out. That was pretty hot."

I grinned. "Yeah. You're a perfect size though. If you were that big, you wouldn't get nearly as much sex from me as you do now."

"So, bigger isn't better?"

"Well, size matters some," I admitted. "But there is such a thing as too big, and Lord Ramirez was almost there."

When we got home, we went straight to bed. I was exhausted after everything. We climbed under the covers and kissed each other good night. Ryan placed his hand in my hair and tilted my head back.

"Good night, slut," he said with a grin.

I smiled back at him. "Careful. Mistress isn't here to stop me from using my teeth right now."

We both laughed as he let go of my hair, and we cuddled until we fell asleep.

*****

The next morning, I woke up before Ryan and went downstairs

to start the coffee. Last night had been . . . a lot. But good. I wasn't sore, but certain parts of my body still remembered the way they'd been used the night before. I was a gift to Mercedes, yet I'd managed to get a two-for-one deal myself when she handed me over to Lord Ramirez. The world of BDSM still confused and intimidated me in many ways, but I couldn't deny how much I'd enjoyed myself.

Ryan came down just as the coffee finished brewing.

"You look like you're thinking hard about something, and I bet it's not the coffee," he said.

"It's nothing," I said, then gave him a quick kiss. We poured some coffee and sat on the back porch, enjoying the cool fall morning.

"What are your plans for Chet's birthday?" Ryan asked.

"I don't know if I can handle a repeat of last night," I said. "Mercedes is intense as a Mistress. I don't even want to think of what Chet would be like as my Master."

"Well, I think you did great last night."

Of course, he thought so. He got to see one hell of a show.

"I don't know if I can do this BDSM stuff," I said, then took a sip of my coffee.

"I feel like there's a 'but' there."

I smiled. "But . . . I do like the intimidation and control, especially when a man does it."

Ryan reached into my hair and grabbed hold. "You mean like this?"

"Ha-ha. I'd hate to accidentally spill this coffee on your lap."

He laughed and let go. Ryan did it jokingly, making me want to let my sass out and joke back. But when it was Lord Ramirez holding my chin, telling me what to do in that firm, controlling way, it was erotic, and I wanted to do whatever he said.

"I like the lust and romance with our lifestyle, but I like a man who wants to get into my head and make me experience things just as much as he wants to get into my pussy."

At that, Ryan raised his eyebrows. But it was the best way I could explain it. When Lord Ramirez said he was going to fuck me hard, and I was physically unable to resist, that did something to me. The mental aspect of it made the physical part that much more exciting. I was getting wet just thinking about it.

"I like a man who can be confident, passionate but in control, and still show just enough restraint to make me hunger for him."

Ryan laughed. "I'll put an ad in the paper tomorrow."

Smart-ass.

"I'm serious. You can do that occasionally, and Kurt is close, but I have yet to find a man who can rock my mind that well. I would love to see what that Lord Ramirez—or whatever his real name is—can do."

"Oh, you were smitten with him, were you?" He raised his eyebrows again as he sipped his coffee.

I grinned into my cup. "Maybe."

He gave me a knowing look but didn't say any more.

We enjoyed breakfast on the back porch and spent most of the morning there, talking and enjoying the weather and the view. I got a text from Mercedes asking how I was feeling and thanking me again for the gift.

"Anything for my best friend," I told her. Then she sent another message that made me grin and stare at my phone, unsure how to respond.

"Who is it?" Ryan asked.

"It's Mercedes." I bit my lip. "Lord Ramirez wants my phone number."

"Go for it," Ryan said. "Maybe he's into swinger's parties too."

I loved that he was all for it. We were secure in our relationship, our love for one another, and that bond had only strengthened through our lifestyle experiences.

"Staring at the phone isn't going to do anything," he said. "Go ahead and give him your number."

I thought about it for another minute before I responded. Then I put my phone down and reached for my coffee.

"What did you tell her?" Ryan asked.

"I told her I'd think about it." I was really curious what he would be like again, but I was still fearful about a lot of BDSM aspects, including much of what I'd seen in the dungeon last night. I needed to sort out my confusion first.

*****

Over the next few weeks, we spent a lot of time with family and didn't attend any lifestyle parties or socials. Every once in a while, when I had some free time to myself, Lord Ramirez would pop into my head—the way he projected power, and how that affected me. I was captivated by the concept of being used, especially by someone like Lord Ramirez.

I wanted to experience something like that again. Very much, in fact.

Finally, I sent a text message to Mercedes. *Feel free to give Lord Ramirez my phone number.*

Will do! Oh, and what are you guys doing next weekend? It's Chet's birthday.

His not-so-subtle reminder to me at the dungeon a few weeks ago rang in my mind. Hopefully, he didn't actually want that from me again. I didn't think I could do it. I told her we were free and hoped for the best.

I was thinking of making some salmon, having some wine, and maybe some time in the hot tub.

Whew. I knew what alcohol and hot tub meant. I told her we were in.

When Ryan got home, we sat down to dinner, and I let him know about the plans with Mercedes and Chet.

"Wine and hot tub," he said. "So, in other words, they want to play?"

We both laughed.

After dinner, we went out to our favorite spot on the back porch to relax with our wine.

"You know how you've always been into role-playing, but I haven't so much?" I asked.

His eyes lit up like he already had scenarios running through his head. He ran a finger down my arm. "Why, yes I do."

"And remember the mansion with Lord Ramirez?"

"Oh, do I ever."

I rolled my eyes. "Well, I've been thinking about it, and what really turned me on was how confident and dominant he was, but soft at the same time. That was one of the most incredible turn-ons I've ever had. If you can pull that off, I'll role-play with you."

He smiled and reached for my chin with his finger. "You've got a deal."

I pushed his hand away and laughed. "I'm serious. I liked that a lot."

"Okay, baby. I think I know what you're talking about, but I'll do more research and prepare, and we can try it out one day."

I couldn't contain my grin. It made me happy that he was willing to give it a try for me, and was also willing for me to pursue that feeling with Lord Ramirez if I wanted. I wondered what it would be like to have two men like that at once? My face grew hot thinking about it. Ryan still had to learn about it, so it's not like it would happen anytime soon. But maybe in the future . . .

Ryan studied me over the rim of his coffee cup as he took another sip, like he could read my thoughts. I just smiled and sipped my coffee.

*****

On the week of Chet's birthday, I got another text from Mercedes asking if it would be okay if another guy friend joined us for dinner and hot-tub time. That was strange. I'd assumed wine and hot-tub meant sex, so who would she want to invite?

What kind of guy? I texted back. Would it be a BDSM friend?

281

Or was it a vanilla friend, and she wasn't really expecting us to get sexy in the hot tub?

Trust me, you'll like him.

I guess that meant playtime was still on the table. Well . . . I told her that was fine, because it was Chet's birthday, and if he wanted another friend there, who was I to say no? I didn't have to play with him if I didn't want to. And I could trust Mercedes—as she and Ryan were always quick to remind me with each new experience. Going to play without knowing someone did make me a little nervous, but if Mercedes thought I would like him, I'd trust her.

On Saturday, we picked up a nice bottle of bourbon for Chet and headed over for dinner. We knocked on the door, and Mercedes answered with a huge grin and a glass of wine in her hand.

"Hi. Come in."

I was immediately suspicious. She seemed really excited about something. Giddy, even. As soon as we walked into the kitchen, there was Lord Ramirez. My mouth went dry. I looked at Ryan.

"Did you know about this?"

He shrugged and shook his head.

"Well," I said, at a loss for words. "Hello . . ." *Should I still call him "Lord Ramirez?"*

He smiled, and those blue eyes melted me. He set down his glass and casually walked over to me, never breaking eye contact until he hugged me.

"Hi, my name is Matt."

That voice . . . Well, hell, everything about this man turned me on.

"Hi, Matt. I wasn't expecting you here tonight." I looked over at Mercedes, who immediately looked away as though she wasn't paying attention at all.

"I enjoyed our role-playing quite a bit. And, of course, I enjoyed the sexual aspect too."

Warmth flooded my cheeks. "Yes, you made that *very* obvious." His face flushed pink. "Oh my, Lord Ramirez, do you blush?"

That made everyone laugh.

Matt continued, "Mercedes passed along your phone number but then said you were coming over to celebrate Chet's birthday and asked if I wanted to attend. I hope you don't mind this little surprise."

"Hmm . . ." I walked around him, looking him up and down as though to inspect him, and ran my fingers through his hair. I came to stand in front of him again and raised my hand to his chin. "He can stay."

Those gorgeous eyes sparkled when he smiled. I was quite proud of myself to mess with him like that.

"Perhaps you need to be reminded who the Master is," Matt said in that smooth, slightly deeper tone I now realized was one he adopted for his role-play. His natural voice was still silky and sexy, just a little bit different. "Or perhaps you really are a switch, despite that excellent role-play a few weeks ago."

I was momentarily speechless. How could just that voice and the suggestion affect me so much? He smirked, likely realizing he'd beat me at my own game.

Dinner was ready, so we moved to the dining room. Matt guided me with a hand at the small of my back. Was he staking a claim?

"I know it was only a role-play fantasy, but you seemed to take to submission quite naturally," he said. "Do you have an interest in pursuing that aspect of kink outside of role-play?"

"No," I said quickly, sitting in the chair he'd pulled out for me. Mercedes and Ryan were on the other side of the table, which left me sandwiched between Chet and Matt. "I mean . . . I like a man who can take control like that sometimes, but I don't want to do that all the time. I wouldn't really say I'm kinky or into BDSM at all."

"That's a surprise to me based on what little I know of you so far," Matt said, sliding his hand over my thigh. "I suppose we'll have to get better acquainted."

Then Chet slid his hand over my other thigh, and my heart thumped in my chest.

We started passing dishes around to serve ourselves. All throughout dinner, Chet and Matt engaged me in slow torture, running their fingers up my thigh, between my legs to tease against my covered mound, and then back down my thigh again. Every time I glanced across at Ryan or Mercedes, they just grinned at me.

We spent some time talking about how swinging was Ryan's and my preferred lifestyle, rather than BDSM. Then we got to talking about Matt and how he came to live in that massive house. He said he'd worked for a man who'd made a fortune on some kind of computer chip, and he had no children.

"I took care of his home, his pets, and anything he wanted. He was a very generous man who paid me well, and I never asked him for anything else. He passed away a few years ago, and he left me his inheritance. I traveled the world and learned a lot. I'd always had a casual interest in BDSM, or what I knew of it, and then I learned much more from some very wealthy friends in Europe. One particular thing I picked up from them was that if you were going to enjoy it and had the means, you should go all out. Hence the decor of my home."

"Do you have it like that all the time?" Ryan asked.

"Yes, but I do have a part of my home that's more vanilla. Even I like to take a break sometimes."

I asked, "When you explored BDSM, what did you learn that was the most fascinating?"

He smiled. "I've seen so many things, including some things I just couldn't bring to my home. But the one thing I found most intriguing is the psychological spell that can be cast from just the simplest touch." He stared into my eyes and brushed his fingers over my cheek in the gentlest caress.

It froze me in my seat for a few seconds, and then I shook my head to clear it. I took a sip of my wine and looked at Ryan and Mercedes, who were grinning yet again.

"Oh, shut up," I said.

We laughed, then Chet said, "How about we take our wine to the hot tub?"

I bit my lip, remembering how big Lord Ramirez—or, Matt—was. But this time, I wouldn't be restrained and could have some measure of control instead of just taking it however he wanted me to.

We took towels and wine outside behind the house. The half-moon cast a gentle glow over the yard. Being fall in the Midwest, it was quite cool already, but that hot tub was steaming. We shed our clothes and all climbed into the hot water.

Chet and Matt, once again, sat on either side of me. Mercedes sat next to Matt, and Ryan was on the other side of her.

Even before I took my first sip of wine, Matt and Chet each had a hand on me. After all that teasing during dinner, I didn't know how much more I could take.

Mercedes, Chet, and Matt talked about ideas for future kink events, and I just sipped my wine and tried to keep from making lustful noises any time a finger slipped through my crevice.

I had my wine in one hand and went searching for some treasure of my own with the other. I slid my hand up Matt's thigh until I found his nearly erect shaft. I slipped my hand around it and slowly stroked him. I glanced over at him, and he winked at me. I couldn't believe I felt so high school. What was he doing to me?

I scooped down and massaged his balls for a moment, and then returned to his cock, which seemed to be fully hard now. I sucked in a breath as I circled my fingers around him and noticed the increased girth from a few minutes ago.

"Ah, I remember this," I murmured.

The conversation stopped abruptly, as everyone looked at me.

I took a sip of my wine and said, "What?"

They laughed, which seemed to finally shift things from talking mode. Ryan kissed Mercedes passionately, grabbing one of her enormous breasts. He loved her breasts, and I didn't blame him.

I hooked one leg over the top of Matt's leg and the other over Chet's, spreading me wide open to receive their attention. I set down my glass of wine on the ledge of the spa and reached over to stroke Chet's cock, so now I had one in each hand. As two hands reached toward my center, Matt turned my head toward him and leaned in to kiss me. We hadn't kissed the first time we met, and anticipation sizzled through me in that moment before his lips met mine. His lips were soft, but the movements were deliberate. And then his tongue demanded entry into my mouth, and I obeyed. His confidence was even evident in his kiss.

Chet kissed my shoulder and neck. Both men hand their hands in my folds, stroking, exploring, working me into a frenzy. I was lost in Matt's kiss and didn't know whose fingers were doing what. I only knew that two hands were clearly better than one. I did my best to stay focused enough to continue stroking both cocks. Then two sets of fingers slid into my pussy. I gasped against Matt's mouth, and my hips rolled with a mind of their own.

Chet then reached around to grab my breasts. I wanted to feel Matt inside me again, but if I did, I'd be done for the night.

I released both men and whispered into Matt's ear, "Sit on the edge of the spa."

He complied, and I stood up and bent over with my legs open. I looked back at Chet and swayed my hips.

"It's all yours, birthday boy."

He grinned and took up position behind me. I glanced at Ryan sitting on the edge of the spa as Mercedes also showed off her expert oral skills.

I stroked Matt's cock and put my lips around his head. He was so big that I barely got my mouth around him. Afraid of gagging on the massive beast, I only slid my mouth halfway down his shaft before coming back up.

Chet stroked the head of his cock against my entrance, slowly working it between my folds, and then finally, he filled my depth. I looked back at him while I continued stroking Matt and smiled, moaning with each of his thrusts.

I returned my attention to Matt and said, "I can't get all of you into my throat."

He cupped my chin and gazed right into my soul. "But you will try, won't you?" he whispered.

The look in his eyes, and the way he asked, I couldn't help but comply. It was like he had some kind of spell on me, compelling me to follow his every wish. I wanted to please this man.

I took him in my mouth again and sucked his beautiful cock, sliding my head down, then up, then down again, taking him deeper and deeper with each pass. I gagged a couple of times and had to pull my mouth off to catch my breath.

"You're doing great," he said. "You're almost there."

I smiled at him and tried again. I had to brace myself so that Chet's thrusts didn't accidentally shove my face too far into Matt's lap and make me gag—or worse. I got down to where the tip of Matt's cock hit the entrance to my throat and forced myself down lower. My throat stretched with the size of his head, and I pulled off, continuing to stroke him.

He smiled and said, "That's about as far as most can get."

He leaned down to kiss me. Chet was still fucking me in a hard, steady rhythm, and I pushed my hips back a little to meet each of his thrusts as I kissed Matt. My body was on fire from these two men.

Chet groaned and announced, "I'm coming."

My two favorite words. I didn't come, but the feel of Chet's cock pulsing inside me still sent fresh waves of pleasure through my body. I couldn't help myself as my kiss became more aggressive with Matt, and I bit down on his lower lip. He accepted it and gave my lip a gentle nip in return as I pulled back. I moaned as Chet withdrew from me.

"Wow, I need to take a short break," I said, panting. I needed to catch my breath and give my body a break from standing in that position. Chet handed me my drink, and I sat down between these two amazing men.

We each sipped on our wine while we watched Ryan fucking Mercedes from behind. His back was toward us, and she was leaning over the edge of the spa. We had a great view of his cock sliding in and out of her. She moaned with every thrust. I was enjoying the feel of hands on my thighs again, roaming around my center.

Soon, Ryan gave one final thrust into Mercedes and held himself there as he came with a groan. A moment later, he pulled out, and they turned around with lust-drunk grins on their faces. They sank into the hot water to sit. Mercedes grabbed her wine and sighed.

"Did everyone get taken care of already?" she asked.

"Not everyone." I reached over to Matt's cock and stroked it. "But that will be fixed right now."

I set down my drink on the ledge and straddled Matt, hovering over his cock. I reached down to position him at my entrance and looked into his eyes as I slid down. When the discomfort as he stretched me open felt like too much, I lifted myself momentarily and then slid down again, a little farther. And a little farther.

"Your expression as you take my cock is priceless," he whispered.

I smiled down at him and then gasped as I finally settled all the way into his lap.

He thrust up, and I grabbed his face to look into his eyes. "Wait."

I could take it easier this time, and I wanted to. It only took a few slow movements, gliding up and down on his shaft, for me to feel relaxed enough to enjoy his size. Then I fucked him. He pulled my head down to kiss me almost roughly, adding another layer to the pleasure.

My body quickly picked up on the thread of ecstasy I'd left off a few minutes ago. Matt matched my motion with his own, thrusting and grinding. My breasts pressed and slid against his chest. His tongue filled my mouth, probing as deeply as his cock inside me. My body shuddered as my orgasm coursed through me. I threw my head back as my inner walls clamped down and squeezed his rock-hard cock.

I was almost immobilized for a moment as he waited for me. I caught my breath, and then looked down at him. "Wow, that was good."

"We're not done yet." He reached around to grab my ass and controlled my motion along with his. He fucked me increasingly harder, working me up to another orgasm. I was his plaything again, as I had been the first time, and my body was loving the sensations.

Then he said, "I'm going to fuck you mercilessly and come deep inside you, and you're going to take it all. Aren't you?"

His demands flooded my brain with lust that overrode the hint of pain from his massive dick pounding me.

"Yes," I cried out. "Give it to me."

His fingers dug into my flesh as he pulled me down each time he slammed up into me. I didn't know how much more I could take, but at the same time, I never wanted him to stop. Being at his mercy as he fucked me harder still was exhilarating.

Finally, he exclaimed, "I'm coming!"

An earthquake shook my body from the inside out as soon as he said those words. I froze in place as the orgasm rocked me. I could hardly even feel his cock stretching me open at that point. All I could feel were the shudders of ecstasy shaking me from head to toe.

When I returned to reality, I opened my eyes to find Matt smiling at me. I looked around, and *everyone* was smiling at me.

"Wow, Ginger, you need to show me how to come like that," Mercedes said.

Slowly, I stood up, feeling like part of my own body was missing as Matt slid out of me. I sat down and grabbed my wine.

"Wow, with that gap you left in me, I hope I don't sink in this hot tub," I said.

Mercedes busted out laughing, and I actually saw Matt blushing again. Making such a dominant, in-control man blush like that was fun.

We emptied the last of the wine into our glasses and talked about the various lifestyles, and I got to learn more about how BDSM isn't just pain and role-play. I may have even warmed up more to the concept by the end of it. Matt even offered to help Ryan learn about projecting that dominant person I enjoyed.

"Come by sometime. I know a few women who would be glad to help you learn," Matt said.

Ryan raised his glass. "Hell yeah! I think that's a great idea."

I stared at him scornfully. "How about we see what you learn on your own first?"

We all laughed. It wasn't that I minded Ryan learning with Matt and other women, but damn it, I didn't want to be left out of the fun.

"Wow, it's 1:00 a.m. already, and I'm about to fall asleep," Mercedes said. "I can't hang out like I used to."

We all agreed that it was time to head home. We stepped out of the hot tub. Ryan helped Chet put the cover on while Matt and I helped Mercedes bring the glasses, bottles, and clothes inside.

I set the glasses on the counter, and Matt walked up behind me, placing his arms around my waist. He pressed himself against me, sliding his dick against my ass. I craned my neck to glance back at him.

"You do know, after you, I can't play again for a while," I said.

He scrunched up his face in feigned confusion. "Why do women always say that?"

I shook my head and laughed.

Everyone got dressed and walked to the front door to wish Chet a happy birthday again before giving goodbye hugs and kisses all around.

Before Matt got in his car, he said, "I enjoy the swinging lifestyle too, so I'd love to see you again."

I felt myself blush.

"Also, let me know if you want some hands-on dom/sub training."

Ryan glanced at me. "I'll let you know."

We held hands as we walked home.

Our relationship with Chet and Mercedes had not only survived the reveal of our alternative lifestyles, it had thrived and blossomed into something more amazing than any of us expected. It remained to be seen whether Ryan and I would take Matt up on his offer, or explore kink more in-depth. Maybe we'd find a kinkier side to ourselves just like we'd found the more sexually free side through swinging. Or maybe we'd stick with the occasional role-play. I knew one thing for sure though.

I looked up at Ryan. "I love you, baby."

The strength of our relationship and the depth of our love for one another were the key to our success in the lifestyle. Whatever new opportunities lay before us, we'd explore them together.

Ryan wrapped his arm around me and kissed my temple. "I love you more."

Our Secret Life: Our Awakening

An ordinary married couple with an extraordinary sex life dares to step beyond the boundaries of monogamy, diving headfirst into a seductive world they've only whispered about. What begins as curiosity soon unravels into a whirlwind of passion, drama, laughter, and unexpected friendships. But as they surrender to the spellbinding allure of this new lifestyle, they discover pleasures—and challenges—they never saw coming.

Our Secret Life: A Happy New Year

Step into a seductive New Year's Eve where Cirque du Soleil meets *The Great Gatsby* with a splash of Jenna Jameson's wildest fantasies. Opulence and indulgence collide in a night so extravagant it demands its own story. Rumor has it, these legendary parties still pulse with forbidden thrills today.

The Firm's Deception

Fresh out of college, Brett lands a dream job at a top engineering firm in California—but the company's seductive CEO has far more than business on her mind. Drawn into a web of power, desire, and control, Brett soon realizes he's not just there for his engineering talents. As the CEO unveils her true intentions, Brett must decide how far he's willing to go to satisfy her demands—or risk losing everything he's worked for.